Contract
Warrior$

TOM RACE

To DONNY BURGH. FROM

HiS COFFEE BUDDY

Tom Race

ISBN-10: 1530707943
ISBN-13: 978-1530707942

DEDICATION

I would like to give a very special thank-you to my wife Charlene for her patience, and to Kathleen Zuris of Bostwick Typing Service for her excellent work in transcribing and typing a hand-written manuscript.

— Tom Race.

INTRODUCTION

"The road to hell is paved with good intentions."

— Saint Bernard of Clairvaux

Many a man has died in vain

Thinking his enemy has been slain.

So, never put away your gun

Until you're sure the battle has been won.

For providence is part of victory as

Well as defeat.

Never be so arrogant as to not

Call a retreat.

For the dead do not care if they were

A coward or a hero.

They only know that their lying in

Their grave, a constant zero.

– ARGO –

You can live your life with strangers and forsake tomorrow for today,

Because you know for certain change is on its way.

You may search for the answer on how to be free,

Only to realize you don't need to buy the key.

For if you follow your faith and stay true to God's way,

You will receive what you need [almost] every day.

    [religious]

You can live your life with strangers and forsake tomorrow for today,

Because you know for certain change is on its way.

You may search for the answer on how to be free,

Only to find it takes money to buy the key.

So, if you follow your desires and stay true to the way,

You will get what you want almost every day.

             – ARGO Poem –

EPITAPH OF AN ARMY OF MERCENARIES

These, in the day when heaven was falling,

The hour when earth's foundations fled,

Their shoulders held the sky suspended,

They stood, and earth's foundations stay;

What God abandoned, these defended,

And saved the sum of things for pay.

—A.E. Housman

United Nations Mercenary Convention

Definition of a mercenary

Article 1 of the Convention has the following definition of a mercenary:

"1. A mercenary is any person who:

(a) Is specially recruited locally or abroad in order to fight in an armed conflict;

(b) Is motivated to take part in the hostilities essentially by the desire for private gain and, in fact, is promised, by or on behalf of a party to the conflict, material compensation substantially in excess of that promised or paid to combatants of similar rank and functions in the armed forces of that party;

2. A mercenary is also any person who, in any other situation:

(a) Is specially recruited locally or abroad for the purpose of participating in a concerted act of violence aimed at:

(i) Overthrowing a Government or otherwise undermining the constitutional order of a State; or

(ii) Undermining the territorial integrity of a State;

(b) Is motivated to take part therein essentially by the desire for significant private gain and is prompted by the promise or payment of material compensation;

(c) Is neither a national nor a resident of the State against which such an act is directed;

(d) Has not been sent by a State on official duty; and

(e) Is not a member of the armed forces of the State on whose territory the act is undertaken.

— UN Mercenary Convention

Privatizing war also changes warfare. Offering the means of war to anyone who can afford it, changes why we fight and for what. Moneyed corporations, cartels, and "individuals" could become a new kind of superpower.

The Modern Mercenary

Private armies and what they mean for world order.
Sean McFate

"Private Military Corporations: Benefits and Costs of Outsourcing Security"
— By Allison Stranger and Mark Eric Williams

Private military corporations serve a necessary function in the execution of U.S. foreign policy. All contracts must be approved and licensed by the State Department of Defense Trade Controls (ODTC), and this licensing can occur at any point in the process of bidding, awarding, or accepting a contract.

Because no U.S. company can operate abroad without a license (the de facto veto), these procedures provide State's ODTC and demonstrates a pronounced instrumental relationship between PMCs and the U.S. government.

[From the Yale Journal of International Affairs]

The Federal Acquisition Regulation is the principal set of rules in the Federal Acquisition Regulation System. This system consists of sets of regulations issued by agencies of the federal government of the United States to govern what is called the "acquisition process;" this is the process through which the government purchases ("acquires") goods and services. That process consists of three phases: (1) need recognition and acquisition planning, (2) contract formation, and (3) contract administration. The FAR System regulates the activities of private sector firms, except to the extent that parts of it are incorporated into government solicitations and contracts by reference.

The largest single part of the FAR is part 52, which contains standard contract clauses and "solicitation provisions," are certifications, notices, and instructions directed for firms <u>that plan to compete for a specific contract</u>.

Paul Bremer's Order 17

"Contractors shall be immune from Iraqi legal process, with respect to acts performed by them pursuant to the terms and conditions of a contract or any subcontract thereto. Nothing in this provision shall prohibit MNF personnel (coalition forces) from preventing acts of serious misconduct by contractors or otherwise temporarily detaining any contractors who pose an injury to themselves or others, pending expeditious turnover to the appropriate authorities of the sending state. In all such circumstances, the appropriate senior representative of the contractor's sending state in Iraq shall be notified."

The Anti-Kickback Act of 1986
41 U.S.C. §§
8701 to 8707
<u>48 CFR 3.502-2</u>
<u>et seq.</u>

Prohibits any payment or gratuity made for the purpose of inducing an award of a subcontract or prime contract with the federal government.

In the nation's capital, <u>crime does pay</u>—for defense contractors.

The DOD has admitted that it has rewarded hundreds of companies convicted of fraud with new deals that totaled more than 1.1 trillion dollars.

Senator Bernie Sanders (I-Vermont) who requested the information from the Pentagon said:

> "The ugly truth is that virtually all the major defense contractors in this country for years have been engaged in systemic fraudulent behavior, while receiving hundreds of billions of dollars of the taxpayers' money."

The special activities division (SAD) is a division in the United States Central Intelligence Agency (CIA)'s National Clandestine Service (NCS) responsible for covert operations known as "special activities." Within SAD there are two separate groups SAD/SOG for the tactical paramilitary operations and SAD/PAG for covert political action.

Special Operations Group (SOG) is the department within SAD responsible for operations that include the collection of intelligence in hostile countries and regions, and all high-threat military or intelligence operations with which the U.S. government does not wish to be overtly associated. As such, members of the unit (called Paramilitary <u>Operations Officers and Specialized Skills</u> Officers) <u>normally do not carry any objects or clothing</u> (e.g., <u>military uniforms</u>) <u>that would associate them with the United States government</u>. If they are compromised during a mission, the government of the United States may deny all knowledge.

Many of the duties and functions of the intelligence community activities, not the CIA alone, are being <u>outsourced</u> and <u>privatized</u>. Mike McConnell, former director of National Intelligence, was about to publicize an investigation report of outsourcing by U.S. intelligence agencies, as required by Congress. However, this report was then classified.

. . . What we have today with the intelligence business is something far more systemic: senior officials leaving their national security and counterterrorism jobs for positions where they are basically doing the same jobs they once held at the CIA, and the NSA and other agencies, but for double or triple the salary and for profit. It's a privatization of the highest order.

Yet, there is essentially <u>no government oversight of the private sector</u> at the heart of our intelligence empire. And the lines between public and <u>private have become so blurred as to be nonexistent</u>.

"You have to grasp the impending change of attitude to stay ahead of the curve and the cutting edge of the future."

Unknown

CHAPTER 1

The place: the Temple Beth Shalom, a synagogue in a predominately Jewish section of Brooklyn.

The Time: Saturday, 10: 15 A.M.

Standing motionless on the dais, Rabbi Levi Jacobs looked out at his congregation. He had just finished his sermon. He was waiting for what he thought might be the right moment to speak to them about a subject that was on everyone's mind, as well as their lips.

Standing in front of him was a wooden lectern whose countertop held a gooseneck microphone. Before he approached it, he reminded himself that his audience probably considered him as nothing more than some interim rabbi from Tel Aviv—an Israeli citizen with no particular connection to the neighborhood other than his status as a rabbi. Therefore, it would be more than advantageous for him to be sensitive to the mood of the congregation—to be respectfully aloof, and not to convey too much opinion, especially when it concerned political matters.

There were, however, a few things in his favor. First of all, he was well aware of the fact that to be a successful speaker, as well as a religious leader, you needed some

1

basic requirements.

It was somewhat imperative to have a belief in what you were saying. You also needed an understanding of what your audience wanted to hear. Another qualification was to convey the proper amount of verisimilitude. All of which he believed he had. In addition to all of that was his general appearance.

He was over six-feet-tall with a stocky build, a distinguished salt-and-pepper beard, deep soulful eyes framed by a pair of dark-rimmed glasses. In addition to all of that was how he made it a point to always wear the accepted attire: a black suit with a matching colored frock, the all-too-necessary yarmulke, and a checkered prayer shawl.

No one would ever suspect or believe he was a working member of the Israeli Secret Service—the Mossad. He had been sent to the United States to monitor and relay any information on the ongoing race for the presidency.

The two perspective nominees for the Republican Party were the senator from New York, David L. Greenberg, and his opponent, the Republican senator from California, Cameron C. Mitchel. The two men had been highly-regarded incumbents in their own states, and this was their first presidential primary.

Jacobs had been instructed to become friends with his congregation's two most noted members: the parents of the senator from New York, Dr. Louis Greenberg, and his wife Rebecca.

The Israeli government via its many connections had arranged for the former rabbi of Temple Beth to leave on an extended sabbatical to the Holy Land. This provided the opportunity to put him in his place and to carry out his clandestine assignments.

It went without saying that the entire Arab world, as well as the state of Israel, was waiting with baited breath as to the outcome of the campaign. Each side knew the election of a Jewish president could change the course of history. This was something radical Islam could not accept.

Jacobs knew if ever his presence was detected, the notoriety could easily alter the outcome of the campaign.

Without waiting any longer, Jacobs approached the lectern; before he got there, he stopped for a moment. Then, with a sideward glance, turned his head, raised one hand towards his audience, then placed the back of his other hand over his mouth and coughed.

He walked over to the microphone and tapped on it, ostensibly, to determine if it was working or not.

All the while the congregation patiently watched in respectful silence to his all too familiar gesticulations. They had seen him do similar things in the past. Most assumed he was like many rabbis. He had a few peculiar idiosyncrasies and this was his way of gaining their attention—They were right.

After excusing himself, Jacobs waited another moment before he decided to speak. He used a pronounced Israeli accent while saying:

"My dear friends, as most of you are aware, a member of our faith and this congregation is the Republican candidate . . . ah, excuse me, I meant to say the perspective nominee for the Republican Party for the presidency of the United States.

"Of course, I am speaking of none other than our own senator from New York, David L. Greenberg."

The mere mention of his name sent a ripple of excitement through the congregation. It seemed that all anyone ever talked about was the senator and his chances of becoming president.

The consensus was if America could accept a black man as their president then they could accept a Jew.

After taking a few quick sips of water from a bottle on the lectern, Jacobs was quick to say, "As an Israeli citizen, and as your interim rabbi, it is not my place to speak to you about political matters. However, since 9-11 and the events that followed, I feel I must . . . no, I feel compelled to say to you, I believe in Senator Greenberg, not only because of his religion or his politics, I believe in the man himself. I feel David Greenberg is a fair and honest person, someone of great integrity, a man of his word."

At that point, Jacobs glanced down at the area where the senator's mother and father were sitting. To his dismay, it seemed their only sign of interest was an innocuous smile.

He had been assured by members of Greenberg's entourage the senator would be there. However, for some undisclosed reason, that hadn't happened. If it had, he prepared an entirely different speech, one that he considered not so obsequious.

Jacobs didn't know the senator; however, on several occasions he tried to meet him, but failed to do so due to conflicting schedules. He wanted to get as close to the senator, and his family, as he could. By doing so he could provide them with his unique form of pro-active security.

He had been sent by the Israeli government to protect Greenberg and his family from a group of terrorist assassins who, until recently, were unknown to the Mossad, as well as any other intelligence agency.

Their presence in the United States was perfectly legal since they had valid passports and weren't on any agencies' list as possible terrorists.

His mission was a simple one: to neutralize them by any means possible before they could harm the senator or any member of his family. The hard part, of course, was he couldn't be found out, or have the Israeli government implicated in any way with the operation.

To accomplish this he was to employ the help of a private military firm called Global Solutions. He had used their services while he was stationed in Iraq. Of course, his activities were supposedly unknown to the CIA or the State Department—at least that's what he was lead to believe. If those agencies had an inkling as to what Global was up to, they most likely would have had their licenses revoked as private contractors for the U.S. government.

He was interested in two of Global's most competent "employees." A couple of ex-army guys named Anthony Robert Gordon, or ARGO as he was called, and his partner "TOJO" Grimaldi. The nickname came from Thomas Joseph; it was a Brooklyn moniker—supposedly he was in the Mafia. The idea being if you were an Italian from Brooklyn you had to be in the Mafia—although, he and Gordon had the reputation as Global's top assassins and probably some of the best anti-terrorists in the Middle East.

After a brief pause he took another sip of water and then continued by saying:

"I feel Senator Greenberg will restore the honor and dignity of the United States. He will place this country in its rightful place in the world. A place where friend and foe alike will respect its commitment to democracy and the freedom of all people."

Then, in a somewhat somber but impassioned manner, Jacobs went on to extoll the conterminous existence between the people of Israel and the people of the United States. He emphasized the historical significance of David Greenberg's candidacy while reiterating the obvious. He did this by pointing out what every person of the Jewish faith knew—as well as every Arab. If Senator Greenberg was elected, it would change the course of history and alter the stalemate of Arab-Israeli relations.

He then warned them how radical Islam would stop at nothing to undo what ever chance the senator had at being elected.

He told them they would have to be ever-vigilant to the nefarious depths that these people would go to while pronouncing their innocence. With no apparent reason he stopped in mid-sentence and slowly turned in the direction of the senator's mother and father. He raised his arm and pointed a finger in their direction.

With a hushed tone of voice he said, "I am quite sure most of you know the senator's parents: the Honorable Dr. Louis Martin Greenberg and his wife, Rebecca."

In unison most of the congregation glanced in their direction, something they would often do whenever the senator's or his parents' names were mentioned.

Sitting ominously on either side of them were two very large men. Jacobs had seen them before and assumed they were private security personnel hired by the senator.

Each man had on a pair of dark-tinted glasses and wore a grey business suit that appeared to be a little too tight in the shoulders. Hanging conspicuously from one ear of both men was a wire that went down into the collar of their suit jackets. From time to time one of the men would raise his wrist up to his lips and speak into his sleeve.

To the congregation it all seemed overly dramatic like a TV show. However, they had gotten used to seeing them every Saturday with the Greenbergs, and their presence gave everyone a feeling of security.

Before he concluded his speech, Jacobs took another sip of water from the same bottle he used before. He then pointed to the bottle and said, "Water is a precious commodity much like our resolve, so we should not waste it. We are too few in number, so we must make every effort count. Before you leave, I would like to make a few announcements. As you know, tonight at nine o'clock in the temple hall, we are having a fund raiser for the senator. I know all of you have given generously. Tonight however, as advertised in our weekly bulletin, our guest speaker will be Joseph Weinshank, the senator's campaign manager.

"He wants all of you to know how the campaign is going and would like to speak to you on the senator's thoughts concerning the future of the country and its relationship with Israel. As always there will be ample refreshments courtesy of Rosenfeld's Delicatessen on 34th Street in Brooklyn.

"There will also be a short documentary on places of interest and where to stay when visiting Israel.

"I want to thank all of you for staying. I hope to see you all tonight at 9:00 P.M. May the peace of God be with you, shalom."

With a noticeable sigh of relief from the congregation they stood up and filed into the aisle. With a united mindset, they pressed anxiously toward the open doors of the synagogue.

In the midst of the procession were the Greenbergs and their bodyguards and a trail of well-wishers in tow. Jacobs watched them leave. He would have been close by their side if he didn't have a very important engagement to attend.

He was supposed to meet with an agent from Global Solutions at an Italian restaurant in Manhattan. Besides, he was starving and looked forward to a good meal with copious amounts of wine.

CHAPTER 2

Standing not too far from the entrance to the synagogue on the opposite side of the street, was a row of parked cars. Sitting on the driver's side of one of those cars was a young man. His general appearance was quite similar to most Jewish men of his age.

He wore the customary black suit with an open-necked white shirt, black-framed glasses, a yarmulke, short beard and long side curls.

However, he was doing something that was decidedly uncharacteristic for someone of his persuasion. He was chain-smoking cigarettes then tossing them out the window onto the street by his car. His action was an obvious violation of the anti-littering law and something no respectable citizen of Brooklyn would ever do, at least not during the day.

The young man's name was Rashid Naid al-Yaya. He was an Iraqi National who had entered the United States illegally. He had purchased a fraudulent Canadian passport and student visa from a group calling itself the Islamic Canadian Brotherhood. The name on those documents was not his, but of another young man by the name of Rashid Mohammad al-Assad. The two men looked almost identical, right down to their height and weight.

Upon entering the United States, he had been transported to New York City by a group of fellow Muslims who told him they were affiliated with CAIR. The acronym stood for the Council on American-Islamic Relations.

Rashid knew little of what their purpose was, and they knew him only by his alias. while in Pakistan he had been instructed never to divulge his real name, or his true place of origin, not even to those he trusted with his life. By doing that, he protected whoever was helping him, and it made it more difficult for law enforcement to identify his remains. Also, by not knowing who he was made it almost impossible to connect him with any group or cause.

Rashid had been parked in the same place for a few hours staring out the front window of his car. He was watching as an ever-growing crowd of people began to gather on the sidewalk in front of the entrance to the temple. On previous occasions he had seen this before. From what he could make of it the people stood in front of the synagogue in hopes to see the senator and possibly shake his hand. Well, today might be their lucky day, at least he hoped so.

Amongst the many people he saw were a few newspaper photographers with their distinctive cache of cameras and press cards that dangled from chains around their necks—the sight of which led him to look down at his own camera that hung from a lanyard around his neck. On the same strap was a fraudulent identity card with his alias name and picture of him with the word "Press" above it.

While he sat there contemplating the appearance of the senator, a flood of thoughts and recollections crossed his mind. He remembered his family and the tragedy of their untimely deaths. He saw the faces of his mother and father and his older brother.

They had been taken from him as he sat in school,

unaware and hopelessly naïve that such a thing could ever occur. They were the innocent victims of what the United States Air Force called an "errant bomb." At least that was their explanation for such a disastrous event. A common mistake at that time in the war the Americans called "Iraqi" Freedom.

They were thoughtful enough to give him a considerate sum of money as recompense for the loss of his family. Mentally he spit on such a thought as if anything could ever replace them.

He used the money to go to Pakistan to be with an uncle who was an imam at a mosque outside Lahore, the capital of Pakistan. His uncle was also one of the leaders of a devout group of Muslims who called themselves "The Lashkar-e-Taiba, the Army of the Pure."

Within the confines of one of their camps were his mosque and a madrassas for studying the scripture of the Holy Koran. It was there that he received his training in the art and purpose of Holy Jihad. In time he found out that the group he studied with were members of "Al-Qaeda" (in Arabic, the base). It was a fact that he most admired and wanted to emulate. He made it known to them that he wanted to adopt their politics and beliefs while he conducted his studies of the Holy Scriptures. With those thoughts, he nodded his head and said a prayer for the continuation of Islamic consciousness, the "TAGWA."

He remembered the night as if it were yesterday that his uncle brought him aside and told him he was to be a martyr for Allah and Holy Islam. He had been chosen above all others for a purpose of paramount importance— the details of which would only be told to him as needed.

He could see his uncle with his head bowed and his hand upon his shoulder with the moonlight shining down into the courtyard in front of the mosque, how he stressed upon him that failure to complete this "fatwa" (Arabic for a legal degree) was not an option.

He recalled how his uncle explained to him the way he was selected. He remembered him saying that it was his study of the Holy Koran that set him apart from the others. His uncanny ability to recite from memory its most difficult passages proved he was exceptional with superior skills.

Another part of the selection process was based on the unspoken belief that he had not slept with a woman or a man—that he was pure.

"Praise be to God," he said to himself as he mumbled a short prayer.

By being pure of heart, he was allowed to receive the solemn vow of "Shahada," the Muslim profession of faith. He was considered by all who knew him to be of superior orthodoxy, a devout follower of the Islamic law of "Shariah." He was considered to be a "Sahabah," a true companion of Muhammad.

"Allah, be praised," he whispered for such a consideration as tears came to his eyes.

Suddenly, without anticipation, a feeling of forlornness settled over him. He couldn't help but think there should be more to life than what he planned on doing.

He thought of how other members of the faith did not conduct their lives as he did. His only anodyne for his misgivings was the knowledge that they were not one of the chosen. He knew above all else to give one's life for Islam in Holy Jihad was to live forever in immortality, so to this end he had pledged his soul.

His one remaining concern was that he wanted it to end, to be free from all that it entailed, free of the anxiety of contemplation. In some complex way his thoughts of death had edged itself into his consciousness as a symbol for his purpose of eternal life, the thought of which still chilled his soul.

He knew he had to dismiss what he knew of life and transform his thoughts so as to find his happiness elsewhere. Of course, the only way that could be done was to accept death and revel in the glory of its finality.

Without further reflection, he knew the moment of truth had arrived. He rolled up the driver's side window and then checked the time on the watch his father had given him.

He swallowed a few deep breaths, then, without any sense of caution, stepped blindly into the street.

As fate would have it, a passing motorist nearly ended his life, but swerved just in time. The man blew his horn wildly as he went by cursing and shouting while he waved his middle finger in Rashid's direction.

After he regained some of his composure, Rashid crossed the street to the sidewalk that led past the entrance to the synagogue.

As he made his way towards the crowd that had gathered in front of the temple, he could feel a great sense of calm pass over him. He had been told to expect such reverie, that it was the presence of Allah guiding his every footstep.

No one seemed to notice his presence as he sidled his way amongst them. While he stood there being as unobtrusive as he could, he began to think why he hated them and their cursed religion. How they had killed his family and friends. The Jews, the Christians they had desecrated the Holy Koran and blasphemed at the name of Allah.

How indeed was he a stranger in a strange land. His only friend was the one he was wearing: his explosive vest filled with 30 lbs. of C-4 and ball bearings.

With monk-like resolve, he waited for the senator and his family to appear. Through the darkness of his muse he noticed a man staring in his direction. The man did not appear to be part of the crowd. He looked quite formidable and aware of what was happening around him.

He had been forewarned that the senator and his family were being protected by some unknown security force. He had been given strict orders to detonate his device if he thought his capture was at all imminent.

Rashid tried not to look at the man. He could feel his knees get weak and his stomach tighten as beads of sweat covered his forehead.

What he had no way of knowing was there were security agents posted on different roof tops around the synagogue. With the use of powerful binoculars, they scanned the neighborhood searching for anything unusual or out of place. They were in constant communication with the other members of their detail inside the temple, as well as the ones outside.

Suddenly, at the doors of the synagogue, a throng of parishioners jostled their way across the threshold. They rushed down the steps into a small crowd of well-wishers asking them if Senator Greenberg was inside. The crowd stepped aside as the senator's elderly parents walked towards the street and a waiting limousine.

Rashid saw that the senator wasn't with them; however, his parents were directly in front of him and that was good enough. He also saw two men try to shield them with their bodies. Out of the corner of his eye he noticed the man who had been staring in his direction pushing his way towards him.

With the deftness of someone who had practiced for this moment countless times, Rashid reached inside his jacket pocket. The inside lining had been removed allowing him free access to the detonating device of his vest.

His last words were, "Allahu Akbar" (God is great) as he felt the pressure of an outstretched hand grab at his shoulder—he flipped the switch.

CHAPTER 3

Sitting in the solemn atmosphere of a dimly-lit room was David L. Greenberg. He sat in a chair behind an ornately carved desk of African Blackwood, the most expensive of its kind. It was a gift from his wife Etta; she had given it to him for their tenth wedding anniversary.

Across from him sat Irwyn C. Roth, a life-long friend and chief counsel for his hedge fund, The Delaware Group. Both men were staring at a large-screen television set, seemingly transfixed at what they were watching.

Greenberg used his remote to channel surf, stopping only at news stations for whatever they said or showed of the bombing. Without saying a word, he turned off the sound, only to sit there, rocking back and forth as he drummed his fingertips on the top of his desk.

The two men had just returned from the funeral for David's parents. He had fulfilled the tenets of the Orthodox Jewish religion and buried them within 48 hours of their death.

Both men were dressed in similar attire: a black suit, white shirt open at the neck, and a black yarmulke. However, that was where the similarity ended.

David L., as he was often called, was six feet, two

inches tall, with a dark tan and a trim athletic build. He had salt-and-pepper hair, an engaging smile, with a thin nose cosmetically altered by one of Manhattan's leading plastic surgeons.

It was well understood that David L. had it all: the money, the looks and charisma to burn. He carried himself with an air of what the French would say, a *"soi-disant"*— his own self style.

On the other hand, his friend Irwyn, or Wyn as David L. would often refer to him as, wasn't as fortunate.

He was short, noticeably bald, and overweight, with a slight speech impediment that manifested itself in the form of a stress-induced stammer. Those facts, along with a few others, left him in dire need for female reassurance and ego enhancement.

This could have been construed as mitigating factors for his inordinate desire to seek the company of young girls. To go along with that predilection was the cumbersome fact that he was married with two teenage daughters.

He worked in a high-profile business as a corporate attorney where discretion and apparently honesty was of the utmost importance. In addition to all of that, his wife was a favorite cousin of David L.

All of this left Roth in a state of elevated vigilance that bordered on paranoid distraction. He had spent a considerable amount of money trying to keep what he did a secret and was relatively sure no one was aware of his "extracurricular activities."

While looking down at the floor, Roth slowly massaged the back of his neck. Without saying a word, he stood up, pretended to stretch, turned his head in the direction of the television set and pointed to it:

"David, why are you watching this?" he asked, his question sounding more in line with a tone of commiseration that being evocative.

With his mind still reeling from the storm of

emotional events that rocked his world, Greenberg stood up, glowered at Roth and said:

"Because I fuckin' want to—that's why." He let the tone of his voice convey more than his words, something he often did whenever his actions were questioned.

He reached down and picked up a Zippo lighter from his desk. The Zippo was the same one his father had used when he was a doctor in Vietnam. His father had given it to him after he had won the senatorial seat for New York. He had wanted that lighter ever since he was a kid and now it held more significance than before.

As Roth went to sit down, he apologized—for what, he wasn't sure. He often did that around people he was familiar with. It was one of those foibles he wished he could control.

In a display of subdued anger, Greenberg glanced over at Roth, held his gaze for a moment, then snapped open the lid of the Zippo and lit a cigarette. He had been trying to quit; it just wasn't PC to be a smoker, especially if you were seeking the highest office in the land.

After exhaling a draft of smoke, Greenberg said, "Sorry, Wyn, you know . . . I guess I'm kind of out of it."

With genuine sorrow in his voice Roth replied, "Yeah, I sure know how you feel. I feel the same way, too. Your parents were closer to me than my own. I still can't believe they're gone."

Roth was well aware of his friend's mercurial moods—how the man could go from being the nicest person you would ever want to meet, to being a cold, remorseless prick.

While they stood there talking, Greenberg poured himself a drink from an open bottle of scotch. The bottle was sitting on a silver tray his mother had given him on his last birthday—off to the side of it was a container of ice cubes.

With a ceremonious flair, Greenberg used a pair of silver tongs to drop a few cubes in his drink. He then raised his glass up to his lips, leaned forward and looked at Roth.

"So, how are Sharon and Lisa doing these days?" he asked, all the while using his index finger to mix his drink. "Oh, I'm sorry. I guess I just forgot. You know how that is, you sort of forget people when you have other things on your mind."

Roth bent forward and pretended to brush some imaginary lint from his pant leg. He didn't like the atmosphere, nor the tone of the conversation. He wanted to go home and have a cocktail and smoke a cigar. He was extremely tired; it had been a harrowing few days. Normally, Roth wouldn't think anything of his friend's question; nevertheless, it was still kind of peculiar since they had just talked to them at the funeral.

Without waiting for a reply Greenberg added:

"Oh, yes, I almost forgot. How's your wife. I'm sorry . . . I mean Silvia?" He followed his question with a quizzical expression, as if there was something else that needed to be said.

"Ah, I . . . I guess she's just fine . . .. You know we just saw her and the kids a few hours ago."

"Well, David," Roth said, "I think both of us have a lot on our minds. I agree with you. I wish I could spend more time with Silvia and the girls. You know I've been real busy lately with the Lloyd Monroe account, he was one of Cliff Van Dameer's victims—the guy lost millions."

"Yeah, that's too bad about all of that. It kind of puts a lot of extra heat on us and everyone else. The SEC has been knocking on my door 24/7. Say, would you like a drink?"

"No, no, I've been trying to slow down; alcohol makes me tired. My doctor thinks I'm pre-diabetic."

"Sorry to hear that," Greenburg replied. "Pre-diabetic, huh? Well, you can never be careful enough when it comes to your health."

"You know, David, your mother and father would

want you to go on, no matter what. You are going to stay in the race, aren't you?"

"Maybe, so; I'm not really sure right now."

"Well, I guess it's up to you," murmured Roth.

The two men stood there for a moment staring at the television, as flashes of different scenes from the bombing crossed the screen.

"Well," Roth said, "I guess I should leave you alone. I'm feeling kind of tired; I should get home."

At first Greenberg didn't answer. He just stood there staring at the glass in his hand, "Well, David," said Roth, "if there's anything I can do for you, you know, anything, uh . . . just ask; you know I-I'm here for you."

"Hey, thanks, Wyn; you're my best friend."

"I hope so."

"Oh, there is a . . . something . . . maybe you can do," Greenberg said as he stirred his drink.

"Just n-name it."

"Well, Wyn; it's like this—I want justice."

"Justice," Roth said, squinting his eyes as he pronounced the word. "How . . . what kind of justice? I mean, like, the guy . . . is dead."

Roth searched his friend's face for some kind of clue as to what he had in mind.

"It's not really justice," Greenberg said. "I want . . . you know, like in the Bible, revenge . . . an eye-for-an-eye type of revenge."

As he finished his sentence, he swallowed the last of his drink, then poured another.

"R-r-revenge?" Roth asked incredulously. "Like in the Bible. David, listen to me; you don't know what you're saying. Jeez, David, I understand how you f-feel and all, but don't go jeopardizing everything with something crazy. Y-you'll . . . end up in fuckin' jail for Christ's sake."

"Not if we do it right," Greenberg said.

"We! Who the hell is we? You mean you and me?"

"None other," replied Greenberg as he lit another

cigarette.

"Are you f-fuckin' crazy . . . you mean-you and me? . . . What are we supposed to do? Go around New York City, shooting at every fuckin' Arab we see?"

"Something like that, but we're not the ones who will be pulling the trigger."

"Oh, is that so? Well, answer me this. Who the hell is going to be doing it?"

"Eric Lowe."

"Eric Lowe, Eric Lowe. You mean that crazy guy from Global Solutions?"

"The same," replied Greenberg as he crushed out the cigarette he had just lit.

"He was at your last PAC meeting. I remember talking to him. He had scary eyes and a funny k-kind of a twitch." Roth sat down shaking his head from side-to-side. "David, do-do you know what you're doing? I hope you haven't said anything to him."

"No, not yet, but . . . I plan to. Well, not me exactly, but you can. I mean you can take him a message for me."

"Not me," Roth answered, his voice an octave higher. "What makes you think I would have anything to do with this?"

"Teresa Williams and her daughter, Natisha, and maybe this CD of you together."

"Who?! Who?! What are you saying?" Roth screeched. "Are you trying to blackmail me? . . .. You had me followed."

"Stop," David L. answered. "I've known about your little dalliances for a long time. When someone works for me and their actions threaten my business, well, I take it seriously . . . you get my point?"

"You son of a bitch . . . y-you had me followed—I'm your best friend."

"Take it easy," Greenberg replied. "I'm not blackmailing you, and stop yelling at me. You know I can't get involved. Don't worry; you'll only act as a messenger and nothing else. Hey, look at it this way, for your assistance I'll give you the biggest bonus you ever had."

"What is this? . . . A bribe? A fuckin' bribe?"

"Call it what you want—I need your help."

"You really are something else—you know that," Roth replied as he poured himself a drink.

"Go home, Wyn. Go home, think it over. Oh, before you leave, you remember Rabbi Levi Jacobs?"

"Yes, of course . . . so, what about him?"

"Well, he isn't a rabbi."

"Oh, yeah? Then what the fuck is he?" Roth asked, his voice an angry rasp of sarcasm.

"He's Mossad."

"Mossad, Mossad. Are you . . . s-serious?"

"Listen to me," Greenberg said. "Listen to me; it's like this." He then went on to explain Jacobs' connection to the Israeli Secret Service and his involvement with Global Solutions and Eric Lowe.

He told him that Jacobs explained how there would be future attempts on his life and the lives of his wife and children. To be safe, his only option was to either drop out of the race and leave the country or fight back.

"Like how?" Roth asked, as he lit another cigarette.

"Well, according to Jacobs, I could eliminate the terrorists who planned the attack on the synagogue."

"As in you could kill them?"

"That's the idea," replied Greenberg. He then went on to tell him that it would cost a lot of money. The point was he was willing to spend it. It would also take the cooperation of certain political friends and a number of clandestine connections.

"Why didn't you say something to me before? I would do anything to-to protect you and your family."

"I would have, but I wanted you to know how I felt about your . . . what you were doing. I was so goddamned pissed at you. Do you know what kind of fucking scandal it would have caused if you were found out?"

Greenberg turned away then walked over to a window and stared at the Atlantic Ocean. He had one of the most expensive mansions in the Hamptons and, like everything else, its views were spectacular.

He stood there for a moment or two then turned to face Roth. "I hope," he said, "that I don't find out you're mixed up in any kind of . . . you know, child pornography."

"So help me, God, David; I'm not. My God, you have to believe me."

"Okay, I believe you, but you understand that your behavior suggests that . . . suspicion."

Roth's eyes teared up as he turned his head.

"Take it easy, Wyn. You know you could have cost me a lot of money. So, what are you going to do about it?"

"I'll stop . . . I'll stop."

"Good," Greenberg said. "So, go home and get some rest . . . you don't look so good."

As Roth was leaving he felt as if a giant weight had been lifted from his shoulders.

When he went to open the door he stopped for a moment, turned and waved at David L. It was more of a salute to tell him he could count on him. With that gesture, he closed the door behind him.

Once again Greenberg sat down and mulled over his friend's transgressions. The son-of-a-bitch was a liar and a fraud—that was something he could put up with. "Hell," he thought, "so was he—as a politician you had to be." The pedophile thing was over-the-top. He hated even the thought of them. If he could he would put a bullet in every "pickle smoocher" there was. However, he knew he couldn't, but he knew of someone who could and would, if the price was right. All he had to do was pick up the phone and send a check—that was something he was more than willing and able to do.

Unfortunately, before he attempted to do what he planned, he needed to grease a few very big wheels. He could do that by giving some very sizable donations in the form of PAC money to a few senators for their up-and-coming re-elections.

There was one in particular, a senator from West Virginia named Harlan Oates. He had close ties to the FBI and the Justice Department. It was crucial that these two agencies did the right thing and stayed out of the way.

However, he was sure of one thing, that money and politics were inexorably intertwined. It was a panacea that cured all ills and Washington had a permanent prescription for it.

CHAPTER 4

For Senator Harlan Oates, the rain that pelted the windshield of his Cadillac Escalade was an uncomfortable reminder of his responsibilities to the citizens of his state.

On his mind were two things: the flooded vicinities of West Virginia and what FEMA was doing to help the victims of those storm-ravaged areas.

There was something else that bothered him. Why was he sitting alone in a parking lot of a 7-11 waiting for someone who used to work for the CIA?

His name was Stanley Hamilton—a fairly reserved, well-dressed, good-looking young man who never seemed to smile. This would be their second meeting. Their first had taken place in his car in Washington, D.C. The funny thing about that: it was raining on that day, too.

He found the coincidence to be somewhat unnerving, maybe ominous, but not problematic—God he hated that word. His "reason" for meeting Hamilton, now _that_ was problematic.

The circumstances of the situation were such that he and a few of his fellow senators had gotten together and agreed something "drastic" had to be done to reduce the threat of terrorism in the United States and elsewhere.

To initiate their plan they would use the resources of an NGO (a non-governmental organization). The idea was to help facilitate the work of the CIA, Homeland Defense and the FBI.

It would be the first time such a group would work within the United States. They would be of such secrecy that only he and the other senators who were involved would know of their existence and what they were attempting to do. Hopefully, the NGO would insulate them and the perspective agencies from the possibility of any legal scrutiny or accusations.

To help solidify that thought would be the advent of no money or paper trails to follow. All transactions or communications would be done face-to-face or by encrypted text messaging. It was kind of a low and high-tech approach to "stymie" the world of government surveillance.

He thought about his Cadillac, how it had been equipped with the latest electronic gadgetry, the type that could detect the use of any device that might be used to record his voice or visual image. The system was good both inside and out; therefore, it would render his meeting with Hamilton a certain amount of anonymity, or at least he hoped so.

Suddenly there was the sound of a reverberating rap against his passenger side window; it startled him into an immediate response. He reached down and pushed the button that would release the door lock on the other side of his car. After sliding into the seat next to Oates, Stanley Hamilton reached over and closed the door. Within that same movement he placed his folded umbrella on the floor beside him.

He then turned to face Oates, extended his hand and said, "Good afternoon, Senator. Nice to see you again; bad patch of weather you're having."

With a soft southern drawl Oates replied, "Yes, sir, raining harder than a cow "pissin'" on a flat rock."

"Is that so? Well, I guess I never really noticed."

He didn't know much about Oates other than he was a "do-gooder millionaire Democrat," with a "good ol' boy" demeanor and a sharper-than-a-tack mind.

As to be expected, he was like so many of his kind: a hypocrite—saying one thing and yet doing another. He also ran the usual political scam of supporting whatever it was that would get him re-elected; of course, that takes money—something all politicians needed. This time his gut feeling told him that Oates might be into something beyond the customary political bullshit.

The two men sat for a while just talking, sort of reacquainting themselves with one another's visual patterns of expression and voice inflections. They used some arcane references and subtle nuances to get their point across. It was the kind of conversation Hamilton was used to, where no one said what they meant or meant what they said. It was a way of doing business while attempting to "cover your ass."

The CIA had let him go for just such palaver, of using his own interpretations of certain directives and agency protocol. To him it was nothing but a bunch of "ho-hum, whatevers." However, he understood their way of thinking: no loose cannons, no loose ends. "Hey," he thought, "not all of us can be a Stansfield Turner."

Since his dismissal from the agency, Hamilton had started his own security and investigative agency. He enjoyed the autonomy of being your own boss and used his former contacts to further his own interests. It was through one of those connections that put him in touch with Oates.

"Do you know who Eric and Conrad Lowe are?" Oates asked.

"Yes, sir! I'm aware of who they are. They're the CEO's of Global Solutions and the World Enforcement Bureau. They're both private military firms or, as of now, they're referred to as . . . uh, security companies."

"Well! Uh, you're . . . kind of right," Oates replied. "The World Enforcement Bureau is mostly an international detective agency."

"I didn't know that," answered Hamilton. Of course, he didn't feel like saying he did.

"No matter . . . I want you to go to their headquarters . . . sort of introduce yourself. Of course you're not to mention my name. You got that? Are we clear on that?"

"Yes, sir, quite clear."

"When you, uh . . . get there, you sort of suggest that uh, you know . . . certain, uh, arrangements can be made in their behalf. That is, if they're agreeable or not."

"Yes, sir," replied Hamilton, "but, will they know what it is I'm talking about?"

"I think so; your brother Lloyd will fill you in on the details."

"Excuse me. Did you say my brother?"

"That's right," Oates said. "You remember him, don't cha? Your brother Lloyd?"

"Oooh, right. I kind of forgot about him," replied Hamilton. "I have other brothers. Lloyd and I . . . well, we don't see one another often."

"Is that so?" answered Oates. "Well, something tells me that you and Lloyd will see more of one another in the future." He then reached up and removed a manila envelope from his overhead visor.

"Say! You know what extrajudicial intervention is?" he asked.

Stanley looked over at Oates searching his expression for the appropriate answer. As he took the envelope from Oates's hand, he nodded his head. "Well, sir, it's a form of legal defense. We called it—that is the company called it—selective intervention or a green light."

"A green light, huh . . . you know what? I kinda like that . . . a green light."

Hamilton didn't bother to reply; instead, he removed a plastic bag from his jacket and placed the envelope inside. He already knew its contents: $20,000 in European currency.

"Thanks," said Hamilton as he slipped the plastic bag inside his jacket, adjusting the pocket to make sure the bag was secure.

"Well, a deal is a deal," Oates said.

With an indiscernible murmur Hamilton replied, "Amen to that." However, underneath his outward nonchalance Hamilton knew he had just stepped over the line. He had done it in the past, and yet it still left him apprehensive.

"Before you leave," said Oates, "when you see your brother tell him there are two more names for him to look into."

"Okay, and, uh . . . does he know?"

"What? Does he know what?" Oates asked with a perturbed voice.

"Well, all I'm saying . . . this entails . . . I mean . . ."

"Maybe," Oates said. "Does it matter?"

"No, not really," replied Hamilton. "Uh, when is my brother going to contact me?"

"Soon. Maybe not tomorrow, but soon . . . you'll probably get some kinda text message to meet him somewhere."

"Well, sir, it's been a pleasure meeting with you," Hamilton said, as he extended his hand.

"Oh. Looking forward to see you again," he added.

Oates looked away as if he was considering his choices. "About our next meeting," he replied, "well, I really don't know . . . uh, when that will be. I guess we'll cross that bridge when we get to it. You take care, you hear? Drive careful . . . roads are pretty bad."

With an emphatic nod of his head Hamilton said, "Yes, sir! I'll take your advice. You know me; I'm always careful."

Once again Hamilton shook Oates's hand then turned and opened the passenger side door and stepped out into the deluge.

He looked up at the sky, popped open his umbrella and walked hurriedly in the direction of his car. The wind and rain lashed against him as a clap of thunder followed in his footsteps. He had a lot on his mind, the least of which was the weather and yet he couldn't ignore the obviousness of its implications.

CHAPTER 5

At a nondescript building outside of Charlotte, North Carolina, was the world headquarters of Global Solutions: the home of one of the premiere private military companies in the United States.

Sitting at his desk in a room filled with military memorabilia and mementos of his past was retired army colonel Eric Lowe. He along with his brother Conrad were its cofounders; they had been in business since 1998. Eric was the CEO of Global and Conrad was the CEO of their subsidiary, the World Enforcement Bureau or the W.E.B., an international detective agency. Ever since the Iraq War they had seen their business multiply many times over. However, business was off due to the withdrawal of the troops in 2010.

As usual Eric went over to a large full-length mirror to see how he looked. He was dressed in his daily attire of a heavily-starched camouflage uniform and a pair of glossy patent leather jump boots. Around his waist was a shiny black leather belt with a flap-covered, military- styled holster. It held a 1911-56 automatic pistol with a scrolled walnut grip and gold inlay etched into the slide. It was a gift from a Saudi prince during Operation Desert Storm.

Resting on his desk was a manila folder containing his business itinerary for the day. Along with his schedule there were encrypted notes and papers concerning sensitive business issues.

Off to his side were a laptop computer and a coffee mug with the words: "trust nothing but guilt" written along the side of it. On its screen was a e-mail from his wife Charlene; it read: "Mystery and reality often come from the same source."

He smiled at her notes of arcane advice and axiomatic wisdom. He remembered how he once told her that if love was blind he hoped never to regain his sight. She was the only person he never took for granted and the only woman he ever truly loved.

Hanging from the wall behind him was a framed, autographed picture of George W. Bush.

Standing off to the side in one corner of the room was an American flag. It was attached to a wooden stanchion with a golden eagle at the top. In the other corner on the other side was a Special Forces flag. It hung from a metal pole with the blade of a spear at its peak. The symbolic significance being that they were considered the tip of the spear: the first to go into combat.

On that same side of the room was an array of assorted photographs. They were of him shaking hands with various dignitaries, both civilian and military alike.

Nestled amongst those pictures was a framed license issued by the State Department. It gave Global Solutions the authorization to conduct business as a private military contractor to assist the United States Army while in Iraq.

As he read over his list of appointments, Lowe saw a one o'clock meeting with his brother Conrad and two other men. One of them was Lloyd Hamilton, a man he had met before. The other was labeled as unknown. Not an unusual occurrence when you considered the nature of the military contracting business and the people in it.

Lloyd Hamilton was a supposed representative for

some undisclosed business in the D.C. area, who, under further investigation, turned out to be a representative for a major lobbyist named Blaze Odom. He was a former congressman from Georgia with a controlling interest in a private military company called Mantis, Ltd.; they had just obtained a $1.7 billion contract with the Department of Defense.

As he sat there mulling over that thought, Eric glanced at his watch; it was six past one.

"Son-of-a-bitch," he mumbled. "They should have been here by noon." If there was one thing he couldn't abide was being late. Of course, he had become used to it dealing with civilians and all.

On the other hand, his brother had no excuse. He was ex-military; however, he did it as a form of one-upmanship and as a way of getting you off your game. He made a mental note of the infraction then let it go to be referenced at some future date.

Another point of consideration was Conrad had been a senior intelligence officer, a major in the air force and graduated from their academy. In addition to that, he had also worked for the CIA in their National Clandestine Service Division. A fortunate occurrence he thought when he reflected on the type of business they were in.

In a reflective mood, Lowe sat there thinking about his brother, then began to notice and admire the timepiece that adorned his wrist. It was a recent gift from his good friend Senator Harlan Oates of West Virginia—Gold Rolex Daytona, an Oyster Perpetual with the inscription "Much Success" engraved on the back; success he thought, could only be measured by one thing—money.

With a sudden sense of annoyance, he stood and marched abruptly over to his office window. From there he caught sight of his brother, Lloyd Hamilton and someone else strolling leisurely in the direction of his building.

For some unknown reason, seeing the three of them

brought to mind something his father used to say that hell was filled with men who thought they were doing the right thing, and the path they took to get there was paved with good intentions.

He went back to his desk, lifted the receiver of his phone, then pressed one of its many buttons. He told his secretary that his brother and two other men were on their way up and to let them through unannounced and unrecorded.

Within the allotted amount of time he had given them to pass through security and to ride up in the elevator, Lowe heard what he expected: his brother's familiar knock at the door. The first to emerge was his brother Conrad followed by Lloyd Hamilton, then the so-called unknown visitor.

As they came through the door, he stood up to greet them making it a point to look as pleasant as possible as they shook hands. A sharp contrast to his usual gruff and somewhat unaccommodating demeanor—a persona he had developed while attending West Point and 25 years in the army.

While they were shaking hands, Eric made a quick study of his unknown visitor. To him the man appeared to be in his mid-forties, good-looking, well-dressed— distinguished with the obvious air of an elitist. The type you might see at any white-shoe legal firm. The kind that didn't cater to Negroes or Jews.

Conrad introduced him as Lloyd's brother Stanley. He made it a point to say that he wasn't associated with Lloyd's place of employment. It was his way of warning him to be cautious as to what he said or alluded to.

At the conclusion of their amenities, Eric motioned for the two brothers to sit in the chairs facing his desk. Conrad stood behind them where he couldn't be seen—an obvious gesture of disrespect, yet something he would often do if he thought it necessary.

"Well, gentlemen, what can I do for you?" Eric asked.

"First, Colonel, I would like to thank you for seeing us on such short notice."

Eric smiled, "No bother; the pleasure is all mine."

"Well, let me say that this visit is a way of an introduction. My brother has told me that you are a businessman first and a soldier second. Is he right?" questioned Stanley.

"Could be! Depending, of course, on the circumstances of the situation."

"Well, Colonel," replied Stanley, "let me see. How should I put this? Uh, this might be one of those, uh, circumstances or situations, but . . . before we get started, I have a request."

Lowe rocked back in his chair then took a moment before he answered. "A request," he said, then with an inquisitive tone he asked, "and that request would be . . . what?"

Stanley fixed his gaze on Lowe. "I would like to sweep your office . . . if you don't mind, that is."

Eric came forward placing his forearms on his desk then stared at Hamilton. "You want to do what?" he asked.

"Sweep your office . . . I mean . . . that is . . . if you don't mind."

"Oh, I don't mind," Lowe answered, "but, correct me if I'm wrong. I didn't see you walk in carrying a broom. So, how pray tell are you going to sweep my office?"

Stanley countered by reaching into his jacket pocket to produce what appeared to be a cell phone with a telescoping antenna.

"With this," he said showing the device to Lowe.

In a voice that belied more anger than curiosity, Lowe asked, "How did you get that in here?"

"Well, Colonel, it's almost entirely made of plastic, and my pocket is lined with a substance that . . . uh, deters metal detection."

"Is that so? Any chance of you telling me what that

substance is?"

"Well, sir, not right now . . . maybe, later . . . I mean at some later date." Hamilton flipped a button on his counter surveillance unit then stood up and pulled out its antenna.

"Hey, be my guest," Lowe said. "You won't find anything, no bugs, no video cameras—*nada*."

"Sorry about all this, Colonel," said Stanley's brother. "I didn't know he was going to do that."

"That's okay . . . no harm done. Your brother is a . . . cautious man," said Conrad Lowe. He then stepped forward to stand next to his brother's desk.

After a few minutes Stanley sat down then put the unit in his jacket pocket. He straightened his tie, coughed into his fist, feigned a smile then looked at Lowe.

"Everything satisfactory?" Eric asked.

Stanley nodded his head then said:

"Sorry, Colonel, but you understand that I'm just a messenger and what I have to say comes from another source."

"No, Mr. Hamilton, I didn't know that . . . how could I . . . did you, Conrad?"

His brother turned his head from side to side. "No . . . I didn't . . . but, maybe?"

Eric interrupted him by saying, "Go ahead, Stanley, please continue. I suppose, that is . . . I guess you're not at liberty to reveal that source . . . are you?"

"Not really, Colonel . . . I'm kind of . . ."

Conrad leaned forward, held up his hand as he looked at Stanley, then sat on the edge of his brother's desk.

"Sorry to interrupt," he said. "My brother and I haven't the slightest idea of what it is you want. You're here as a matter of courtesy to . . . your brother Lloyd. So, if you don't mind . . . maybe we should discuss whatever it is you're interested in—you know . . . at some future date."

While reaching into a box of Cohiba cigars, Eric said:

"Take it easy, Rad, maybe we should listen to what

Stanley here . . . has to say. Who knows, he could be selling something we might want to buy."

With that being said, Lowe lit his cigar then puffed a stream of smoke in Stanley's direction.

"Sure, why not?!" uttered Conrad.

"Well, as I was about to say," said Stanley, "you are aware that your business like so many others needs contracts. So, to that measure, I'm at liberty to say, for you, that is, it could be a *'fait de complete.'"* — (a completed fact)

Peering through an exhaled cloud of smoke, Eric replied:

"I think the correct phrase is a *'fait accompli'* (an accomplished fact) . . . no matter, please continue," he entwined.

"Well, sir, my French is a little rusty."

"No need to apologize . . . I'm listening," answered Lowe.

He then picked up a pen and flipped open the cover of his manila folder—an obvious gesture of intimidation toward Lloyd and his brother. The idea being he might jot down whatever was said—a flagrant violation of decorum in a meeting of this type.

"Sorry, Colonel, I can't go on with that pen in your hand."

"Oh! I'm sorry," replied Lowe as he placed the pen he was holding on his desk.

"I didn't know . . . please continue."

"Well, sir, the future of the PMC industry, or the 'circuit,' is under congressional scrutiny. The main concern is . . ."

After sitting on the edge of his brother's desk, Conrad said, "Is what?" swinging his leg in obvious annoyance as to what Stanley Hamilton had said.

"Well, for starters," Stanley replied, "uh, like the defense contract auditing agency over in Smyrna, or for that matter . . . POGO."

"Say, what?" Conrad asked.

"You know, uh, the Project On Government Oversight."

"Oh, that POGO," replied Conrad as he threw a glancing smile at his brother.

"Yeah, that's the one alright," Stanley said. "They're looking into private military firms for fraud and noncompliance. At least that's what I've been told."

"You mean corporate whistleblowers?" Eric asked.

"Well, kind of, to name just a few," replied Stanley.

Both Eric and his brother knew the game, the innuendo: either do what we say or run the risk of being shut down. Of course, pretense and obfuscation was the coin of the realm in the shady world of private military firms.

"Okay," asked Conrad, "what is it you want us to do?"

"Not much—my brother Lloyd can fill you in on the details."

Lloyd went on to explain how he and Stanley were interested in the possibility of a feasibility study on a select group of people.

"And, of course, with the possibility of a completion," said Stanley.

"A completion?" Eric asked as he puffed on his cigar.

"Yes," replied Stanley, "or, to put it another way: a 'green light.'"

"A green light—whatever that is. You know, Mr. Hamilton, I haven't a clue as to what you're talking about. However, I'm sure . . . uh, you and Lloyd can explain it to my brother Conrad. He handles minutiae better than I do."

"Of course," answered Stanley. "I think maybe that should be left up to my brother. He's far better at details than I am. Isn't that right, Lloyd?"

His brother glanced over at him and said:

"If you say so." He then stood up abruptly and stated,

"Uh, you know, not to be rude, but . . . I think my brother and I will be going. I'll be in touch, Colonel . . . sorry for the inconvenience. . . . You ready, Stanley?" he asked.

"I'm with you."

Lloyd looked at Conrad and said:

"I'll be talking to you, Major. . . . So, Stanley, are you ready or what?"

Following his brother's lead, Stanley stood up. "Sure thing," he said. He then gazed over at Eric Lowe. "You know, Colonel," he stated, "when the irrational is slighted, the unreasonable takes its place."

"Oh, to be sure," answered Lowe. "I take it then you're a student of Edmond Burke?"

"No, not really," replied Stanley. "I just like quotes whether their appropriate or not."

Using a tinge of unmistakable sarcasm, Lowe replied:

"An admirable quality."

"Well, Colonel . . . it's, uh, been a pleasure . . . hope to see you in the near future."

"Major, it's been nice meeting you. So, until we meet again, I hope both of you have a nice day."

"And you have a better one," said Eric Lowe, as he stood up to shake hands with Stanley and his brother. The two men shook hands with him and then with his brother. As they walked towards the office door, Conrad said:

"Oh, I forgot. A Sgt. Matthews will be escorting you back to the parking lot."

"Hey, Stanley," Eric asked, "before you leave, you mind telling me where you went to school? College, that is."

"Well, you know what, Colonel? I really can't do that. I can't divulge any personal facts about myself. My brother can—although, he's been asked not to. Of course, I realize you have your ways of finding out."

Then with a conciliatory smile and a wave of his hand he followed his brother Lloyd out the door.

After watching the door close behind them, Eric sat

down and looked over at Conrad. He then picked up his cigar that had been smoldering in his Special Forces ashtray, took a quick puff then slowly crushed it out. With a look of disgust Conrad sat down in the chair previously vacated by Lloyd Hamilton.

"Do you mind telling me what the fuck that was about?" Eric asked.

"Beats the hell out of me," replied Conrad. "But! I'll tell you what. You can bet your ass I'll find out."

"Is that so?! Well, I certainly hope so because that guy and his supposed brother are trouble we don't need. He's either from the fuckin' FBI or the CIA or . . .!"

"Or from a hundred other government agencies," snapped Conrad. He then stood up and walked behind the chair he had been sitting in. Before he decided to say what was on his mind, he leaned over the back of the chair and watched his brother shuffle through some of the papers in his manila folder.

"You mind telling me what the hell you're looking for?" he asked.

"Ah, it's this . . . I mean I have a letter here somewhere . . . it's a newspaper article about Van Dameer."

"I already read it. By the way, I've got something for you, too."

"Like what?" Eric asked as he handed Conrad the article he was looking for.

"Like Lloyd or one of his men delivered the rest of that one million you were waiting on."

"When?"

"Yesterday," Conrad replied, as he swung around the back of the chair so he could sit down.

"Yesterday, huh? Well, why the fuck didn't you tell me yesterday?"

"You were busy."

"I'm never that . . . mother-lovin' . . . busy."

"Hey, you know how it is," Conrad said. "I had to

have the bills scanned for marks."

"Well, were they?"

"No, they were clean," Conrad said.

"So, tell me about the drop."

"Okay, well . . . they didn't do it like the last time. GPS-it to Stone Mountain State Park. You know they buried it with a GPS locator. We followed the signal . . . that's the . . ."

"Skip the rest of it," Eric said. "Let's get back to Lloyd and his so-called brother."

"Alright, it's only a thought mind you . . . no proof, but I think their working for . . . Mantis."

"Mantis . . . Mantis—why them?" Eric asked, as he poured a small shot of bourbon into a glass with no ice.

"Blaze Odom. He doesn't like you or me."

"Or anyone else," Eric said as he downed his drink.

"You got that right; but he's the honcho at Mantis. He's always looking to get rid of any competition. So, what better way to get rid of us then to send us a bomb like a hit on a prominent citizen—a.k.a. Clifton 'fuckin' Van Dameer—then turn us into the FBI or the Justice Department."

"Nah! Sounds too far-fetched," replied Eric.

"Ok, so how about this? Odom or someone in his organization worked out a deal with some senator, or with someone in the intel-community."

"Yeah, and to do what?" his brother asked.

"Maybe do a little house cleaning in the financial world. The guy's a hedge fund honcho; he's up on SEC charges for massive fraud and money laundering. The guy's got a lot of enemies in high places. So, think of it this way: he gets rid of Van Dameer and us—a two-for-one shot."

"If that's so, somebody's got a lot of money just to find out," Eric replied as he lit another cigar.

"You know, Rad, you might be right. I'll have to give it some thought."

"You do that," said his brother.

"Oh, in the meantime, did you read over that article I gave you? It came in the mail the other day; it's from *The Wall Street Journal*. Some of it's been redacted. Why?! I don't know."

"Yeah, I read it over. We all know the drill. The question is: who do you think sent it to you and why?" replied Conrad.

"Well, you're the intel-guy . . . got any ideas?" his brother asked.

"To be honest with you . . . no. If I had to guess . . . probably Lloyd Hamilton or his phony brother . . . Stanley."

"Why them?" Eric asked as he walked over to one of the office windows to open it.

"Thanks," Conrad said, "that cigar smoke was starting to get to me. Anyway, to answer your question . . . to shake us up . . . to let us know: I know what you know."

"So?"

"Well, it's a reminder to do what we're being paid to do . . . or else. A way of saying if it ever gets out about Van Dameer, you and I are toast."

"That won't happen," Eric said.

"Oh! And why's that?"

"Because Lloyd and his supposed brother know they would end up DOA—that's why."

"Well," said Conrad, "that's reassuring."

"Well, I have to be. What do you think we're playing here? Don't bother; I'll tell you . . . fuckin' darts and chess at the same fuckin' time . . . that's what. Reminds me of the time I was out on an 'op' in Iraq."

"No! That reminds me," said Conrad.

"Reminds you of what?"

"Elizabeth asked me to tell you to have Charlene call her."

"What for?" Eric asked.

"You know . . . for that fund raiser for your good

buddy Senator Greenberg. She told me to tell you she has some new contributors . . . big-money types. They want to see a Jew in the White House."

"Well! Why not?" Eric said. "Look what we have in there now."

"Hey, he's politically correct," answered Conrad.

Shaking his head in apparent disgust, Lowe replied:

"Big deal," then added an additional insight by saying: "So's fuckin' toilet paper."

"You're a racist," answered Conrad.

"Yeah, so what? Everybody is. Say, did you tell Bentley this hit on Van Dameer was sanctioned?"

"What do you think? I had to. He needs to know it's a legitimate intervention . . . like in Iraq . . . that way he can pass it on to Gordon and Grimaldi . . . and the others. He needs a pretext. Every soldier does. Sort of clears their conscience . . . you should know better than anyone."

"Somehow I don't think that's the case, and yet I know the nature of your cynicism."

"Well, let's not get into one of your philosophical diatribes," replied Conrad.

He then stood up, picked up his briefcase, walked over to the door and said:

"Will I see you at the club tonight?"

"You bet. I want to hear more about Blaze and your thoughts on this Van Dameer thing; something tells me there's a lot more we should discuss."

While Conrad was walking towards the door he turned and said:

"Oh! By the way, before I go, there's something else."

"What's that?" his brother asked.

"Who did you want for a back-up and a go-between for Bentley, Gordon and Grimaldi?"

"I don't really know. Who do you want?"

"I was thinking: Orlando Stokes."

"Good choice. He's like the rest of them."

"How's that?"

"Crazier than a shit-house rat."

Conrad pretended to laugh at his brother's assessment of Stokes. It was something he would often do just to placate him. If anything he knew his brother wasn't too tightly wrapped and prone to volatility.

"Hey!" he said. "There's something else."

"Oh, and what would that be?" Eric asked.

"Don't be late."

Eric smiled then flipped him the finger. It was something he would often do so as to exercise the economy of scale.

Conrad took a moment then opened the office door. Before he shut it, he turned and blew a kiss in his brother's direction. Eric didn't bother to reply. He knew that Conrad would always try to get in the last laugh; he always did ever since they were kids.

Instead, he decided to open the manila folder that lie in front of him and contemplate a letter that had been sent to him the day before.

Dear Sir, it read:

> It is my belief that "PMCs" are the future of asymmetrical warfare or at least a support system. Your company Global Solutions and the World Enforcement Bureau provide a much needed logistical service. You are an integral part of national and world security.
>
> I feel your services are desperately needed within our own borders as a counter measure against our obvious enemies.
>
> I hope we can meet in the near future. Until then, however, feel free to discuss anything you wish with my representatives Lloyd Hamilton and his brother Stanley.

The letter was unsigned and the envelope had no return address or postage. It had been hand-delivered to the company mailbox. Of course, he would have the letter and the envelope scanned for fingerprints. He knew there would be none, but it was SOP so you had to do it.

Over the years he had read many such letters; usually they were of little or no consequence. This letter had the makings of some unknown future developments and its mystery left him with an uneasy sense of intrigue.

He put the letter in his folder then sat back and pondered where it would all end. One thing was for sure, he and his brother were about to cross a very big line. A line that could lead them into a very small cell in a very big jail.

CHAPTER 6

"The human body has 7 trillion nerves and some people manage to get on every one of them."

– The Condescending Wonk –

While driving along the tree-lined entrance way of the Field Stone Country Club, Eric Lowe mulled over a few of its varied amenities. He wasn't an avid golfer; however, he could play a respectable round or two, so the lure of the Field Stone's prestigious links held limited appeal.

He was more interested in the club's gourmet cuisine and its opulent dining rooms, which, when needed, could be united into one lavish banquet facility. A convenience he would use when he hosted political fund raisers or company affairs.

He was also quite partial to the indoor pool and adjoining eucalyptus sauna. In addition to that was an attending female masseuse who was always busy; but, for the right price could find the time to accommodate you.

They had the other kind as well; however, the idea of having some man touch him, when all he had on was a towel, creeped him out.

Unfortunately, he had to meet his brother and spoil a

nice dinner by discussing business with him, which, of course, was the main reason for him to be there, although Conrad did mention that there might be the possibility of him meeting someone else.

When he pulled up to the club's plantation-styled portico, a uniformed parking attendant ran over to his car and opened his door. "Good evening, Colonel," said the valet. Lowe glanced up at him and smiled then slowly slid from behind the wheel of his E-Class Mercedes. While standing next to its open door, Lowe looked the man in the eye and said:

"So, how was your day, Curtis?"

"Oh, not bad, Colonel. How was yours?"

"Ah, about the same, I guess."

As he stood there scanning the parking lot, Lowe said, "Say, is my brother here?"

"Who? Mr. Conrad?" said the valet. "He sure is."

"Was he with someone?"

"No, sir," replied Curtis. "But, later on this well-dressed man showed up, said he was a guest of your brother."

"Really!" Lowe replied. "What did he look like?"

"Well, sir, he was kinda tall, had a moustache, with sandy-colored hair. He kinda spoke with one of those English accents . . . like in the movies . . . you know what I mean?"

Lowe handed the attendant a ten dollar bill then murmured, "Yes, Curtis, I certainly know what you mean."

"Why, thank you, Colonel!" said the attendant as he took the money from Eric Lowe's outstretched hand.

"Hey! Don't mention it," Lowe exclaimed. He then started to walk in the direction of the club's revolving entrance doors and the marble stairs that led up to them. To most people the idea of giving someone a ten dollar "cumshaw" just to park your car might seem extravagant. To Eric Lowe it was money well spent. He was well aware of the fact that Curtis knew everyone at the club and the gossip that followed them. He was a source of information that might prove far more important than any ten dollar tip.

In addition, the man wore gray velvet gloves so he wouldn't leave any fingerprints on your car when he parked it. It was a nice touch and something he appreciated. It exhibited class and an attention to detail, something most people didn't bother to do.

While walking down the hallway towards the bar he happened to meet a woman whose husband had recently died. He was a French businessman named Louis Jongleur which meant jester in that language . . . something he most definitely wasn't.

Her name was Cozzette Jongleur. She was a lot younger than he which might lead you to believe she married him for his money, or so it would seem. He tried not to make assumptions. Besides, she had that quality about her, a certain *"je ne sais quoi"* that would preclude such a thought. He had his eyes on her for some time; however, he hadn't the audacity or impudence to approach her—at least, not until now.

She stopped for a moment to talk to him. Their conversation lasted long enough for him to allude to the possibility of them getting together for a drink. She acted coy, but somewhat interested. When they shook hands and said their "goodbyes," it seemed to him she let her fingers linger a little longer than they had to.

As he watched her walk away his eyes drifted over the tight pair of golf pants she was wearing. To him they appeared to enhance the outline of her heart-shaped ass. A consideration he was often drawn to. He loved his wife, but yet he wanted to hold on to the idea that he still had it. The part that bothered him was the feeling that perhaps he might go farther than just looking. Something he swore he would never do.

When he entered the club's bar, known as the "red room," the obviousness of its title became apparent.

Especially in the soft light of its surroundings, when its deeply-polished mahogany gave off a muted vermilion hue.

Lowe stepped back for a moment when he happened to see his brother sitting at the end of the bar. He had his back towards him and was having a conversation with a man named Lincoln Asbury. His real name however, was Leland Crawford the Third.

Supposedly, he was a good friend of Blaze Odom; at least that was what he had heard. The guy had a somewhat spurious past, and from what he could ascertain, wasn't to be trusted.

He had been a captain in the British Army and worked with MI-6 (Military Intelligence, Section 6)—the English version of the CIA—what they called their foreign intelligence service.

Supposedly, he had taken part in an ultra-secret operation called rip-flash. The purpose of the mission was to infiltrate and bug certain Iraqi businesses and military facilities. In addition, his team was to purloin whatever they thought was of military value. Some of what they considered to be of military value was large sums of cash, drugs and jewelry.

In addition to all of that, he heard while conducting the operation his team had taken out a few Iraqi security personnel—an obvious violation of coalition protocol which led to Asbury's dismissal from the service.

He had to make the assumption that Lincoln was the "someone else" Rad had alluded to back at the office.

When he sat down next to his brother, Asbury stood up and went over to him to shake his hand. They exchanged the usual insincerities [good to see you, how have you been?, etc.]

After a brief conversation between the three of them, Asbury excused himself by saying he had to use the men's "washroom." Lowe couldn't help but think he knew why; the guy was so full of shit his eyes were brown.

When Asbury walked away Conrad leaned over and

47

filled Eric in on the gist of what he and Lincoln had been talking about. While he was doing that, Eric decided, as an act of supplication, to order another round of drinks. Conrad told him that Lincoln said that Odom was going to outdo Global by any means necessary to obtain government contracts.

As he sat there listening to his brother, Eric sipped on his drink then interrupted him by saying:

"Okay, so what else is new?"

"Yeah," answered Conrad. "Here's the kicker . . . He told me that Odom might have recruited some senior members of that Salvadorian drug gang . . . the Mara Salvatruca, you know: MS-13."

"I know who they are," Lowe said with a scowl. "Are you sure they're the ones who are supposed to take me out?"

"That's a could be. I don't really know . . . yet."

"Are you wearing a wire?" Eric asked.

"Yeah . . . but, so is he, and he had on a RF detector as well. So, we both agreed to turn our stuff off."

Eric put his drink down on the bar and sighed, then looked at his brother and said:

"I don't buy it and neither should you. Asbury is a fuckin' bullshit artist. Besides, Odom's crazy, but not that crazy. How many times have I told you? Assessment, then divestment."

Conrad leaned forward and spoke to him under his breath:

"Hey! I believe you . . . but still and all, we have to take anything he says into consideration . . . it's an in—the guy wants to be a fifth column."

"Okay. What else?"

"You know the story . . . he wants money . . . says he can give us details on what Odom is up to."

"Mmmm . . . that's more like it," Eric said with a smile and a slight nod of his head. "How much?"

"It's negotiable—probably . . . three 'k' a week."

Lowe took a moment to sip on his drink then said,

"So, here's the deal . . . you know, negotiate with him, play him along . . . tell him we're on board . . . we'll take it from there."

"Okay, that's what I thought . . . that's why he went to the little boys' room . . . so we could talk . . . Hey, here he comes now . . . so, stoway the words way."

Eric looked askance then shook his head. "Jeez, Rad," said Lowe, "when are you ever going to learn how to speak pig Latin?" He let his words trail off just as Lincoln strode up beside them.

With an awkward smile and a quick glance at Eric and his brother the Englishman asked:

"So, did I miss anything?"

Using his usual up-and-down nod of his head, Conrad replied:

"Nah . . . not a thing."

"Well, then, knees up," said Asbury. "How about we do a few more 'nozzles' . . . they're on me." He then sidled his way closer to where Eric was sitting.

In an annoyed tone of voice Lowe answered:

"Sorry, old boy," then made it a point to move his leg away from the presence of Asbury's thigh. He went on to explain how he would like to stay, but he had a previous engagement with his wife, "Dinner reservations and all that."

Asbury clinked his glass with Lowe's then told him he understood.

Eric stood up and said, "I'll have to leave you in the capable hands of my brother Rad." He then patted Conrad on the arm saying:

"Oh, and Rad, put Lincoln's bill on mine, and yours, too."

He then turned toward Asbury, shook his hand, wished him well, then walked off in the direction of one of the dining rooms.

He made a brief stop at the men's room to wash his

hands, thinking that only God knew where Asbury's hands had been before.

When he entered the dining room, one of the waiters "moseyed" his way over to where he was standing. "Good evening, Colonel," said the waiter with a toothy smile. "Nice to see you again; I have your table ready and waiting for you . . . right next to the window just the way you like it."

"Thanks, Freddy," Lowe said. "Where's Louis tonight?"

"Oh, he had to take the evening off . . . had some family issues to attend to."

When he sat down at his table, Lowe said "goodbye" to the waiter . . . thinking Freddy had to be the blackest man he ever saw.

He remembered what his father used to say about Negroes, that some of them were darker than the inside of a Hollister. What he never explained: was he referring to the color of their skin or the content of their character?

Before Freddy departed, Lowe told him to hold off on the menus until later, that he was waiting for someone else to join him.

It wasn't long until his brother arrived in a state of visible exasperation, shaking his head as he sat down.

"Christ all lovin' mighty," he complained. "That son of a bitch wouldn't shut up . . . He kept rattling on about Iraq and all that war story shit."

"Well, Rad," Lowe said, "you gotta forgive him."

"Oh yeah! Why's that?" his brother asked.

"He was an unwanted baby."

"How do you know that?"

"Well," replied Lowe with a snicker, "he was born with a coat hanger in his ear."

Conrad pretended to laugh, then said, "Hey, Eric, don't quit your day job . . . anyway, Asbury agreed to take my offer of a thousand a week."

"That was nice of him," answered Lowe. "Hopefully,

the son of a bitch will give us something we can use. You know . . . I don't trust him . . . as far as I can throw him."

"Hey, me too," Conrad said, "but I've got other things I want to go over with you."

"Such as?"

"Well, for starters, Lloyd Hamilton sent me an encryptic with two names on it . . . one is an ex-con named Richard Carroll Spencer. The other is some lowlife pervert named Fulton Bates."

"So?"

"He wants a compilation on the two of them."

"Where is all of this coming from?" Eric asked.

"I don't know . . . all I know is I gave him a price: $65,000 a piece . . . He agreed."

"Okay . . . what else?"

"Uh, there's something else that's more to the imperative—it's the other."

"What the hell are you talking about? The other . . . the other what?"

"If I'm right . . . I think," Conrad said, "if we green light these two assholes . . . we get the okay on a few contracts from the DOD and the State Department."

"Really?" answered his brother. "Well, we'll have to wait and see, won't we? Until then, let's eat."

Lowe waved to the waiter for him to bring two menus.

"What are you having?" asked Conrad.

"The rack of lamb."

"If you already know what you're going to order, why do you want a menu?"

"Curiosity!" answered Lowe. "I kind of want to see if it changed any."

"Well," replied Conrad, "I'd save some of that curiosity for the future . . . you might need it."

"I'll take that under consideration," Lowe said. He then turned his attention to Freddy, who was standing patiently by their table. In the process of giving him his order, Lowe noticed Cozzette and another woman at a table nearby.

He remembered she had a fondness for chardonnay wines so he told Freddy to bring her a bottle of Montrachet. As he was doing that he noticed his brother smiling at him. When Freddy left, Conrad leaned forward then pointed a finger at him and said:

"So! You like Ms. Cozzette, do you? You know, Eric, you're a hopeless Francophile—that's what you are—hopeless."

"That could be . . . let's not talk about me. Okay? Let's get on with what we came here for."

"Alright, as you well know, Odom and his boys at Mantis will go to any length to get contracts . . . we have to do the same."

"I know you're right and yet I can't help feeling as if we're going to be."

Lowe paused for a second then picked up a swizzle stick and bent it in half. While Freddy was placing his appetizer of oysters Rockefeller in front of him, Conrad said:

"Jeez, Eric, don't you think I know that . . . sometimes you have to do what you have to do?"

"Okay . . . so, let's get down to a few specifics, shall we!" Lowe exclaimed.

"Like what?"

"Like how much are Bentley and the other two getting for this Van Dameer thing?"

"Oh, something in the neighborhood of $65,000, plus expenses. Of course, with the advent of the other two names . . . I figure about the same."

"Pretty expensive neighborhood," answered Lowe as he cut off a piece of lamb.

"I know, but look what we're asking them to do . . . so I . . . ."

"So, they owe us a favor . . . Hell, they've been on the payroll for months while they were out of the country."

"But . . ."

"But nothing . . . send Bentley a confirmation on Van Dameer . . . tell him we'll be in touch . . . no cell phones unless it's encrypted. Got it?"

"You seem to forget I've done this before," replied Conrad as he pointed his fork in his brother's direction.

"Don't you know not to point?" Lowe said. "Oh! Before I forget . . . what about Max Geiger and Trevor Jacks?" Lowe asked.

"What about them?"

"Well, are they still on board . . . or what? You know . . ."

"As far as I know, they are; of course, that's subject to change . . . They've been in contact with Chris Bentley."

"Sounds good . . . keep me posted . . . you know what I mean—I want updates."

"Will do, Jefe," said Conrad. "Don't look now, but I think Cozzette and her friend are trying to get your attention."

"I've got eyes," Eric said.

"Well, why don't you invite them over?"

Lowe glanced over at his brother, then in a low and menacing tone said:

"You ain't too bright, are you? Why don't we invite your wife and mine while we're at it?"

Conrad sat back, took a sip of wine, then leaned forward and smiled.

"Relax," he said, "don't be so serious—where's your sense of adventure?"

"I've got none," Lowe answered, "especially when it comes to Charlene and my kids."

Conrad knew he had touched a nerve so he let the moment subside. He was well aware of his brother's quixotic nature. How he could turn on a dime from being the nicest guy in the world to the worst. On top of that, at times he was hopelessly delusional about himself and others.

Moreover, there was something else. His wife Charlene had told his wife that Eric had slapped her a few times. He had also hit the children when they were small. He had never said anything to Eric about it; at times, however, he wanted to. He hated the hypocrisy of his brother's pretense of being holier-than-thou.

After taking another sip of wine Conrad looked over at Lowe and said:

"You know, Eric, this stuff is pretty good."

"It's an acquired taste."

"Is that so?" replied Conrad. "Sorta like some of the women I've known."

"I doubt it," said his brother, "and yet you know, Rad, at a distance . . . perception often becomes a matter of expediency."

"Okay, spare me, will you?" Conrad replied. "I already know the rest of it."

"And that would be?" his brother asked.

"Or the insolence of disposition."

"Well, Rad, nice to see you've been paying attention to someone else besides yourself."

"Thanks . . . you know how you always said to me if you could stand in the right place you could move the world."

"Of course," Eric said, "like Lee Harvey Oswald or those Saudis in 9-11. They were nobodies who found the right place and time and changed history."

"Well," Conrad said, "right now you have a small group of Lee Harveys at your disposal—the quintessential assassins—just think what they can do?"

"I already have."

"Good, and to make things even better, I have some good news."

"What's that?" Lowe asked as he sipped on a glass of wine while watching Cozzette watch him.

"We received that shipment of bullet-resistant clothing from Maelstrom Clothing."

"I think they said their clothing was bullet-proof."

"I stand corrected. I meant bullet-proof."

"How much?"

"About 60k."

"This stuff better be good or it's going back. Anyway, how's it made?"

"It's the best," Conrad said watching Eric's eyes shift from him to Cozzette's. "They've combined nano-tubles with Kevlar . . . It's light and very flexible."

"Did you talk to Bentley about it?" Eric asked.

"Just the other day."

"Good. When is Bentley having that meeting with ARGO and Grimaldi?"

"I think the day after tomorrow."

"Yeah, well keep me informed . . . don't forget . . . I want updates . . . they're the tip of the spear."

"I agree," said Conrad. "They're also . . . shall I say, a liability."

"How's that?" his brother asked.

"Well, they could open Pandora's box."

"Oh! Is that so?" Eric said, with half-a-smile. "Well, I know how to shut it."

CHAPTER 7

Resting comfortably on a chair in his New York hotel room, Christopher Graham Bentley scanned through a series of photographs on his iPhone. Some of them were of himself and of his ex-wife Adiba, which meant well-mannered in Arabic. While he was sitting there thinking how he should have deleted those pictures of her, he contemplated some of the reasons why he couldn't. One of them was the way she died and how he felt about it.

It wasn't his place to ponder the spuriousness of her demise; however, the memory of her had left a smattering of feelings he couldn't dispel—the kind of awareness that questioned his intent to never think of her again.

He remembered the police report and how it stated that the brakes on her new BMW had been tampered with. There was also the matter of her million dollar life insurance policy being left to her husband. The obviousness of its implication had never been resolved. "*At least*," he thought, "until now."

He came across one photo that caught his eye. It was of the two of them on a beach off the coast of Greece on the island of Santorini, framed against a background of sugar white sand, azurean water and spectacular rock formations.

She stood there smiling at the camera looking just as serene as her surroundings. She was wearing a postage-sized bikini and a jade necklace that he had bought for her at a shop next to their hotel. The sight of her being all tan and fit with her long black hair shimmering in the summer sun conjured up the thought of some Greek goddess from the pages of mythology.

He looked at himself. He was standing somewhat obliquely by her side, his fingertips barely touching her arm. It was as if he was admiring some fine piece of artwork. His body was taut and muscular with the image of a temporary tattoo spiraling down his left bicep. The picture made him appear the way he wanted it to: ominous and yet forgiving.

He had to admit those were good times. He was in love and making a lot of money and so was she; at least, that's what he believed. While he sat there mulling over the past, clouds of bitterness darkened his muse.

She was a Jordanian barrister working in London mucking about in law and commercial real estate. Supposedly, she was making quite a go of it; or so it seemed. "Why not?" he asked himself, "how could she fuckin' fail?" especially when you considered the size of the Arab population of London. He started to chide himself even more as he thought over how he should have bloody-well known better.

She was a bloody lawyer and like all lawyers she had a fuckin' devious mind. The kind of mind that never questioned what an SAS officer was doing in Iraq working for MI-6. The kind of mind that knew enough not to ask why her husband was shipping large amounts of U.S. currency to her. "Why would she?" it was bloody-well more than the anemic paychecks he had been sending her!

The other part of the equation was the fact that he was in the bloody-fuckin' army. So, as anyone would suspect, he would be abroad a good share of the time. Of course, as most young army wives, she became desperately lonely. As it would follow she decided to mitigate her condition with a diversion.

His name was Samir Al-Sayyed, an Iraqi businessman of "questionable character"; at least to the police, that is. Ironically, he was just the type of Arab the British Army was paying him to kill. A job he had become highly proficient at.

He remembered her letters asking him for a divorce. How she refused to accept his phone calls. Her only explanation for her decision was she had fallen in love with a man of her own culture and religion.

She also reminded him of an affair he had when they were first engaged. "Well," he thought, little did she know he had many of them, mostly prostitutes, but still a matter of deferred fidelity.

All of that would have been acceptable if it weren't for the money he had entrusted to her. The agreement was he would decide what to do with it when he returned from the Middle East. The assumption being that he returned at all. In that case the money would have been all hers and probably something she wished for.

She told him in a letter that she had "lost most of it" while investing in commercial real estate and the commodities market. He knew better; Arab men were notorious for making off with anything a woman had. They controlled their women with an iron hand and twice that if it pertained to money.

In addition she wrote to him that she and Samir were leaving for the States. She apologized and asked for his forgiveness and yet she still had the "bullocks" to warn him not to follow them.

He reflected on how he felt at the time. His only thoughts were that someday he would see them again, and when he did the pictures of Jack the Ripper's victims, as well as some of his own, entered his mind.

Unfortunately, to make matters worse, he couldn't do

anything about it since he was under investigation by the FBI and MI-6. He had been restricted to his area of operation and couldn't leave Iraq. He was also confined to his quarters, akin to being under house arrest.

As it all turned out, he was never formally charged due to the nature of some very sensitive information he had in his possession. It was the kind of information neither the American nor British governments wanted to go public.

He was asked to leave the service for conduct unbecoming an officer and given a general discharge under less than honorable conditions. It was under those conditions that he sought employment with Global Solutions, one of numerous private military firms that dotted the Iraqi landscape.

He was like so many ex-army types who found work with some PMC doing what they did in the service, except for a lot more money. Of course it carried the stigma of being called a mercenary, or as one wag put it: a contract warrior. A distinction he sort of wore with a certain degree of pride.

With a feeling of dejection Bentley dismissed his thoughts, gazed at his watch, turned off his iPhone, stood up, then walked into the bathroom. He looked into the mirror. It was time to rearrange his appearance, but first he had to pee; after that he would work on his transformation.

Ever since Iraq he had become adept at the art of disguise, pretense and moral ambiguity. He attributed those feelings to some hidden desire to be an actor. He enjoyed the freedom of being someone else—an obvious psychological ploy to excuse his actions.

He reached into his leather valise and removed a black hairpiece, moustache and a pair of non-prescription glasses. In addition to that he took out various shades of make-up and eyeliner.

While he set about preparing his "look," Bentley kept

an ear out for a ring on his hotel phone. The call would be from Orlando Stokes, another "employee" of Global Solutions—he had worked with Stokes in Iraq and other places. This time he was to be a back-up for his team and a physical go-between for Conrad Lowe and himself.

When the phone finally rang Bentley answered it in Arabic. The caller responded in kind; their greeting was a way of insuring who they were.

The sound of the anticipated knock on his door sent Bentley scurrying towards it. He then pulled up sharply only to peer carefully through the eyepiece. After seeing who it was he opened it and ushered Stokes in with a quick wave of his hand.

To dramatize the seriousness of their meeting Bentley slammed the door behind him. To Stokes it was just another example of Bentley's mercurial personality—a demeanor he had become accustomed to.

Forgoing the customary handshake, Bentley placed his right hand over his heart then bowed his head. It was a gesture of spiritual reverence called a "Namaste"; Stokes did the same. He then walked over to a desk which was situated close to a large-screened television set. The picture was on, but the sound had been turned off.

To Stokes it seemed kind of weird since it was a porno channel. As anyone would know . . . half the attraction to porn was the sound; however, he knew Bentley. The guy was strange so he tossed the observation aside and concentrated on the reason for him being there.

They spoke for a while reminding one another of the various situations they shared while working for Global in Iraq. One of those involvements was when they happened to meet in operation Rip-flash—a joint exercise between MI-6 and Global Solutions whose mission was to take down illegal banks and terrorist money strongholds.

Since both men spoke fluent Arabic they interspersed their conversation using Arabic words and phrases. Stokes did his best to have Bentley divulge how much money he "appropriated" while raiding those illegal banks. However, his efforts were to no avail because Bentley was never the type to say anything he didn't want you to know, either in Arabic or English.

"Hey," Stokes said, "I'm into disguises myself," pointing to the wig Bentley was wearing.

"Oh! That's good," replied Bentley using the Arabic phrase: *hada shay'un Jameel!*

"Yeah," answered Stokes, "I did some in the A.O., pretended to be a convert, dressed up like one of them . . . grew a beard. Did some work . . . took down some serious cash . . . you know what I mean?"

Bentley responded by using the Arabic word for "really" (*haggan*) then with a disdainful gaze Bentley said:

"From what I remember you were highly effective at uh . . . acquisitions, and as well at pretense."

Not sure how to respond to Bentley's remarks, Stokes countered by saying:

"Hey, whatever . . . you know . . . I guess you could say that about the both of us . . . right? Couldn't you?" He let the tone of his voice infer his own brand of antipathy.

Not wanting to extend the flavor of their conversation, Stokes turned in his chair, snapped open the latches of his attaché case, lifted the sides and pointed to the contents. Inside were stacks of neatly bundled money wrapped in mustard-colored bands with the number 5000 written on them.

"What's the count?" Bentley asked.

"Oh, about 200k," replied Stokes. "It's to cover your expenses, that is, for you and your associates."

"I know what it's for," replied Bentley.

"You said about!"

"Whoa, don't worry about it," Stokes replied. "It's all there." He then handed one of the bundles to Bentley. "There's more if you need it," he said. "All transactions are to go through me, you dig? No direct contact with the office. Oh! Yeah, by the way. I got two names for you to look into, same price as your 'principle.' That is . . . I mean, if it comes down to a green light. I won't know that until I've been advised . . . you understand?"

"Are they sanctioned?" Bentley asked.

"Damned if I know," replied Stokes as he shrugged his shoulders. "I guess they are, but what the hell does it matter, as long as you get paid, right?"

Bentley nodded his head then slowly counted the number of $100 bills in the bundle; when he finished, he then mumbled the number "50."

"You satisfied?" Stokes asked as he stood up from his chair closing the lid to the attaché case. He then walked over to Bentley's bed and put the case on it. "Oh, as you can see I got this heavy-ass suitcase for you. I don't know what's inside the mother fucker, but HQ wants you to have it."

Bentley knew what it contained: various-sized, bullet-proof clothing.

"You mind if I use your bathroom?" Stokes said.

Bentley gazed at him through a squint-eyed smile. "Use it later," he said. "I have a request of you . . . a private matter . . . I want you to look into it for me."

"Oh, I'm sorry, maybe you didn't notice, but I'm kinda busy right now."

Bentley walked over to Stokes and handed the stack of bills he had counted.

"Find the time," he said. "I want you to do a feasibility study for me or find someone else to do it."

As Stokes slid the money into his jacket pocket he said:

"Hey! I'll do my best."

"Mmm . . . I'm sure you will," replied Bentley.

A feasibility study was a preliminary study as to the best course of action for the future possibility of an intervention. The intervention was a way to "neutralize a target," i.e., kill an individual. It could be in the manner of a long distance sniper shot, car bomb, a drive-by shooting, whatever appeared to be the best way to get it done.

"Ok," Stokes said. "So, you mind if I use your facility now or what?"

"Sorry! Old boy, be my guest."

"Maybe while I'm in the can you could write down the subject's name and address."

"I've already taken the liberty," Bentley said as he handed Stokes a slip of paper.

"How did you know I'd . . . you know . . . accept?"

"I never underestimate the rapacious nature of the perfidious or the profane."

"Wow! I'm all of that?" Stokes asked as he gazed at Bentley with a slightly bemused grin.

"And, then some," Bentley replied.

When Stokes returned from the bathroom he looked at Bentley and said:

"So, the guy's an Arab, huh?"

"Is that a problem?" Bentley asked.

"Nah! Not really, just making an observation. Hey, are you meeting with Grimaldi and Gordon?"

Bentley looked at his watch. "Later tonight," he said as he glanced at his watch one more time.

"Oh, yeah? Where's that?"

"At a restaurant in Brooklyn called Scalzo's . . . do you know it?"

"No . . . never heard of it . . . I'm the wrong color for Italian."

"So, what is it you want me to . . . say to them?" Bentley asked.

"Oh, not much, just tell them to sit tight," Stokes said, as he glanced at his watch.

"You might be getting an encryptic for a 'go ahead.' Oh! And tell Gordon he and I . . . uh. . . . have to get together sometime."

Bentley nodded his head as he showed Stokes to the door. He was well aware of enmity between the two of them. He couldn't care less; but, dissension in the ranks could spell disaster.

As Stokes was leaving he turned to Bentley and said:

"Hey! Have a meatball for me."

Bentley pretended to smile then shut the door. He didn't like Stokes. He wasn't fond of black people. They were emotional and loud: bad characteristics for a soldier. Of course, Stokes was never a soldier, just a hired gun and operative.

What bothered him was the people of interest. Who were they and why were they singled out? He knew enough not to fill his mind with conjecture. It led to doubt and hesitation, then possible failure—an outcome he wasn't about to contemplate. He walked over to his bed picked up the attaché case then placed it on the desk.

His thought was when he left for the evening he would take it with him. He would give it to the manager at the front desk; have him put it in the hotel safe. "No need for undue risk," he thought, "even the best hotels harbored disreputable guests."

Bentley grinned at the rumination knowing that most likely he would be the first amongst that ilk. He looked at the case, patted the handle and then thought about its contents: money. How it was considered the root of all evil . . . the great motivator . . . the stuff of dreams. The disturbing part was he really couldn't bring himself to believe all of that.

He referenced something he once heard: that money couldn't buy what the heart desired. He smiled at the thought then said the word "rubbish" as he set off for his dinner engagement in Brooklyn.

CHAPTER 8

The casual atmosphere, large portions and the quality of food made dining out at Scalzo's Italian "ristorante" one of the more popular places in Brooklyn. For "TOJO" Grimaldi it felt good to be back in familiar surroundings. His given name was Tomas Giuseppe Grimaldi, in English it would be Thomas Joseph, but everyone in his neighborhood called him "TOJO." He had just returned from Naples and was there to meet two of his partners, Anthony Gordon and Christopher Bentley. It wasn't customary for the three of them to be seen together in public places. This time the consensus was maybe a little get-together would be a good thing. It would be the first time they had seen one another since they left Afghanistan six months ago. Besides all of that, they had some urgent business to discuss and face-to-face was always a better way to communicate.

While waiting for his two "associates," Grimaldi ordered a bottle of Chianti, the best the house had to offer. After sampling its flavor he sat back and mulled over what he knew of them. When he thought about it, he really didn't know very much except what they told him. Of course in their line of work maybe that was enough.

Gordon's full name was Anthony Robert Gordon. He was often referred to by the acronym "ARGO." He was kind of good-looking with a "me first" attitude; a quick temper, yet highly reliable. He liked to work out a lot, sort of a physical fitness nut, with a black belt in two different styles of martial arts. According to him, he was from Bogotá, Columbia; his father was German and his mother Spanish. At first he denied having any siblings, but later let it slip that he had a twin brother named Ernesto. Supposedly, as a kid, he had been kidnapped by the military wing of the communist party called the FARC— the revolutionary armed forces of Columbia. His father had been killed by them while attempting Ernesto's rescue. From what Gordon let on, his mother paid a heavy ransom for his return, and then sent him to live in New York City with his uncle in Queens. The rest of his story was relatively normal. He said he had gone to college at NYU, had a degree in English and another in philosophy. His plans were to become a teacher, but history got in the way; a short time after 911, he joined the army.

Grimaldi remembered how Gordon made a point of telling him he didn't do it for the sake of patriotism. He said he did it for a higher calling—for the sake of curiosity. What didn't make sense was why Gordon hadn't tried for Officer Candidate School. He was more than qualified. Instead, he went to sniper school then on to become a ranger.

As he sipped his wine he thought about it. He had seen it before. A guy with a good education passing up OCS. From what he could tell, it probably had to do with responsibility or a fear of failure, or both. Whatever it was only Gordon knew and that was all that mattered. As his father used to say: "*Ad augusta per angusta*," Latin for "to high places by narrow roads."

Grimaldi took another sip of wine and studied the menu. He was certain he knew what he wanted; however, he had to look over the specials just to make sure.

His thoughts returned to the other man in their association, Christopher Graham Bentley. He was English, well-spoken, kind of reserved, and a good dresser. But, he was a stone-cold killer, with strange wolf-like eyes that were ice blue and never seemed to blink. He had a jagged scar along the side of his jaw. It was an old shrapnel wound he picked up in Afghanistan, compliments of the Taliban. He had graduated from Sandhurst Military Academy, England's West Point. Supposedly he was a captain in the SAS—Special Air Service—the Brit's version of the US Special Forces. According to Bentley, he had done some highly secret stuff in Iraq; but for reasons he "couldn't reveal," had to resign.

There was no reason for Grimaldi to confirm or accept any of what the men had told him. He didn't care. It was their business. All he knew was they had better never cross him or sell him out. "If they did, well, *arrivederci*." Grimaldi dismissed the thought. They had all been in the army and done multiple combat tours in Iraq and Afghanistan. When they left the service they went to work for Global Solutions as private "security" contractors.

In all their time together neither of them gave him any trouble or tried to rat him out. But, as the saying goes, "there is a first time for everything."

When he spied the men entering the restaurant, he checked his watch. As always they were right on time. He stood up and waved them over. They put aside the formalities of shaking hands and patting one another on the shoulder. It wasn't their style. Instead, they all sat down and picked up their menus, talking as if no time had passed since they had last seen each other.

Bentley spoke first, "Well, gentlemen, I have it on good authority we will be conducting operations somewhere within the immediate vicinity." Before he could continue, Gordon interrupted him, "Really?" he said. "I thought we weren't to do anything with the United

States. I mean, did something change while I was away or what? The last time I checked, an operation had to be a legitimate foreign target sanctioned by the agency or the State Department."

Without so much as a sideways glance, Bentley replied, "Yes, what you say is correct, but that was then, this is now."

Grimaldi set aside his menu and looked over at Gordon. "Hey, Antonio, what do you care, huh? Whatsa matta for you? Fuggetaboutit, as long as you get paid, *smetalo* (so cool it), you know?" Grimaldi would frequently use Italian dialect or Brooklyn-ese to express his feeling, emphasize his point, or even lighten the mood. He finished his statement by dragging the back side of the four fingers on his right hand upward along his neck to a point under his chin with a flip. It was a common Italian gesture of contempt for either a situation or for something that was said. "*Vaffanculo,*" he uttered—Italian slang for "fuck it."

"Oh, is that right?" Gordon said. "Well, you know what? Maybe I DO care. So maybe you ought to *vaffanculo* yourself, you *Mameluke.*" TOJO threw back his head and snickered. He considered Gordon to be his *fratello,* a brother, but he enjoyed the banter.

With a show of obvious disregard, Bentley interrupted them by saying, "Gentlemen, I'm sure we will have enough time to discuss our differences." He considered Gordon and Grimaldi's petty squabbles as just superfluous verbiage. However, after living with various Arab factions, he was quite used to it; amongst them it was a daily occurrence.

TOJO turned his attention to Bentley and said, "So, Christ, what's the story? I mean are we supposed to just sit around and wait, or what?"

"Precisely," replied Bentley. "I will clue you in on details when needed. So, until then . . .."

"Until then, I'll think about it," said Gordon. "I

didn't sign on to hunt Americans."

Neither Bentley nor Grimaldi replied or gestured. To them it was a done deal. The remainder of their conversation revolved around the past with varying degrees of speculation on future scenarios. However, like most ex-soldiers, they would often slip into some minor embellishments while recounting some of their battlefield exploits. The difference being their stories were often about what they had done while working for Global Solutions, not what they had done in the military. What most Americans don't know or care to realize was what private contractors did. First and foremost they provided a support system that gave real soldiers the time and wherewithal to do their jobs. It stopped them from being bogged down with menial tasks or having to participate in something that might be considered illegal, or, at best, questionable. This is where the corporations such as Global Solutions came into use. They hired highly-trained ex-soldiers to carry out certain sensitive operations; not so much for the military but for the CIA or State Department. It gave these organizations a great deal of latitude to do what they wanted without congressional interference. To accomplish that, Global Solutions would select a few of their handpicked men to carry out what might be seen as assassinations, theft and coercion. These men were paid a king's wage. However, they would bristle at the word mercenary; to them they were doing a job that others couldn't or wouldn't do.

Finally after getting a few things off their chests, they got around to ordering what they wanted. Grimaldi decided on mussels Fra diavolo with osso buco as his entrée. Osso buco in Italian means "hollow bones." He often thought of himself and the others being just that: "hollow bones."

Gordon and Bentley considered themselves to be epicurious, so they went with the Caesar salad with polenta croutons. For their entrée they wanted the flank steak for two, with sides of gnocchi cavofioré (potato dumplings with cauliflower, cheese, eggs and flour).

TOJO began to pour himself another glass of wine. Bentley reached over and touched his arm and told him to take it easy, or as he stated it: "to tuck his wattle."

"Why?" TOJO asked.

"Because," Bentley replied, "we have a job to do after dinner."

"Oh, is that right?" said Gordon. "Like where?"

"The Club Climax," answered Bentley.

"The Club Climax! You mean that couples swing club? What's there?"

"A person of interest," replied Bentley.

"Any fruit flies?" Gordon asked.

"Hey, what'd you care for?" TOJO said, pointing his fork at Gordon. "You're getting paid; don't be *antipatico*" (Italian for unpleasant). "Anyway," he added, "your *condottire*" (Italian for contractor or mercenary).

"I don't like homos," answered Gordon.

"They're not homosexuals," replied Bentley. "They're gay."

"Oh, I forgot! That's right. We're not mercenaries; we're 'security specialists.'"

All three of them laughed. Euphemism and verisimilitude were endemic to the military. It provided an accepted way to mollify or obscure the true nature of a group and what they did.

"So, what's the poison in there," Gordon asked, "the usual booze and coke with a little BDSM thrown in for spite?" Bentley took a sip of wine, smiled and then nodded his head in the affirmative. "Yeah, that figures," Gordon replied, "a bunch of perverts standing around shading glasses and bumping rails."

Without saying a word, Bentley turned away from them and took out his cell phone that was vibrating in his pocket. Both Grimaldi and Gordon knew it was probably an encrypted text from Global; Bentley was one of their chief field operatives and it was their way of communicating. Encrypted text messages were virtually impossible to intercept or decipher by the FBI or NSA. Without an explanation, Bentley told them to finish up, they had to go. "When we leave I want both of you to follow me to my car." He motioned to their waiter for the check which he paid for in cash. He handed him the money, turned back to the two men and said, "Listen up. I'll give you a lift to the city. When I let you off, take separate cabs to the club."

As they made their way through Brooklyn, Bentley asked Gordon what his intentions were. Was he in or out? If he was in, he had to see it through. If not, Bentley said, "no hard feelings." He would drop him off somewhere in mid-town, after that he was on his own. He was to have no contact with Global, and that included himself and Grimaldi. Without hesitation, Gordon told him he was in. Why? Gordon thought to himself, he didn't really know. It was a mystery he could reflect on later. However, he guessed, it must be he felt he would be missing out on something. Whatever it was, it would probably remain another personal enigma.

With Gordon's intentions clear, Bentley felt free to divulge some of the operation's particulars—mainly who and what the target would be and most importantly how much they would be paid. He gave each of them a picture of the so-called person of interest. He was the CEO of a hedge fund in Greenwich, Connecticut, with offices in Manhattan and London. His name was Clifton Van Dameer. That's where the Club Climax came into play. Bentley wanted them to see who he was, sort of up-close and personal. It was all part of what they referred to as a feasibility study. He told them that Van Dameer liked to party a lot and was under indictment by the SEC for securities fraud. What was worse, he was on somebody's hit-list or what was known as a green light. Bentley told them the price on the guy was $65,000 a piece, plus expenses. They would stay on Global's monthly payroll whether they worked or not. It wasn't a lot considering the risk, but enough to keep them in the game.

Gordon thought back to the last "person of interest" the three of them did. He was a Saudi businessman in Lagos, Nigeria, a silent partner in a multi-national oil drilling company, supposedly connected to Al-Qaeda, but who knew if he was or not. It wasn't their responsibility to ask why, just to do the job, get paid and fade away until the next job came up. TOJO was the one who took the Saudi out. He used what was called a proximity bomb. Grimaldi was an EOD guy in the army and probably the best bomb disposal man in Iraq, or at least that's what was said of him. He also had the ability to build a bomb out of anything. His favorite mode of delivery was the use of a cell phone connected to a shape charge. All you had to do was ring up the right number and "goodbye tomorrow."

On the way to the city, they crossed over the Williamsburg Bridge. In Gordon's eyes the panoramic skyline of Manhattan was as spectacular as ever. To him it was home. But he knew for all the hype it could be treacherous. The place had a way of seducing you into believing if you played your cards right, you could get whatever you wanted. Assuming you didn't get caught or die trying.

CHAPTER 9

"To be free you must uncover the conflict between the unconscious fiction and conscious thought. What counts is to see the depiction of unconscious forces that drives the person in a certain direction and to recognize through his conflict the contradiction between the drama and his conscious goals."

— *The Anatomy of Human Destructiveness*, Eric Fromm

"All forms of sexual persuasion have one thing in common: their roots reach down into the matrix of a natural and normal sex life."

— Albert Eulenburg, German neurologist

A few hours later, Gordon found himself on his way to the Club Climax. He was staring out the window of a taxicab wondering what might be in store for him. He had been to a few of the club's sexual soirees in the past, but neglected to mention that at dinner. "Sometimes," he thought, "discretion can be the better part of a conversation . . . especially amongst inquisitive friends."

When he arrived at the club he did as they had planned: before leaving the cab he made sure neither Chris nor Grimaldi were anywhere to be seen. Manhattan was a sea of security cameras and, even though they were in disguise, the less exposure to surveillance the better—the idea being that law enforcement was based on suspicion, due to intelligence and conjecture.

Gordon knew from the past that the FBI and the Department of Justice had their eyes out for them. It all started while they were working for Global in Iraq and Afghanistan. He remembered one agent in particular—a persistent bastard named Tom Starr. "Someday," he thought, "I'd like to meet up with him—alone."

When he left the cab, he walked up to the club's front entrance and approached one of the bouncers. He was standing behind a roped-off area checking IDs. The guy asked to see his so Gordon took out his wallet and showed him the Canadian driver's license Bentley had given him on their way into the city. It was a masterful piece of forgery with his picture, height and weight, date of birth, where he lived, and, of course, his name: Anthony Austin.

After returning his license the bouncer proceeded to use a hand-held metal detector to scan him. The device was called a Garrett Security Wand. It was the same type used by TSA personnel in airports. It seemed to Gordon that kind of security procedure had become common practice at many public events. Of course, when he thought it over and when you considered the state of how the world was, he could definitely understand the club's precautionary reluctance on who they should let in.

When he was done the bouncer gave him a quizzical look and said:

"Not for nothin'; don't I know you?"

Gordon looked straight at him and slowly turned his head from side to side.

"No, I don't think so," he said. "I've never been here before."

"No, not here!" exclaimed the bouncer. "Some other place." Then, with a snap of his fingers he said, "Yeah, now I remember. You used to work out at a gym I used to go to. It was over in Hoboken. It was a place called The Extreme Fitness Center . . . you remember? Yeah . . . that's it. You used to spar with some of those mixed martial arts guys. If I remember right . . . you were pretty fuckin' good."

"Sorry," replied Gordon, "I'm from Canada. I've never been to Hoboken and I don't do mixed martial arts. However, my brother does. He owns a karate school in Englewood. We're identical twins—you probably have us confused. It happens a lot."

"Wow! Sorry about that," said the bouncer. "You know you really look a lot like him. You know what I mean?"

Gordon stood back and smiled. "Yeah, buddy," he thought, "I know what you mean. That's what identical twins are all about, being identical. But what the hell," he mused, "not everybody is cut out to be a Mensa student."

As he moved away from the bouncer he stopped for a moment and looked back at him. He had a sudden urge to give the man a cursory salute. The only thing he could think of was the guy reminded him of a soldier he knew in Iraq who had been killed by an IED. Gordon then turned sharply, as if he was performing a military about-face and moved swiftly through the club's front door.

Once inside he strolled over to a makeshift cashier's table. Sitting on a chair behind it was a garishly made-up woman collecting money and explaining a few of the "what fors." He knew the "spiel" but listened to it anyway. She told him it was $100 for a single man, $50 for couples, and for unescorted women no charge. She ended by saying he could purchase tickets or poker chips in different denominations. He could use them for drinks or tips or "for whatever."

Gordon knew from his previous experiences what

she meant when she said "for whatever." The poker chips were usually given to some women as a form of payment for the pleasure of their company—the accent being on the word pleasure. The chips weren't legal tender, so technically no money changed hands. The scam being if you happened to have sex with her there was no basis for a charge of prostitution.

From what he was told the club used women from the various escort services to add more action to the general activity. They made their money by hustling patrons for drinks and tips, as well as offering sex behind some strategically placed room dividers.

In addition, the girls would often hand out their cell phone numbers to perspective clients for the possibility of some future hook-up. At the end of the night, or before they decided to leave, the girls would turn in whatever amount of chips they collected for cash.

It was a stretch, but to his knowledge the poker chip ruse seemed to be working since no legal proceedings against the club had been initiated. Of course, you had to believe that somebody in law enforcement had to be in on it. It was standard operating procedure that any pay-for-play scheme or business had to share in the profits, if they didn't want to be shut down.

He didn't know but suspected that the management probably kept a percentage of whatever the girls made as a fee for working there. The kicker was not only the professionals could hustle chips, but the amateurs could do so as well. All and all it seemed to him to be a win-win situation for everyone involved.

So the regular swing couples did their thing with other couples or with anyone they wanted to get it on with. Usually, it was in the form of some innocuous grab-ass or dirty dancing, although a number of them would venture off behind some movable partitions that had been strategically set up, so as to accommodate for the comfort of their "concupiscence."

From what he could recall each cubicle had a cloth-covered couch and a chair of the same fabric, a mirrored ceiling and a tacky lava lamp to throw some subdued lighting on the experience.

Knowing all of that and that nothing in NYC was ever cheap, Gordon decided to buy $500 worth of poker chips. He didn't really plan on using them, but experience told him to be prepared for any . . . unexpected contingencies. His line of thinking was that since he was already there he might want to sample some of the clientele. Gordon slipped a few of the lower-priced chips in the front pocket of his pants. The rest he stowed away on an inside compartment of his jacket that had a zipper on it. It was an effort to thwart any would-be pickpockets from getting to his "pelf"—a situation he had fallen victim to the last time he was there.

Before he moved away from the table, Gordon asked the cashier if she knew who the bouncer at the door was, "the one with the long hair and the leather jacket." Her only reply was to ask him:

"Why?"

"Ah, nothin' much," he said, "just curious. He looks like someone I used to know." He then glanced around before placing a $20 bill in front of her.

"Sal DeMarco," said the cashier, as she put the twenty in a small shopping bag by her side.

"Hey, thanks," Gordon replied with a smile as he walked off in the direction of a makeshift corridor. The passageway had an array of tiny overhead lights that led to a set of heavy swinging doors; they were the kind you would often see in restaurants, the kind that went into the kitchen. While walking towards them he could hear the house music in the background. It was the type that was popular in the '70s and '80s. It had that disco beat that made you want to dance.

When he pushed his way through the doors he was hit by a barrage of sight and sound set off by flashing strobe lights—a mosh pit of body heat and perfume. Before he had a chance to acclimate himself to his surroundings, a young woman nudged up against him. She was wearing nothing but a smile and a pair of high heels. In her hand was a small yellow purse indicating she was a club girl, an escort; at least that's what he thought. The last time he was there they carried white ones. If you checked their contents you would most likely find poker chips and a few condoms and a pack of business cards.

She tugged at his sleeve and then pulled herself close to him, all the while grinding her thigh between his legs. "Hey!" she said. "You want to dance?"

Trying not to shout above the noise, Gordon replied in a voice you could hear, "Not right now . . . maybe." No sooner had the words left his lips then she moved away only to disappear into the swirling crowd.

People appeared to be everywhere, either slouching suggestively on a sofa or canoodling on some overstuffed chair, while others were dancing frantically, their faces and bodies glistening with suggestive sweat.

Off to the side he could see others milling around a long buffet table filled with cold cuts, baskets of bread and fruit. The main point of interest was a large coffee urn he knew to be laced with LSD. He found that out the hard way. The last time he was there, after a few sips of coffee, the place turned into a sparkling mirage of color. As he was doing that he passed up a few come-ons by various women and some overly-sexed couples.

His task of trying to find his two partners wasn't easy considering the size of the crowd and the on again/off again strobe effect of the disco lighting. Gordon was sure it had been set up that way to obscure the identity of the patrons and what they were doing.

The thing of it was . . . everybody had cell phones, which they weren't supposed to use—yeah, right, he thought as he pushed himself right through the "bacchanal." He decided to take some time and meander his way for a while, just to get his bearings, while staying on the lookout for Grimaldi and Chris Bentley.

Finally he caught a glimpse of Bentley. He was leaning up against the bar looking over his shoulder; behind him was a wall of people two or three deep. Standing next to him was a tall, thin man in a grey sharkskin suit. He was holding a drink in one hand and talking on a cell phone with the other. From what he could see of the guy he sort of looked to be their "person of interest"—Clifton Van Dameer.

Bentley finally turned away from the bar and saw him standing a few feet from where he was. Immediately, he rubbed the side of his neck with his left hand. It was a prearranged signal that he was either standing next to Van Dameer or close to him. Gordon signaled back by rubbing the side of his neck with his left hand meaning he got the message.

Suddenly he felt someone behind him pressing an elbow into his back; it was Grimaldi holding a drink pretending to be one of the crowd. "Having a good time *'cafone'*?" he asked, then walked away.

Gordon didn't bother to answer him and moved off in the opposite direction. He used whatever space he could find to absorb some of the action, making sure he stayed in sight of Van Dameer and Bentley.

After a short interlude, he saw Van Dameer move away from the bar. He watched him push his way through a jumble of people into the waiting arms of a gorgeous woman.

She was wearing a tight mini, tube top, and a pair of "come fuck me shoes" or "CFMs," the kind of high heels with the open toes and tiny ankle straps. She had curly black hair, a cute nose, heart-shaped lips and an awesome set of "yabos."

An intriguing sight Gordon mused as he watched the couple move off in the direction of the club's infamous fetish room. It was a separate place set up to accommodate the more adventuresome of the club's kinkier patrons.

Standing outside the entrance were two security personnel, next to one of them was an upright box. The irony of it was that it looked to be a lot like a collection coffer, the kind you might see in the vestibule of a Catholic church. The difference being it had a glass window that allowed you to see what was inside of it— poker chips. There was an iridescent sign that hung from its peak that read: Donations Required.

Off to the side was a marquee showing the price of admission. As usual it cost a single man $100 to get in, paid for in the form of poker chips of that value. Using the same type of currency . . . couples were charged $50 and unescorted women were let in for free.

Gordon watched Van Dameer and his raven-haired escort make their way over to the entranceway. He knew she was a club girl because she carried a yellow handbag. He could see Van Dameer pay the admission fee and then saw the two of them disappear from view. Within a few short minutes he was following after them. As he went through the doorway, he slid a $100 poker chip into the slot of the donation box.

The atmosphere of the fetish room was a stark contrast to that of the club. It was quiet and dark, almost eerily subdued. Hanging from the ceiling was a small number of spotlights. They were focused on a few of the bondage sex scenes being played out in front of a fairly silent crowd.

As a rule he wasn't into paraphilia, BDSM or, as he thought of it, sado-misogyny. He really couldn't grasp the idea of wanting to hurt someone while trying to have sex with them. The thought of it seemed to be more than incongruous, although he could understand the nature of its appeal. The idea of having control over someone, be it a man or a woman, while having them acquiesce to your demands could be more than compelling.

Of course he was capable of something far more

poignant than that. He could be on the outside looking in and manufacture a situation to his own liking. He could end the life of anyone he wanted. In itself that was enough control for the most jaded of the club's participants.

Gordon searched amongst the crowd until he came across Vandy and his lady friend. They were standing close to where a naked woman was laying face down on a leather upholstered B and D bench. Her wrists were shackled on both sides of the table with her outstretched legs glistening, butt strategically positioned behind her— the intention being to make it easy for someone to fuck her. The someone was a powerfully built white dude with a porno-sized dick who was vigorously doing just that.

Off to his side Gordon heard a man say the guy who was banging her was a professional wrestler named Zach Farnak. The scene was such that the wrestler would fuck her for a while . . . then step away. When he did that he would drizzle a small amount of baby oil on her ass then smack her with a belt he was holding.

The oil gave each hit a kind of wet slapping sound that seemingly excited the audience as well as the woman. In response to each swipe of his belt the woman would give out a low sensuous moan. She would then arch her back in the apparent request for more of the same.

Gordon could sense the crowd's enthusiasm as they extolled every slap of the belt with sounds of their own. To him it all seemed an elaborate piece of psycho-drama, a contrivance for people in need of an outlet for their own sick fantasies.

Suddenly, without warning, he saw Van Dameer's girlfriend pull away from his side. She hurriedly pushed her way through the people around her and walked towards the exit door which led into the club.

Instinctively Gordon recognized an opportunity to get closer to their target by getting close to her. He followed the woman into the club then moved swiftly to where she was standing. Without hesitating he leaned in close to her just enough to whisper in her ear:

"I've been watching you," he said.

She turned slightly in his direction then waited a moment before she looked up at him. She answered him by saying, "I'm with someone," then finished with a flirtatious smile. "But, since you're already here, why are you watching me?" she asked.

Without shifting his gaze Gordon kept a discernable eye out for her boyfriend. "I like beautiful women," he replied, "and you are a beautiful woman." Off to his side and sequestered within the crowd he could see Grimaldi furtively gesturing in his direction. He was nodding his head in an apparent attempt at conveying his approval as to what he was doing.

Gordon pretended not to see him and stayed focused on the subject at hand.

"So," she asked, "what else can I do for you?"

"Well, how about your name?" he asked as he pressed a hundred dollar poker chip into her hand. She glanced at its denomination then put it into her purse. "And what's yours?" she asked.

"It's Austin, Anthony Austin," Gordon said, letting his hand touch her thigh.

"Of course you are," she answered, "and I'm Renee Bardot." She slipped a business card into his hand making sure to let her fingernails slide across his palm up to his wrist. As she did that she looked into his eyes and ran her tongue over her lips. Within that moment she pulled away and he knew why. She saw Van Dameer and so did he.

As she turned away she looked back at him and said:

"Call me."

Gordon just waved thinking . . . she could count on it. He didn't bother trying to find TOJO or Bentley. He knew they would find him sooner or later. What he wanted most was to go back to his apartment, take a shower and get some sleep.

When he left the club he said a quick goodbye to Sal

the bouncer. He then trudged along to wait on the corner for some passing cab to come along and pick him up.

While he was standing there Gordon began to contemplate the future. It occurred to him that maybe . . . he wasn't as hip or as good as he thought. He had seen it before . . . a guy loses his edge . . . starts looking over his shoulder.

Or, maybe . . . it was how he was feeling about working in the United States. The idea of pulling the trigger on a civilian didn't sit well. He wasn't sure he wanted in . . . it was an unknown. Whatever the fuck it was, he knew he had to deal with it.

On his ride uptown Gordon saw a large neon dollar sign; it made him think about their target. He wondered why someone like Van Dameer with his vast wealth would risk what he had for more. With that thought he remembered something his father used to say to him:
"You can lose what you have, but not what you are" . . . and Van Dameer was: greed.

CHAPTER 10

"Money isn't the root of all evil: the love of it is."
— 1 Timothy 6:10

While standing in front of the mirror fixing his tie, Gordon began to stare at his reflection. "Ah, what the hell," he said, shrugging his shoulders at the thought of his own vanity. Maybe, his brother was right when he used to tell him that he never met a mirror he didn't like. It wasn't his fault he was born good-looking, at least that's what women told him, and who was he to argue with the better half.

Without bothering to shift his gaze, Gordon slowly drew a comb through his shiny black hair. With a twinge of self-satisfaction he began to admire what he saw: his deep blue eyes, thin nose, hollow cheek bones. As he stroked the side of his face his only comment was to say "yeah, he could have been a model instead of a soldier-for-hire—some kind of contract warrior."

Yeah, he was handsome alright; however, there was a down side to his supposed good looks. It seemed gay men found him attractive also. It was a thought that left him feeling somewhat agitated as well as homophobic. With a wave of his hand he walked away from the mirror.

"Fuck all that," he said. He had more important things to think about than fags and bimbos. For starters, how in the hell was he supposed to stay one jump ahead of the police, the FBI and their ubiquitous minions?

As he crossed the room towards his bed, Gordon removed his 9mm automatic from its shoulder holster and then placed the pistol on the mattress next to its custom-made silencer. From a dresser drawer he took out a box of ammunition then dumped a few rounds on the bed. From the same drawer he removed a pair of latex gloves.

With the dexterity of someone who had done it many times before, he snapped them on his hands. He made it a point to wear them whenever he had to handle bullets; it kept his fingerprints off the brass. Anyway he kinda liked the way the gloves made him feel; it was as if he was a doctor or something more than what he was.

He had made it a habit to inspect each bullet before he loaded them into a magazine—you could never be too careful; sometimes the slightest flan could spell disaster. He was afraid that when it came time for that critical moment and he had to pull the trigger, he didn't want some fucked-up embarrassing equipment malfunction to ruin it. How would that look, especially when he had taken the time to send his very best.

Sitting on the edge of his bed, Gordon tried to relax while he thought about the evening ahead. He pondered the different possibilities and how it would all turn out. Who wouldn't when you considered what he was going to do. He aimed the pistol at the wall and thought about the fact that sometimes you had to trust your instincts. If you didn't, well, probably you wouldn't be around long enough to worry about it anyway.

"Well, guess what?" he said to his imaginary listener; he planned on being around for a long fuckin' time. As that thought crossed his mind he remembered what his mother often said to him, "You want to make God laugh? Tell him your plans." Gordon smiled when he recalled what he would say in return, "Thank God, I'm an atheist."

He fluffed up the pillows on his bed then laid back on them, then stared up at the ceiling. He thought about his intended target and how well he did know the man.

There was always a doubt, that nagging doubt, on how well had he planned things out. No, he wouldn't allow himself to go down that road. He had been down it many times before, too many stop signs, detours and dead ends.

Gordon sat up abruptly then grabbed the pistol from the bed. He began to work the slide back and forth; whenever he cocked it he aimed at something in the room and pulled the trigger.

He had resigned himself to the fact that he was different. When he was honest he could see who he really was. He saw the anxiety and the depression, the desire for self-preservation against the desire for self-transformation. One side said stay the same and avoid the unknown. The other side said change—not only that, but act differently.

That was the scary part. He was comfortable with his actions even though they brought emotional chaos and unfathomable terror. He knew in the court of last resort he would be judged for what he was. He was a killer.

Comforted by the mindfulness of his actions, Gordon stopped and placed the automatic next to him. He lit a cigarette, took a few quick drags then crushed it out. He hated cigarettes, but sometimes smoking felt like the right thing to do.

On a nightstand by the side of his bed was a manila folder. He reached over and opened it. Inside were a series of photos he had taken of his intended target. In addition to the pictures was a list of notes and observations that he had jotted down during his two-month surveillance of the man he would be paid to kill.

That man was none other than Clifton Van Dameer. He was one of those financial avatars with the all too familiar biography. He had the usual litany of personal accomplishments starting with the fact he was considered a financial genius, a gifted attorney with a Harvard MBA, a friend of the rich and famous and CEO of Van Dameer and Wade (a small but extremely successful hedge fund with a reputation for creating sizable wealth to its investors).

What was left out of his biography was the part about him being a cheating, lying scumbag—how he had destroyed the lives of many people who had used him as their investment guru. His hedge fund was under investigation by the SEC for defrauding a number of its clients out of millions of dollars. Of course, Van Dameer claimed he was totally innocent of all charges. He knew nothing of what was happening behind his back.

As he sat there thumbing through his notes, Gordon mused, "Yeah, some things never change." However, this time there was going to be a difference. It seemed that, or appeared to be, one of his clients had taken great umbrage at being cheated out of his money. This time there was a client who wasn't willing to just sit around while the so-called law took its course—although he remembered an age-old adage that whenever you plan revenge make sure you dig two graves: one for your victim and one for yourself.

That's where he came in, that is, Anthony Robert Gordon or ARGO, or whatever name he chose to use. Gordon felt somewhat elated knowing his actions would sort of even things up. He lit another cigarette and gulped down a small bottle of energy drink.

He looked at a picture of Van Dameer talking to his partner Jason Wade. They were standing in front of a building in Manhattan, one that held some of their mid-town offices. This put Vandy and his partner in close proximity to their favorite kind of fish: the financial whales of Wall Street.

These were the type of guys that invested millions and didn't pay attention to details—as in how could a hedge fund give you 17% of your money instead of the usual seven. I guess they never heard of Charles Ponzi, Gordon quipped as he laughed at his own remark.

Another photograph was taken at some distance; it was of Van Dameer's wife Loren and his daughter Sharon. The two of them were playing ball with their dog in the front yard of their home. The place was a spectacular Tudor mansion on Long Island Sound; it was in the Bellport section of Greenwich, Connecticut, where only millionaires could reside.

Gordon laughed at the bucolic scene. He knew Van Dameer's schedule—the guy spent very little time at home. He was far too busy at his office or entertaining clients at his multi-million dollar apartment on Sutton Place.

What no one was aware of, least of all his family and friends, was on every Thursday night he was busy entertaining at another apartment—one that was leased to his very private secretary Mrs. Cynthia McBride. The apartment was located in a non-descript building on 72nd Street on the upper east side of Manhattan.

There was no doorman, no security cameras and was easily accessible from the street. All anyone had to do was walk into the front entrance, ring the buzzer and talk to the tenant. The tenant had the option to buzz that person in or not; all without seeing if that person was alone or with someone else. After that, all you had to do was go in, find the right apartment and knock on the door.

These conditions, as well as others, helped him in his feasibility study as to how was he going to gain entrance to the building and leave without being seen. Fortunately, he had been able to hook up with Renee Bardot the hooker he had met at the Climax Club. It cost him three grand for three bedroom dates and a thousand for some fancy dinners at a few high-end restaurants she wanted to go to.

However, it was all worth it. She liked to talk a lot, especially when she was high on booze and cocaine. She told him Vandy liked to party with her and "whoever" she brought along. Her exact words were: "he was eclectic and enjoyed numerous women." She also told him that she and "whoever" would go to his place on 72nd Street around 10:00 pm and leave around one. The rest was critical that she told him that when they left Van Dameer he was usually very drunk and stayed in the apartment until late the following day.

Another favorable continence was the building had a no pets allowed clause. This meant no barking dogs or an accidental encounter with the owner of some amorous pooch who wanted to make friends. When he thought about it, he liked dogs. Nevertheless, they tended to be somewhat obtrusive, a lot like the people who populated the Big Apple.

Before he decided to leave his apartment Gordon placed an envelope in his jacket pocket. Inside the envelope was an article about an anonymous letter written to a reporter who worked for the *New York Post*. According to the article, the letter was written by the supposed killer of two ex-convicts who had just recently been released from prison.

Both men had been murdered under similar circumstances, one in Albany, the other in Rochester. They had been shot at long range by someone of exceptional ability—maybe, a hunter or a military sniper.

According to the letter, certain details of both cases were only known to the author and the police. These details would be divulged if the newspaper promised not to print them. The *New York Post* declined any such request.

The article went on to say that the shooter was aware of what these two criminals had done. The article also stated that due to the nature of their crimes the shooter was left with an overwhelming sense of outrage and anguish for the victims and their families. The shooter felt that further retribution had to be taken against these two individuals.

Gordon smiled at the idea of how he could write such

lofty bullshit and mean every word of it. The article went on to say that the shooter felt he shouldn't be judged too harshly. He too had been the helpless victim of crime; he had been so traumatized by his ordeal he was left with no other alternative but to give in to his dark side—hence, the title for the article "The Dark Side Shooter." An imposing "sobriquet" Gordon thought, somewhat theatrical and yet quite acceptable.

The notoriety that followed after the article had been published fanned the flames of his ego and perked his interest in the possibility of further acts of "justice." For what was justice, anyway? Just another way of imposing an acceptable form of vengeance on people that society deemed as unacceptable.

Furthermore, the public seemed to be taken up with the fact of some unknown avenger striking back at crime, a real-life comic book hero "The Dark Side Shooter"—had to be worth a book deal or a movie. But, however, who would play him? Of course, only he could.

From the recesses of his mind came a familiar voice, one that warned him not to give in to such self-destructive ideas. He had heard that voice many times before. He didn't listen then and he wouldn't listen now. He did what he wanted to do and whatever happened, happened. An old army buddy of his used to tell him "you can change your life, but you can't change your fate." It didn't make any sense, but it sounded good.

As usual Gordon took the subway up to the 70s—the number 6 train to be exact. Before leaving the apartment he made sure he had the envelope with the article in it.

When he emerged from the subway, he walked a few blocks to where he knew Grimaldi would be waiting for him. He was driving a company car, one that Chris Bentley had given him to further the Van DaMeer operation.

To make sure they weren't being followed, they rode around aimlessly, critiquing the eye candy, fantasizing on how good their sexual ability might be. Mostly they talked over what Bentley had told them, of there being the possibility of future operations in the Northeast.

It seemed that Global, as well as the W.E.B., had a number of moving parts and one of them was Orlando Stokes—a someone that Gordon didn't like or trust. According to Bentley, Stokes was on to some major "work" in the Muslim community. The inference being that some high-ranking Muslims could be targeted for intervention—a concept both Gordon and Grimaldi could totally agree on. He also let on that the Mossad might be involved, mainly their special operations division: the Metsada (a group of highly-trained operatives that conducted assassinations, sabotage and espionage). It came as a surprise to the two of them since the only time they had any dealings with that group was in Iraq.

Bentley also emphasized that the Van Dameer operation should be as quiet as possible. He would prefer the man had a serious auto accident, a possibility that wasn't plausible. He left it up to Grimaldi and Gordon to do what they thought best, with some understated influence pushing their decision the way he wanted.

There was a proposal to have Grimaldi leave a package under Van Dameer's car with a cell phone as a detonator. The plan being when Clifton entered his car TOJO would call that particular cell phone number, then ka-boom. It would be Vandy's last hello and an eternity of good-byes.

The drawback with that idea was bombs made a lot of noise and drew the ire of multiple law enforcement agencies, whereas gunshots in NYC were an everyday occurrence and considered inconsequential or, at best, a passing irritant.

Gordon knew it was time for him to get into character and become his alter ego: ARGO. Grimaldi sensed it also; so, he let Gordon off a few blocks from Vandy's pay-for-play hideaway.

His next course of action was to wait for Gordon's phone

call to pick him up at a prearranged address close to the apartment building.

Gordon drifted around wasting time. He was in complete disguise; a full beard, dark glasses, a hoodie and a shopping bag. He looked like any other down-on-your-luck white guy in that neighborhood.

Finally, at around quarter to ten, he saw Renee and another woman walking towards the entrance of the apartment building. They looked like two bookends wearing similar clothing, matching hair-dos, same height and weight—so much for Van Dameer being eclectic. He watched as they walked up the stairs into the front vestibule, rang the buzzer and waited to be let in.

The next part of his plan was to be patient and wait for them to leave. When they did, he would give them another fifteen minutes just to make sure they didn't double back.

Now, Gordon mused, all he had to do was be patient and wait for them to leave; after that it would be his turn to entertain Mr. Van Dameer. With that thought came three boring hours of tedious anticipation and hanging out, walking around, looking in windows and drinking club soda in a few of the local bars.

With a sense of relief Gordon watched as Renee and her girlfriend put on a ribald display of apparent drunkenness as they sauntered down the sidewalk laughing and talking on their way to who knows where. To be sure that the two women didn't double back, Gordon gave them what he considered enough time to leave the area.

With an anxious gate, he crossed the street and then walked up the front stairs into the lobby of the apartment building. Once inside, he pressed the buzzer for apartment 4A, believing that if Van Dameer happened to be asleep the sound would wake him up.

To his astonishment he was buzzed on through. He had been quite prepared to use his electric lock pick to let himself in, something he had done many times before.

With measured steps, Gordon padded lightly down the hallway to a staircase that would take him up to the fourth floor and Van Dameer's apartment. As he hiked his way up, he started to feel as if each stair challenged his resolve and questioned his reason for being there.

While he stood there staring at the door to apartment 4A, Gordon took a deep breath, then decided to do what he was being paid to do. He then used a piece of chewing gum he had been working on and placed it over its aperture, thereby obscuring his presence to the person on the other side.

With a steady hand Gordon reached down inside his shopping bag and removed his silenced automatic and a spring-loaded blackjack. He used the blackjack with its lead-filled tip to rap on the sheet-metaled door creating a distinct sound that was both loud and intrusive.

Within a very short time he heard a voice from behind the door asking him who he was. Gordon answered him in Spanish, the predominate ethnic culture that lived in the building. The man told him to go away or he would call the cops.

Gordon knew Van Dameer would never do that, mostly out of fear of unwanted publicity and a lot of awkward police questions. So, once again, he rapped on the door and once again spoke to him in Spanish.

It wasn't but a few minutes later that he heard Van Dameer fumbling with the door as he set about trying to open it; when he did, he stood in the gap with the security chain stretched across it.

"What do you want?" he asked angrily, all the while staring out at Gordon with a look of pretentious aggravation.

This time, however, it wasn't Anthony Robert Gordon who answered him, but ARGO and he did so with his silenced automatic. The steel-jacketed bullets cut through the billionaire as if he was made of paper, sending him crashing to the floor in a haze of blood-splattered residue.

Gordon didn't wait around to see if Van Dameer was really dead or not. Instead, he reached into his jacket pocket and removed the envelope with the "Dark Side Shooter" article in it. He threw the envelope through the opening in the door close to Van Dameer's body, he then shut the door knowing the article would be a tantalizing bit of false evidence the police would find more than intriguing to ponder over.

He met TOJO waiting for him at a spot they had agreed upon. With an air of tension they rode around Manhattan listening to a police scanner for any response of the shooting; there wasn't any.

Grimaldi didn't ask him any annoying questions; he didn't have to. He already knew the answers; besides that, he really didn't care. His only telling comment was to say to Gordon, "you did what had to be done," that he was *Condottieri.*

Grimaldi took him back to where he was staying; it was an apartment building on the upper east side. As he was about to step from the car TOJO leaned over and said to him in Italian:

"Hey, you had better get some sleep and then you better get the hell out of town."

It was a piece of advice Gordon was more than willing to follow.

CHAPTER 11

"Some obstacles are borne of fate, others are man-made. Only God knows the difference and only he has the power to decide their outcome."

The Unknown

Place: An apartment building on the Upper West Side of Manhattan in an area called Spanish Harlem.
Time: 6:00 a.m.

Gordon rode the musty elevator up to the eighth floor and then walked along its linoleum-covered corridor toward his apartment.

He was tired, a little hungry, and he hadn't had a shower in a few days. He was looking forward to one. A nice long, hot one, just the thought of it made him feel better. Afterwards, maybe he would make something to eat and get some sleep; God knows he could sure use it.

Before he opened the door to his apartment, Gordon looked around to see if anyone else was in the hallway with him—there wasn't. Quickly he bent down and ran the tips of his fingers along the bottom edge. He had made it a point that whenever he left the apartment to place a small strip of Scotch tape at the bottom of the door, right next to the threshold. His thought was to set up a protective seal, so whenever he returned he would know if anyone had entered the apartment or tried to enter it while he was away.

From what he could tell, the Scotch tape hadn't been tampered with—mindful of what might lay behind any door. He felt somewhat reassured that it was alright for him to proceed, so he placed his key into the lock. As usual, he had trouble opening the door. Ever since he rented the apartment, he had difficulty with the lock. Apparently, the lock was old and the key's teeth were worn. Of course, he would never have another set made, that might expose him to some sort of scrutiny from a locksmith—a situation he cared to avoid. So, true to form, he stood there awhile jiggling the key in the lock, twisting impatiently at the door knob until it relented and let him in.

He reached inside along the hallway wall and found the switch for the light, then turned it on. Immediately, he sensed something wasn't quite right. He couldn't put his finger on it; but, if he had to guess, it seemed the hallway smelled different, like cigarette smoke.

Common sense told him not to go any further. Of course, he wouldn't let that interfere with his curiosity or with his type of bravado, so he had to go on. However, he did feel a little apprehensive as he slid past the door into the hallway, taking care to silently shut the door behind him.

Without moving another step, he removed his 9mm automatic from a shoulder holster inside his suit jacket. Within that same period of time, he took out its custom-made silencer and screwed it to the muzzle. He knew if he had to use his gun he sure as hell didn't want to wake up the neighbors, although in that neighborhood you frequently heard gunshots. More importantly he didn't want the attention of the NYPD; they really looked down on guys with guns, especially unlicensed ones with silencers.

With his back pressed firmly against the hallway wall, Gordon inched his way towards the darkened living room. Halfway there he stopped in front of the bathroom door. He didn't remember how he had left, so, with his pistol at the ready, he slowly pushed it open. Gordon felt for the light switch, and then flipped it on. He took a quick look around; everything seemed copasetic enough, and at least everything as he remembered.

Satisfied as to what he had seen, Gordon slowly backed away leaving the light on and the door halfway closed. He hadn't taken but a few steps when he heard a slight noise behind him. Before he had a chance to turn around, a man's voice said, "Drop the gun, motha-fucker, or I'll cap your punk ass."

In a small mirror that hung on the wall, Gordon could see the partial reflection of the man behind him. He was holding a gun. He couldn't tell the make or caliber; but it looked big enough to end his career.

Sure as hell he didn't want whoever it was behind him to get trigger happy, so he did what he was told. Without saying a word and ever so slowly, he bent forward and placed the weapon on the floor by his foot. As he rose up he made sure to hold his hands at shoulder height making it clear he wasn't about to try anything.

In a wavering tone of voice, the man told him to move away from the gun. Gordon knew the drill; he had been there before. Something told him the guy was probably an amateur. They were the worst kind; out to prove something and crazy enough to follow through.

"Go on," said the man as he stepped up closer to where Gordon was standing, pushing the automatic aside with his shoe. He picked up the automatic then shoved the muzzle of his own pistol into Gordon's back, telling him to walk on. As soon as the two of them entered the living room, the man behind Gordon skirted to his left pointing both weapons at Gordon's head.

Sitting in the semi-darkness of the living room was a heavy-set black man slouching on the sofa. He was smoking a cigarette and holding what appeared to Gordon to be a Glock 9mm automatic. In a nonchalant manner, he waved the weapon in Gordon's direction motioning him to stand where he was.

"Hey, how you doin'?" asked the man on the sofa as he puffed on his cigarette, blowing smoke rings in the air. Gordon did not respond. He knew it was often better to say nothing; it kept the intimidation factor at bay. He needed to figure things out so silence was a good stall tactic. "Hey, what the fuck took you so long? Me and Pickles thought you'd never get here. Ain't that right, Pickles?" "Damn straight," answered the man to his left.

So that was what he smelled, said Gordon to himself, as he stood there contemplating what he was going to do next. A fuckin' cigarette, wouldn't you know. He should have known, he hadn't smoked a cigarette but a few times since he rented the apartment a few weeks ago.

The next question was where did the guy from behind him come from, and then it dawned on him. He hadn't checked the fuckin' broom closet. The guy called Pickles was short and very thin. So, the son-of-a-bitch was able to squeeze himself into that narrow space.

"You stupid fuck," said Gordon as he berated his stupidity and obvious carelessness. The man on the sofa must have read his mind because he smiled a big toothy grin at Gordon's predicament. Before he said another word, the man on the sofa leaned forward and slowly crushed out his cigarette in an ashtray that was sitting on a coffee table in front of him. The man made it a point to stare up at Gordon long enough and hard enough to let him know who was in charge.

Gordon couldn't help but notice that the ashtray was overflowing with cigarette butts. In addition to that, there were a few empty wine bottles on display along with a box of Kentucky Fried Chicken. He saw some empties lying on the floor next to a few bags of potato chips and some leftover jars of salsa dip.

So, these guys were having themselves a little party while they were waiting for him. The observation brought a smile to his military mind. He had to believe that these two assholes were probably drunk or close to it and that made them vulnerable, at least he hoped so.

One thing was for sure: he didn't want to get into some sort of sanctimonious diatribe with these two assholes unless he had to. More than that, how could this be happening to him, especially after all he had gone through with Van Dameer? His mind wrestled with the implausibility of his situation and yet he knew he didn't have the time to think about it.

The man on the sofa stood up them walked around the coffee table and stood in front of Gordon.

"Hey, asshole, I'm like fuckin' talking to you. I said, how you doin'?" "Yeah," said the man called Pickles, "How you doin'?"

"Yo, Pickles, shut the fuck up, will ya? I'm talkin' to our guest here."

Gordon didn't respond to the man's query. He just stood there reticent, looking over the man's shoulder. He knew from previous experience sometimes the less you said the better. Anyway, he had to stall for time. At the moment time was all he had. He had to figure a way out of this or else things could get ugly real fast.

From what he saw of his two adversaries they looked to be no older than their late teens or early twenties. They were wearing the typical gangbanger uniform: the gold chains, baggy pants, baseball hats cocked sideways, their shirts hanging over their belts.

Out of all his momentary thoughts, he couldn't help but think that gangbangers had to carry a lot of guilt for their sartorial mayhem. He would have found the situation somewhat amusing if it wasn't for the guns and the apparent seriousness of their undisclosed intentions. Most of the time he didn't like black men; he liked them even less now. He never considered himself to be a racist. He just found black men to be uneducated, ill-mannered, and atavistic, with a perpetual chip on their shoulder. They also displayed a penchant for gratuitous violence. They seemed to enjoy knocking off people who didn't deserve it—other than that, they were probably okay. Unfortunately, they gave high-end shooters like him a bad rap. The thought irked him to the fuckin' max that people might see him in the same light as these two pieces of shit.

With a hawkish sneer, the man in front of him said, "Hey, you seen that little punk-ass Puerto Rican Alfredo Vacca around?"

With a condescending sneer of his own, Gordon replied, "No, I haven't seen him in a week or two." He lied. He saw Alfredo on the street in front of the apartment building as he was walking in. Without thinking, Gordon lowered his arms down to his side.

The gangbanger known as Pickles stuck the muzzle of his Glock against Gordon's face. "Who the fuck told you to drop your punk-ass hands? Huh? Who?" He punctuated his last words by shoving the muzzle of the Glock into Gordon's cheek.

Gordon responded by immediately raising his hands above his shoulders. "Sorry," he said sheepishly, trying hard to hide his growing sense of rage. "So, what do we do now?" asked Gordon of the man in front of him.

"Well, we wait for Alfredo to come back. Ain't that right, Pickles?"

"You got that right. You know what, Carnie? This mother is sun-dola, man. I know it; he's sun-dola."

"Easy, Mr. P. Don't mind, Pickles. He's kinda like edgy around you. It's like he thinks you're not straight. He thinks you're some kinda faggot. You're not a faggot, are you? I mean faggots don't carry heat with silencers."

"Hey, Pickles, turn on that light by the radiator, will

ya?" asked Carnie pointing to a standing lamp in the corner of the room.

"I gots to take a better look at our friend here. Hey, you can drop your hands now. Ain't that right, Mr. P.?"

"What the fuck," sneered Pickles while turning on the light. He then staggered to a loveseat in the center of the room and sat down.

"So, what's your name?" asked Carnie.

"Ernesto Rivas," replied Gordon, giving him his brother's name. It was the same name he gave Alfredo Vacca when he rented the apartment. Somehow he knew Vacca was behind all of this. It just smacked of some kind of setup—the kind of scam a punk like that would try to pull off.

"So, Ernesto, you work with Alfredo or what?"

"No, I just sublet the apartment from him. You know what I mean?"

"Oh, yeah. Well, let me tell you what's going down. Like you know, your partner Alfredo . . . he jacked us for twenty grand, you dig? So, me and Pickles are here to get it back and we don't give a fuck how we do it or who we get it from."

Suddenly Carnie stopped talking, letting his eyes slowly drift up and down giving Gordon the once over. It was an obvious ploy of intimidation, but Gordon still found it unnerving.

In a graveled voice, Carnie said, "Ain't that right, Mr. P?"

His partner's only comment was to say, "fuckin' eh, and he better do the right thing, or else," making sure to overly dramatize the conviction of his statement by brandishing his Glock in Gordon's direction.

Carnie stepped closer to where Gordon was standing. He then ran a hand over his suit jacket. "So, Ernesto," he said, slurring his words as he spoke, "I gotta like pat you down, you know what I mean? So, don't go doin' nothin' stupid or Pickles will have to bust a cap in your dumb ass."

Gordon's only response was to smile weakly then

bow his head in abject compliance. The atmosphere was contentious. Knowing he had to get the two thugs to relax, he decided to act as docile as he could. Later, however, rest assured, his demeanor could be quite different.

Gordon could see the affects alcohol was having on Carnie. When he leaned forward to frisk him he sort of lost his balance. His breath reeked of cigarettes and wine. Besides all of that, when Carnie felt his jacket he stopped only long enough to inspect his pockets and nothing else—a sure sign of someone who didn't know what he was doing or didn't care.

He told Gordon to take off his suit coat and hand it to him. With an acceptable degree of deference Gordon obliged his request. He took his time and folded the coat neatly before giving it to him. When Carnie went to take the jacket he missed something in the transaction and let it fall to the floor.

Gordon bent down and picked it up then handed it to him. "Thanks," said the gangbanger as he gave it back. Before doing so Carnie stopped for a second, pointed to Gordon's shoulder holster, and said, "Whoa, Ernesto, nice fuckin' holster, man. You must be some kinda drug dealer or somethin'. Where are you from, anyway?"

"Columbia," replied Gordon as he slipped into his suit coat. "You know where that is?"

"Yeah! I know where it is. What the fuck? You think I'm stupid or somethin'? Hey, how come you got no wallet on you?"

"I don't like to carry one, too many pickpockets around," replied Gordon, letting one of his hands touch his crotch, a sign of disrespect for that type of criminal.

"Yeah, me, too," said Carnie while he switched gun hands so he could wipe his nose.

"Yo, Carnie, man, this guy is fuckin' O.C.," interrupted Pickles from the other side of the room, ending his statement with an audible fart.

Gordon turned his head in the direction of the so-called Mr. P. and stared at him for a second or two. The gangbanger looked back at him with an expression that said: what, what you never heard a fart before? Gordon smiled with a contemptuous sneer of his own letting the gangbanger know what he thought of him.

"Hey, Ernesto, you O.C., or what? You got organized crime on your jacket. You know what I'm talkin' about? Like on your manila folder down at the precinct?"

"No, not really, not at least in your country," answered Gordon as he stuck one of his hands into the front pocket of his trousers.

"So, what's in your pockets?" asked Carnie shifting his stance from one foot to the other— another sign he was losing his concentration.

"Not much, just this," said Gordon, removing a wad of cash from his pocket. He then held the money in front of him so Carnie could take it.

He didn't want the gangbanger to make another attempt at patting him down. For one simple reason: he was wearing an ankle holster with a double-shot .22 Magnum Derringer in it. He often carried the weapon in the anticipation that someday he might need it; apparently that day had arrived.

From where he was standing Pickles interjected his own observation on Gordon's character.

"Yo, Carnie, this dude is the fuckin' berries. He's holdin' all that jack and he's got this fancy-ass biscuit for a gun."

Gordon could see that the gangbanger was showing signs of gastric distress. He couldn't stand still; he kept stepping from side-to-side as if he needed to use the bathroom. Apparently he was the victim of too much pizza, wine, spicy chicken wings and possibly vanilla ice cream.

Carnie paid no attention to what his partner said, or his obvious need to relieve himself.

"Hey, Ernesto, how come you're like carryin' a nine

with a silencer?"

"I don't like noise," replied Gordon with a tentative smile, all the while studying his two antagonists for some sign of weakness.

Carnie snickered, "Yeah, I get you; that's cool, that's cool. You know, you're like us. I mean, you know?"

"Yeah, I know," said Gordon keeping an eye on Pickles. "Say, Carnie, I think your friend isn't feeling so well."

"Is that so? Who asked you?"

"Well, I'll tell you what I'm going to do for you, Ernesto. You come up with some more Jing, and we'll get out of your face."

"Yeah, like a lot more. Your friend Alfredo took us for twenty grand. You think you can get that up, E-R-N-E-S-T-O?" barked Pickles, who looked as if he was about to explode.

Carnie glanced over at his partner then asked Gordon if he thought he could get the money.

"Sure, it might take a little time, but . . ."

"There ain't no buts. Like the man says, 'you got the watch, we got the time.'"

"Sure, but answer me this: what do I get in return?" asked Gordon.

"How about your life?" answered Carnie, while swaying slowly back and forth.

"Sounds fair to me," said Gordon.

"Ah . . . answer me this."

"Yeah?"

"What's your name?" asked Gordon. "Like your real name." This time he said it with a smile, hoping to stall him just a little bit longer.

Before Carnie could reply, Pickles said, "Yo, Carnie. Man, I got to sit down; I ain't feelin' so good."

Gordon watched as Pickles dropped himself down in a large loveseat that occupied the middle of the room.

"Hey, Pickles, what the fuck you doin'?"

"I gotta sit down."

"Well, get your ass on up, nigger. We got business here; you can sit the fuck down later."

"No, man, I gotta take like a wicked shit, like, I'm dyin'," said Pickles with a plaintive moan, holding his stomach as he spoke.

"You gotta what . . . how come you didn't shit before?"

"Because I didn't have to, that's why."

"So, go use the toilet. How you going to act, and don't take all fuckin' day, and gimme Ernesto's nine. You don't need two guns to shit with."

Gordon could sense his time was at hand, but not quite yet. It would come soon enough and then he would exact his own type of fairness. He would follow the criminal code of self-interest to approve to any means to facilitate your own ends.

While he waited for his moment of opportunity, Gordon thought over the scam that Carnie and Pickles were trying to pull off. When he rented the apartment from Alfredo, he gave him his brother's name. Alfredo checked it out, found out some guy named Ernesto Rivas was connected to the Colombian Cartel. So, he figured he'd make a quick score, and shake him down, knowing no drug dealer would ever go to the law. So, he set up a scene with the two gangbangers playing the heavies.

Somehow he figured out the Scotch tape on the door trick, then let Carnie and Pickles in the apartment with a spare key, replaced the tape and then waited outside for him to return. He used his cell phone to call the two thugs in the apartment to tell them that he was on his way up. Not bad, not bad thought Gordon as he stood there watching Pickles run down the hallway to the bathroom.

"Ernesto, pay attention. Go over to where Mr. P. was sitting and kneel the fuck on down. Don't go fuckin' around on me or I'll shoot your spic ass."

Gordon did as he was told and knelt down toward

the back of the loveseat. From that position he watched and waited as Carnie kept looking in the direction of the hallway towards the bathroom.

"Hey, Pickles," shouted Carnie. "Pickles, you hear me? I gotta take a piss. So hurry up and use the spray. I don't want to go smellin' your nasty ass."

Gordon timed his move perfectly. He waited for Carnie to turn his head in the direction of the hallway. With one quick move, he threw himself behind the loveseat. As he did that, he brought his knees up to his chest.

With the swiftness of a man who had practiced that maneuver before, he snapped open his ankle holster and took out the Derringer. After witnessing what Gordon did, Carnie stood there laughing.

"Hey, Pickles, Pickles, man, you gotta see this. You ain't gonna believe it. Ernesto is fuckin' hidin' behind the couch you were sittin' on. What a fuckin' . . ."

Before Carnie could finish what he was about to say, Gordon reached up from the floor using the loveseat as a blind and fired a single shot from his Derringer.

The bullet hit Carnie just below his right eye. The jolt sent him flying backwards as if he was hit by a baseball bat. It was a .22 Magnum hollow point that went in small, but mushroomed as it went into his brain. Carnie was dead before he hit the floor.

Gordon scrambled from behind the loveseat and went to where Carnie had dropped his automatic. He heard a terrified Pickles shouting from the bathroom asking what was going on.

As quickly as caution would allow, Gordon made his way down the hallway towards the bathroom, and the unsuspecting Mr. P. In a matter of a few seconds, he positioned himself to the side of the bathroom door. He did that just in case Pickles decided to use his Glock and shoot through it.

He then fired six muted gunshots from his automatic.

The nine millimeter bullets tore holes in the door doing the same to their intended target. Gordon heard the cry and familiar moan of a man who had been shot. The next sound was the heavy thud of Pickles' body hitting the bathroom floor.

Cautiously, Gordon pushed open the bathroom door; the gangbanger's body was in the way. He lay there grasping for breath, his eyes wide beseeching him not to shoot, his lips quivering as he tried to speak while blood oozed from his wounds.

Gordon looked down at the dying man. For an extended moment he started feeling pity for him. However, he knew what he had to do. His face became a mask of unfeeling derision. Slowly, he turned his head from side-to-side, "Sorry, Mr. P," said Gordon as he pulled the trigger of his automatic, shooting the gangbanger in the head. A fountain of blood spurt from his temple covering his body while it spread across the bathroom floor. Not wanting any of Mr. P.'s blood to touch his shoes. Gordon quickly backed away. He didn't need any telltale signs of what happened following him around.

He shut the door behind him, re-holstered his automatic, and then slipped his Derringer into the side pocket of his suit coat.

Gordon spent the next half-hour going through the apartment with a bucket of bleach wiping down everything he could. He tossed a few cigarette butts on the floor. (He made it a point to pick up cigarette butts off the street and keep them in a jar.) He then sprinkled some urine around which he had collected from a few homeless guys he had paid to piss in a bottle.

Every crime scene told a story and he did his best to tell a lie. No sense making it easy for the crew from CSI and forensics to figure things out.

He then put all his clothes in a duffle bag. When he was about to leave, he heard the phone ring. Gordon knew it could only be Alfredo wondering what was going on. Well, he would soon find out, Gordon thought, hoping someday he would run across him again.

Gordon followed the stairwell down to the bottom floor of the apartment building. He left through an emergency exit that led to an alleyway on another street— one that wasn't in front of the building. He knew Alfredo was probably there somewhere looking at everyone leaving the front entrance.

His most pressing issue was to get as far away from New York City as he could. He knew that sooner or later the cops would be all over this and Alfredo was sure to implicate him or whoever he thought he was. It wasn't until months later that Gordon found out who the two gangbangers were. The guy called Carnie was Carnival Jones and Pickles was a man named Marcus Heinz. Their bodies were found in a shallow grave outside Philadelphia. They ended up in a cold case file under the heading of homicides of an unknown origin murdered by unknown assailants or assailant. Cause of death: gunshots to the head and torso.

CHAPTER 12

Since the incident at Alfredo's apartment Gordon spent the last five weeks drifting throughout the northeast. He would travel from one small town to another, the more obscure, the better.

His reasoning was to avoid what he considered the consistent professionalism and the watchful eyes of big city law enforcement. He had this notion that small town cops were lackadaisical. Whether or not his assumption held any merit, he really couldn't say. The fact being that he never had any encounters with any of them and wasn't sure of what they were capable of.

Whenever he found himself on the run Gordon preferred using mass transit as his mode of travel. He never stayed in one place for more than a few days, a week at best. He used that old cliché as his impetus: that a moving target was hard to hit, adding the thought, and also hard to find, especially if you don't know what you were looking for.

Always the consummate chameleon, Gordon changed his looks and his name as he saw fit. He used different colored wigs, glasses, and would shave or not shave depending on the situation.

He used cash only whenever he had to make some type of monetary transaction. Whenever he was asked if he could use a credit card Gordon would use the excuse that they had been lost or stolen. Most of the time cash was acceptable; however, on a few occasions motels would want a credit card as a form of insurance for any damage a guest might cause while staying in one of their rooms.

Most of the time Gordon tried to find an out-of-way bed and breakfast to stay. Another place he would often use was state or national parks. They were perfect to hide in and bury caches of money and equipment. He felt at home in the woods. His four years in the Rangers gave him the confidence that once he was there, it would take God to find him and an army to take him out.

All and all he was satisfied as to the success of his surreptitious journey; it was uneventful, and at times downright boring. Of course, that was the way he wanted it: no fuss, no muss and no one the wiser.

As part of his daily routine, he often checked his laptop for any mention of the two gang bangers he had killed. He found nothing about them on any of the news websites or their blogs. In addition to that, he couldn't find anything about them on the law enforcement sites, either. The only explanation he could think of was after Alfredo found his two dead buddies lying on the apartment floor, he went into panic mode knowing he would have to do a whole lot of explaining to the cops and everyone else. So, he did a Houdini, and somehow, someway had them disappear.

If that was the case he was home free and could return to New York City. He could take up where he left off and catch up on some very urgent business. In the meantime, he thought he would go on to just one more place. A place he hadn't been to since he left the university eleven years before: Bar Harbor, Maine.

The thought brought back a few memories, one in

particular. He remembered a certain co-ed he took there with him, Cynthia Audrey Martindale. He hadn't thought about her in a long time. Still, he could see her standing there, her long auburn-blond hair, her dark-colored eyes, and her dead-white skin. He remembered how she liked to wear white turtleneck sweaters; he thought wistfully about her skin-tight jeans and hiking boots. Strange how faded memories can linger in the mind; Gordon remembered how she was convinced he was what she wanted, and was willing to do anything to have him. They went camping in Acadia National Park; she was willing to experiment and followed his sexual desires to a tee. He could still feel her body under him, the taste of her perfume as he sucked on her neck; he could still hear her gentle moans of passion that left him quivering with uncontrolled desire.

"Ah, what the hell," he said to himself; that was a long time ago, no use thinking about that now. Anyway, that was before the army, before Iraq, before Global Solutions and all that went with it. Still and all, he thought what if he had stayed with her; where would he be now?

Gordon went to Bar Harbor by bus and then used a local cab to travel around in. The driver took him to four different bed and breakfasts before he found the kind of place he was looking for—a quiet little hideaway called Shady Isle; it was situated on a spit of land that extended into the sea. It had a beach made of small stones, a white picket fence and a few rose bushes, and a large poplar tree that sat next to the entrance. The name of the place, Gordon guessed, came from the shade given by that tree.

The proprietor of Shady Isle was a matronly woman by the name of Mrs. Virginia Wolff. He put her age around fifty or so with what he considered one of those effusive personalities that could become somewhat annoying once you got to know her. Besides all of that, he didn't think she was much to look at either: kind of plain with long gray hair tied in a ponytail, no makeup and a stocky build in a print dress.

However, true to his mission and for acceptance sake, he put all that aside and decided to let the chips fall where they may. On his first night at Shady Isle, Gordon decided he would pass up going out to dinner and would try his luck in Mrs. Wolff's overly hospitable dining room. At first glance, it looked to him like a picture out of *Town & Country* magazine. It had a high ceiling with a well-polished wooden floor that was partially covered by an oriental throw rug. On one side of the room was a very large fireplace surrounded by an elaborate mantelpiece made of mahogany. On the other side was a magnificent grandfather clock that chimed softly on the hour. In the center of the room was a table large enough to accommodate eight to ten people. Across its surface was an embroidered white tablecloth made of fine Irish linen. To round out her picture of convivial bliss, her *pièce de résistance* was she used real china plates, genuine crystal glasses and fine silverware as place settings.

Gordon rarely fraternized with the guests when he stayed at a bed and breakfast; he found them to be a little too tedious and overly inquisitive. This time, however, he would make an exception and try to make himself a little more gregarious. Being the perfect host, Mrs. Wolff introduced her guests to one another by the first and last names and where they were from. The first on her list was Mr. and Mrs. Frank Campbell and family; there was Frank, his wife Charlene and their two children Elisabeth and Nick. They were from Rhode Island—Narragansett to be exact.

The second couple to be introduced was Steve and Patricia Brodski from Hartford, Connecticut.

Gordon himself was the next on her list of introductions; she said his name, that he was from Ottawa, Canada, and that he had recently returned from the Middle East. He forgot that he happened to mention that to her when he checked in. Gordon swore at himself; he hadn't been there but a minute and already he was telling people his life story.

The next person was the introduction he was waiting for. He noticed her immediately when she walked into the dining room. Her name was Dr. Donisha Danville, a psychologist from Boston, Massachusetts. She had an uncanny resemblance to his long-lost co-ed, the same auburn hair, the dark eyes, and the white skin. It was all too unsettling for him to take in. Maybe there was a thing called destiny; whatever it was, he swore he wasn't going to talk to her, but he knew he would. Unfortunately, she happened to glance in his direction; their eyes met, she smiled and he knew he was dead.

The dinner conversation was the same old chitter-chatter, "How do you like Bar Harbor?" "What do you do for work?" "How's the weather?" and so on. While he sat there trying to make polite conversation with the other guests, Gordon couldn't help but steal a few furtive glances in the direction of Dr. Danville. He was sure she was aware of his interest in her since it seemed to him she was returning his gaze with one of her own.

Of course it might have been a case of wishful thinking and he misinterpreted her come-hither expression as a flirtatious invitation to a more insightful discussion.

Other than that he was taken up with the thought of what was under her mint-green sweater. He was caught up in the idea that every time she moved, her overly-ample breasts appeared to sway ever so slightly leaving him in a state of forgetting why he was there in the first place.

That was the meal their host Mrs. Wolff had prepared for them. Her menu consisted of a generous portion of corned beef and cabbage with boiled potatoes and carrots, a poached salmon dish with a honey mustard demi-glaze and rice. For dessert she made a lemon chiffon pie, as well as a peach cobbler that she served with vanilla ice cream. All of it quite scrumptious, but he really wasn't interested in the meal.

Before they sat down to eat, Mrs. Wolff gave them

the option of having wine with their meal, something most bed and breakfasts didn't do. She left the obvious unsaid, that the cost of the wine would be added to their bill. Gordon purchased four bottles for the table, one for himself and one for Dr. Danville. As a courtesy, she openly acknowledged with a smile and a nod, while mouthing the words "thank you." The other guests also thanked him for his generosity, but left their bottles half full, preferring to drink ice water instead.

Gordon didn't mind what some people might consider a slight—since the wine was only intended for the doctor and himself in the first place. After the meal was over everyone at the table exchanged the customary pleasantries of saying goodnight, see you in the morning, etc. Gordon was glad to see them leave, and even more pleased that Donisha had decided to stay behind.

Mrs. Wolff offered each of them a cup of coffee and a complimentary after-dinner drink of cognac. His feelings about Mrs. Wolff had changed from someone he didn't like to someone he did like. He criticized himself for being so impulsive, for judging people at first site. It was a character flaw he couldn't seem to mitigate; of course, if the truth was told, he didn't really want to.

Since he was old enough to know the way things were he knew you had to trust your gut feelings. If you had to change the way you felt you could always do that at some later date. Besides, he never liked to stray from his nature to shoot first and aim later.

Gordon's conversation with Dr. Danville hadn't gone too far, when he noticed that she was beginning to show signs of how much she had been drinking. Her words weren't coming out right and she had that expression on her face that said "I'm loaded."

In the course of what she was saying, she told him that she wasn't much of a drinker and maybe it would be best if she just called it a day, went upstairs to her room and got some sleep.

It was a thought that Gordon wholeheartedly agreed with knowing that upstairs was the place he wanted her to be. He told her he was tired also and would probably do the same. When it involved a woman that interested him, he would often play the role of the gentleman. He found out from previous experience that a little politeness could often take him where he wanted to go. In this case, the destination was her bedroom.

Before she left the dining room table, he stood up, walked to where she was sitting and held her chair for her. When she attempted to stand up, she lost her balance and stumbled into his outstretched arms. While she stood there struggling to gain her composure, she begged his forgiveness for being so clumsy.

"Think nothing of it," he said with a rakish grin, all the while contemplating the thought that maybe she was just drunk or trying to send him a message? Either way it was okay by him. He often followed the mantra: "romance was best, but liquor was quicker."

He told her that he would be happy to follow her upstairs to her room just to make sure she was alright, as she stood there holding onto one of his arms with one hand, while massaging the side of her head with the other. She told him that he really didn't have to do all that; she was quite capable . . . to do it by herself.

She looked up at him, closed her eyes for a second then nodded her head in agreement. With an "I'm so hopeless" smile, she said that maybe it would be best if he did follow her upstairs. Out of the corner of his eye, Gordon could see Mrs. Wolff standing near the doorway. She looked like one of those medieval guards with her arms folded in front of her, a supercilious scowl on her face—it was the type of expression women would often get when a man was doing something they disapproved of.

He knew what she was thinking. "Well, that was too damn bad," he thought as he walked Donisha past her. He made it a point to look her straight in the eye as he said "goodnight." She said the same back to him, with the added refrain, "Oh, and pleasant dreams." Yeah, right; he knew what she meant, but he didn't care. What the hell, he thought, maybe he would get lucky and her words would follow him upstairs—all the way into Dr. D's bedroom.

When they arrived at the door to her room, Gordon took her keys from her hand and opened the door for her. She invited him in saying, "I don't feel good and I don't want to be alone; so, if you don't mind staying with me for a minute or so." Gordon was pleased to see that no one else was in the hallway with them when they went inside. That would eliminate any of those awkward glances or mumbled comments that he was sure would follow if they were seen going into the room together. He watched as Donisha staggered over to her bed then flung herself face down on her pillow. She rolled over and placed a forearm over her face then motioned for him to sit next to her by patting the space on the mattress. She told him that she felt like the room was spinning.

As soon as he sat down she asked him if he would mind holding her hand. When he did that, she asked if he thought she was pretty. He told her she was more than pretty, simply beautiful. Taking her words as a come-on for more than a verbal answer, he bent forward to kiss her lips. She put a hand up to stop him; he didn't force the issue, the last thing he needed was a scene. With a sob in her voice, she asked, "You don't hate me, do you?" "Of course not," he whispered, while attempting to console her by rubbing her shoulder, hoping she would respond in a more positive manner if he touched her. "I mean, you don't hate me because I'm drunk, do you?" "No, I think you're just . . ." she interrupted what he was going to say by tugging on his sleeve and asking him to kiss her. Once again, he bent forward to oblige her request, only to be stopped halfway to her lips, again.

"No, don't," she whispered and then pulled herself on his arm. With her head resting against his shoulder, she said, "I think I'm going to be sick." He knew that was coming, so he picked her up in his arms, rushed over to the bathroom and put her down if front of the toilet. He couldn't leave her alone, so he stood there with her and held onto her as she bent over and threw up.

Gordon laughed at his situation; wasn't that the fuckin' way? His plan of getting her drunk worked just fine, but, as usual, the ugly head of unintended consequences popped up and once again bit him in the ass.

After a short while of watching her heave herself dry, she finally stopped and went over to the sink and cleaned herself up—washing her face, brushing her teeth and gargling with Listerine. Without facing him, she turned away, put one hand up to cover her eyes and began to cry.

Gordon smiled at the sight of her predicament, walked over to where she was standing and wrapped his arms around her, kissing the tears from her face. She told him all she wanted to do was lie down and could he stay with her. "Sure," was his only reply as he lifted her in his arms and took her back to bed. As soon as he placed her down and her head hit the pillow, she rolled over and passed out. Gordon stood there staring down at her. He was tempted to do what he wanted to do: take her clothes off, see her naked and helpless. It didn't get any better than that; maybe play with her awhile, just enough to get him off—the thought of it made his dick hard.

However, he knew the code; it was bad karma to take advantage of a drunken woman. He decided to take the right road. He bent over and kissed her on the cheek, letting one of his hands run along the side of her thigh. He knew if he kept on going he wouldn't stop; so, he pulled away, cursing his luck and the code. He left the light on in her bathroom. When he walked out of her room and into the hallway, he made sure to lock the door behind him.

Gordon returned to his room where he lay on his bed trying to read himself to sleep, only to end up staring at the ceiling thinking about his life. He thought about Donisha;

it had been a long time since he had any feelings for a "normal" woman. He was a cash-and-carry type of guy. Mostly he stuck to the incidental kind, the pay-as-you-go girls: escorts, pole dancers, massage parlor types. They were easy, and most of all they didn't ask questions; at least none you felt you had to answer.

Gordon turned to his side then rolled back again, closed his eyes, then put a forearm over his face. He remembered his childhood in Colombia, his mother, father and brother.

With quiet footsteps Gordon padded his way along the hallway towards his room. Somewhere in the back of his mind he contemplated the thought that maybe he would knock on Donisha's door, just to see how she was feeling.

Of course, he knew that was what he would use as his excuse. The real reason would be he wanted to strike up another conversation with her; possibly take up where he left off from the night before, and do what had planned on doing: "fuck her to death, or at least until she couldn't stand up."

Suddenly, he saw the door to her room open just wide enough to see her standing there. She was wearing a terrycloth bathrobe that stopped somewhere around the middle of her thighs. On her feet was a pair of satin pumps with wispy white feathers that covered the toes—a visual aphrodisiac that left him in a lurch.

She was holding the door open with one hand and beckoning to him with the other. Instinctively, he looked around to make sure he was alone. Satisfied that the "coast was clear," he followed her command and once again entered her room sight unseen. Gordon could see she was wearing makeup and shiny red lip gloss—the kind that left him thinking how her lips might feel on certain parts of his anatomy. Her hair was a lustrous cascade of soft, auburn curls which fell seductively around her shoulders.

Without saying a word she shut the door behind him. He turned and smiled at her, but before he had a chance to ask her how she was feeling, she said in a low, sultry voice, "I want to apologize to you about last night; I don't know what got into me, and I am so embarrassed."

"No need to," Gordon said while trying to avert her eyes so he could look around her room. "We all do that from time to time; kind of goes with the territory." He noticed her bed was made and the phone on a table next to it was off the hook.

"I never drink a lot; I'm sort of going through some emotional issues," she said while dabbing at her eyes with a tissue she was holding.

Gordon held up one of his hands with the palm facing her, "You don't have to explain; I understand."

With a tearful smile, she reached out and touched his arm. "Thank you for saying that; I really appreciate your kindness. I hope you and I can be friends."

"Friends?" Gordon asked as he searched her face for some telltale clue as to what she might have on her mind.

"Yes, friends. Well, you know, acquaintances."

"Acquaintances, sure, that's do-able," he said, hoping after uttering those words she didn't recognize the obviousness of his Freudian slip.

Her lips parted slightly as if she was about to laugh; instead she murmured, "Did anyone ever tell you you are very good-looking?"

"Excuse me?" said Gordon, pretending he didn't hear her.

"You are very good-looking."

"Mmmm, no, not lately," he said with a grin, "but thank you for saying so. Ah, would you mind if I took off my jacket? I was out jogging and it's kind of hot in here."

She gazed into his eyes and said, "No, not at all; be my guest," then pushed her hair from the side of her face just enough to expose the whiteness of her neck.

Ever mindful as to body language, he interpreted the gesture as a come-on; at least, he hoped it was. However he had "jumped the gun" before and paid the price of rejection.

"I saw you from my window."

"You saw what?" he asked.

"That you were out jogging. Do you do that a lot?" she asked.

"Well, I try to," Gordon replied as he unzipped his jacket noticing that Donisha seemed to grow tense as she watched him take it off. Underneath he was wearing one of his old army t-shirts; it was soaking wet from sweat and stuck to his chest like a second skin.

Gordon ran his hands over his chest, and then said, "I'm sorry that I am such a mess, I didn't know I would see you. If I had I would have looked a lot better."

Her only reply was to say, "Do you know you are very muscular?"

"Well, I try to work out a lot; I like to keep in shape, and it helps with the stress, kind of like sex."

"Sex?" she asked.

"You know, sex; they say it helps reduce stress."

"Oh, I must have missed that class in medical school," she said while holding out her hand so Gordon could give her his jacket. She then folded it neatly and placed it on a chair next to her.

"Thanks," said Gordon, "you know you are very nice for a psychiatrist and all; I thought you would be . . ."

"What? Stuck-up?" she asked.

Gordon didn't reply.

She laughed then touched his chest with her fingertips. "You are all wet. Would you like to take a shower?"

"Here? You mean now?"

"Of course. I have plenty of towels, shampoo and conditioner; anyway, you won't have to use that community bathroom at the end of the hall."

"Well, that's very kind of you. Are you sure it's okay? I mean, you don't really know me."

"I know you well enough," she said.

She let her eyes say more than her words as she looked him up and down and said, "I know you well enough."

"Oh, if you insist, but I might be in there a long time; so, if you have to, you know, do anything."

"Don't worry, I'm fine. Would you like a glass of ice water? I have a pitcher Mrs. Wolff gave me this morning."

"No, thank you; I'm not thirsty," said Gordon as he proceeded to walk in the direction of the bathroom with Donisha in tow. In the light of what had gone on between the two of them, he decided to let it go and see where it would end up.

When they crossed through the entranceway of her bathroom, Donisha flicked on the light switch and closed the door. She backed up against the side of the sink with her legs stretched out in front of her. The look on her face said enough for him to know she wasn't there to brush her teeth.

In a scene out of some Hollywood movie, they stood there looking at one another, waiting for the right moment to transpire.

"So, what's next?" he said, using his best Clint Eastwood voice. "Are you going to make my day?"

She said nothing, but a faint smile crossed her lips to tell him all he needed to know. As they stood there languishing in the suggestive atmosphere of the moment, her eyes never left Gordon's penetrating gaze.

With a decided air for the dramatic, Donisha took a deep breath, then pressed her back against the side of the sink, letting the well-defined muscles of her thighs stretch out in front of her.

"Well," he murmured as he cleared his throat, "I guess I should ask you . . .." Donisha finished his sentence by asking, "What's next?"

Gordon stepped a little closer to where she was standing and said, "Yeah, something like that—I guess."

"Don't worry, it's nothing much," she intoned, her voice lingering as if she really didn't want to continue.

"However, I do have a small request, if you don't mind. A strange one."

Before he answered her question, Gordon glanced at his reflection in the mirror behind her. He looked the way he wanted to be: aloof, but sensitive; approachable, yet mysterious. He touched the side of her face with the back of his hand, letting his forefinger trace the contour of her cheek.

"A strange request?" he said, his voice far off, but

questioning, "I like strange requests, especially from beautiful women."

Obligingly, she nestled up against him, her head down with the fingers of both her hands resting on his chest.

"You know I like you, don't you?" she purred, knowing that more than a glimmer of understanding had come between them.

"Oh, I kind of got that impression," replied Gordon, wondering when that next shoe was going to fall.

"I know this is going to sound ever so crazy, but would you mind if I watched you take a shower?"

His corresponding thought was "bingo."

"No, not at all," Gordon said as he bent forward to kiss her lips when suddenly she pulled away from him, turning her head as if she was embarrassed by what she had asked of him.

"I mean, if you do, I'll leave—really I will—I swear I will, really," Donisha stammered.

Before he could say anything, she untied the sash to her bathrobe, letting it drop to the floor. Without any hesitation she opened both sides of her robe so he could see all of her. Instantly, his eyes swept over her naked body. As he already knew, she was heavy-breasted, with a semi-muscular waistline, but better than that, she was clean-shaven. A noticeable formality, however, one he was glad to see considering the fact that pubic hair turned him off. More to the point it would have stymied his desire to go down on her—a sexual easement he wanted to follow.

Donisha pulled him from his reverie by saying, "See anything you like?"

His only utterance was, "Where have you been all my life?"

A childish cliché but apparently an acceptable one; she flashed him a look of haughtiness that let him know that things were about to get a lot better.

Once again she did the inexplicable and closed both sides of her robe around her as if to say "you saw enough."

Sensing that maybe she was about to change her mind, Gordon yanked off his t-shirt then slipped out of his running shoes. As he was about to untie the string that held up his sweatpants, she stopped him by touching the tattoo on the left side of his chest.

"What's this?" she asked.

"Oh, that, well . . ." replied Gordon.

She interrupted him by saying, "I know what it says: Latin for 'an eye for an eye,' *lex talionis*."

"Then, I guess you know this phrase, also," he said as he touched the right side of his chest.

"Of course, it is Latin for 'strength through loyalty' . . . *fortius quo fidelius*."

With a somewhat distinct tone of annoyance Gordon replied, "Well, you sure know your Latin."

"I should, I took it for four years in girls' school." She wrapped her arms around him then pressed her lips against the muscles of his chest.

"Sorry," she mumbled, "I don't mean to be so pretentious; it's my nature, it's in my DNA and my father was a judge."

"Are those your sentiments?" she asked. Gordon sensed that the mood between them had suddenly grown somber.

"Sometimes," he replied.

"Are you a violent man, Anthony?" she asked as she reached down and squeezed the bulge inside his sweatpants.

"Only when I have to be," answered Gordon.

Without waiting any longer, he pushed his sweatpants and underwear to the floor. With a look of unabashed confidence he stood there looking at her as if to ask "see anything you like?"

"Well, look at you," she said with a slight smile as she pointed to his semi-erect penis bobbing in front of him like some type of sexual compass pointing the way to the object of his desire.

"Mmmm," she cooed as she shrugged off her robe, "You have a very big dick, Mr. Austin."

"Well, all the better to fuck you with, my dear," Gordon replied as he reached inside the shower to turn it on.

Donisha moved close to him and his embrace then slid her hand around his erection.

"Do you know any more nursery rhymes?" she asked, as Gordon maneuvered the handles of the shower to get the temperature right.

"Does that feel like a nursery rhyme?"

"Only if you are the big bad wolf," she said with a girlish giggle.

Gordon pulled her into the shower with him where they were to spend the better part of a half-hour exploring each other's bodies.

The combination of heat and the pounding wetness against their bodies added to arduousness of their love making. Gordon used his hands and fingers to delve into the intricacies of her gender. At different times Donisha would slide down his body to her knees with her hands on his hips then envelop his massive cock into her mouth. When the feeling became too much for him to bear, he pushed her away telling her that if she persisted he would cum in her mouth.

With Donisha leading the way, they left the confines of the shower, toweled off quickly and then went straight to her bed. Once they were there, the two of them spent the rest of the morning into the early afternoon whiling away the hours with amorous talk and using one another in what could be called an eclectic display of sexual ebullience.

At one point in their Homeric tryst Gordon told Donisha that he enjoyed dominating a woman with mild forms of S&M; would she mind if he tied her up? She thought it would be intriguing and agreed only if he promised not to hurt her. His only response was to bathe her ear with his hot tongue and whisper he would be extra gentle.

She turned her face and kissed him, then said, "Well, you don't have to be that gentle or I'm not going to feel it."

With his eyes half-shut and a lecherous leer, Gordon told her to lie on her stomach with arms extended in front of her. He then used a sash from one of her other robes to tie her hands to the bedpost. In a playful mood, Gordon told her not to go anywhere, and then went to the closet to find a belt to a pair of her pants. When he went back to the bed, he asked her if she missed him; Donisha looked over her shoulder and asked if she should have. With a slight smile Gordon said, "Wrong answer," and then tapped her lightly with the belt.

While laughing in the privacy of her mind, she said to him "Is that the best you can do?" He was what she wanted: strong, muscular, and good-looking, not like her overweight, philandering, stupid husband.

With a bemused grin Gordon smacked the cheeks of her ass over and over again. She twisted and turned straining at the leash that held her hands to the bed. She pretended to moan in the pleasure of his forcefulness. The sight of her writhing in the apparent throes of masochistic ecstasy made him want her even more.

With their mouths slightly open, they French kissed one another; their tongues intertwined in symbiotic accord. After a minute or two, she pulled away then searched the side of his face with her lips, stopping long enough to use her teeth to tease the lobe of his ear.

Satisfied with the thought of what he had just done, Gordon decided to back away from his administrations, and maybe contemplate something else he might want to do with her.

In the meantime, he thought it would be fair to emolliate some of the sting from Donisha's well-worn butt cheeks and kiss them for a while.

Using a small measure of benign supplication, Gordon pressed his lips against her skin. The thought of her vulnerability sent another idea across his mind. Perhaps, he would pursue the possibility of filling the space between the cheeks of her ass with his dick. It was a sexual pleasure that he enjoyed more than any other, and it would definitely cement the idea of his will over hers.

So, in no uncertain terms, he asked her if she would mind if he could do that to her. Donisha wondered why he had even bothered to ask and not just do it. She knew the answer; he wanted her acceptance—that was the key to his fantasy of control; his supposed dominance over her. The thought of her being restrained and being in the hands of a strange man fucking her ass was as intimately visceral as she could imagine.

Donisha tossed the visual around for a moment then rationalized her situation; asking herself what other choice did she have? She had to do it. She turned her head to the side and looked over her shoulder and said, "I'll do whatever you want me to do."

Her answer left Gordon searching for one of his own. Should he do what he wanted, or should he do what he thought she wanted him to do? It was a distinctively male quandary, and one he didn't feel like dealing with.

So, he turned her over. She had one of those languorous looks of weakness: her eyes wide and expressive, her lips soft pillows of want. The picture left him feeling more sexually insatiable than he was before.

Gordon positioned himself on his knees between her legs; from there he could bend over and kiss the inside of her thighs. With due diligence, he worked his way towards his goal: the labial folds of her cunt and the door to her libidinousness—her over-stimulated clit.

The sensation of his tongue pushed Donisha into a series of undulating thrusts of her pubic bone against his face. Her body arched to the point that only the back of her head and the heels of her feet touched the mattress. In the midst of her gyrations, Donisha's only words were a number of "oh, Gods!" and a number of "fuck me's."

Gordon gave into her demands, and from his kneeling position between her thighs, he put his arms under the back of her knees; he lifted her up so he could push his cock into her. He looked down and watched himself sliding rhythmically in and out of her, the sight of which sent him over the edge.

He pulled out of her, and then jerked off, spewing copious amounts of hot cum across her stomach and breasts. He fell by her side panting as if he had run a marathon.

With that done, he kissed her face and told her how beautiful she was without a clue as what to do next. Donisha just lie there staring up at the ceiling struggling with the thought that he was done. He untied her hands asking her did she come. She lied and told him she had, many times, swearing at herself for not telling the truth.

In the bedroom of her mind, Gordon had done what she had wanted. He was handsome, muscular, a sexual maven, and overly endowed—a distant thought from her out-of-shape, piece-of-shit husband who was having an affair with her underage cousin.

No, this guy, Anthony Austin, or whomever, was the perfect outing for her overwrought feelings and a most useful foil for her revenge.

They talked for a while. He told her he was going to go back to his room, clean up and maybe lie down for a while and take a nap. She told him that was a great idea and that she would probably do the same. They discussed going out to dinner that evening, having a few drinks and return to her room for a more intimate nightcap—the idea being to go over the same subject matter with better production values.

Of course he knew he had no intentions of doing that. He knew he had to leave. She would ask questions—

the kind of questions he couldn't answer. Anyway, she was a trained psychologist and could easily see through his lies.

Gordon went back to his room, dressed quickly, packed his bags and made a phone call to a local cab company, asking that a taxi be sent over to Shady Isle. Gordon paid his bill at the desk and gave Mrs. Wolff an envelope to give to Donisha. The note in it was short; he simply told her he had to leave on urgent business. He said he would try to get in touch with her at a later date at her office. Instead of signing his name, Anthony Austin, he signed it ARGO. Why he did that, he couldn't say, maybe he wanted her to wonder who he really was. Gordon shook his head at the thought. Without wanting to admit it, he knew the truth and it wouldn't set him free.

CHAPTER 13

At Manhattan's Mid-Town North Precinct on 47th St.

While they stood there thumbing through a pack of police reports, Detective Jimmy Egan and his partner Sergeant Eddie "Gloves" Moran were in no mood to do what they were doing and to be where they were.

It was late Friday afternoon and getting close to quitting time and close to what they wanted to do. Their minds were on going to their favorite bar, have a few drinks and chow down on some king size prime rib. Although they had been cops for a long time, they were new to the vice unit, meaning they only had a year on the squad. They found out vice was a lot of paperwork and sitting on cases hoping to make some valuable connections.

As in all police work they both sought and used confidential informants. The secret was to give as little as possible while trying to get what you wanted from them.

"Hey, Jimmy," said Moran. "I forgot to tell you."

"You forgot to tell me what?"

"Well, for starters, you know that CI Sal DeMarco?"

"Yeah, what about him?" Egan asked.

"Well, he came by the other day with some pictures from the Climax Club."

"Pictures of what?" Egan asked as he popped the top of a soda can he was holding.

"Pictures of these three guys."

Egan laughed and said, "Oh, yeah, what were they doing? Banging one another?"

"Nah," he said, "they all had Canadian driver's licenses."

"So, what?"

"So, he tells me they didn't look right . . . you know, like they didn't fit in."

"How the fuck would he know? He's always high on something."

"Hey! You going to listen or what?"

"So, how did he get the pictures?"

"You know, off the security camera at the front entrance."

"Okay. You got my attention."

"Oh, and another thing." said Moran, "He told me his sister Renee had a few dates with one of these guys."

"So, big deal, that's what she does for a living."

"Well," replied Moran, "she told me she didn't believe he was who he said he was."

"Oh! Is that so? Well, Renee ain't no icon of veracity," Egan said, knowing that Eddie was well aware of the fact he had a sexual encounter with her himself. It was something they talked about but didn't discuss.

"Well, what else?" Egan asked.

"So, I sent them over to Intelligence. Well, guess what? Intel . . . sends them over to the FBI . . . you know . . . Tom Starr's office."

"I'm listening," replied Egan as he sipped on his can of soda.

"So, what do you think . . . Starr gives me a call . . . tells me he wants to see the two of us at Scrumpy's tonight."

"What time?"

"Somewhere around six or so," replied Moran.

"Anything else?"

"Yeah, he finished up by telling me not to . . . uh, you know, say anything to anybody . . . about you and me meeting him."

"Oh, yeah? Like who did he have in mind?"

"Who else . . . but Desmond 'Fuckin'' Tutu, our fearless fuckin' captain."

"Oh, I almost forgot. There's something else I meant to tell you," said Moran.

"Oh, yeah? Like what?"

"Well, did you hear?" he replied.

"Hear what!?"

"They're planting trees in Harlem."

"What for?" asked Egan with a bemused grin.

"Public transportation."

As he stood there trying not to laugh, small driblets of soda bubbled from his lips then ran down his chin. He wiped at them with his sleeve while pointing at Moran.

"You're a fuckin' racist," he said with a grin.

"Yeah . . . I know," replied Moran. "Please forgive me for not being fuckin' PC . . . sometimes . . . you gotta tell it like it is."

"Is that so? Well, let me tell you like it is," Egan said. "I can forgive you, but you'd better not let Tutu hear you tell that joke . . . you know how he feels about racism in the department."

"Uh, huh, the same way he feels about most white people—he doesn't like them."

While he was slipping into his sport jacket, Egan said:

"Fuck all that . . . so, you ready . . . or what?"

"I was born ready," answered Moran. "You know, Jimmy, we'd better get over to Scrumpy's before Reno gets there. Hey, did you ever wonder how Tom Starr got that moniker: Reno?"

"No, Eddie, I never did . . . did you ever wonder how the fuck you made detective?"

Moran threw back his head and grinned at Egan, then slapped him on the shoulder as they walked out the door.

CHAPTER 14

Located in midtown Manhattan close to the 20th Precinct was an Irish pub and restaurant called Scrumpy's. The name had been derived from a form of hard cider that originated in England, but over the years had been adopted by the Irish as something uniquely their own.

Amongst the bar's better-known patrons were Detectives Jimmy Egan and Eddie "Gloves" Moran. The two men were known as stand-ups due to their penchant for telling off-color jokes—the kind that could be considered politically incorrect.

As usual the place was jam-packed with patrons of the same stripe—the majority of which being a mixture of off-duty cops and firemen. While struggling to find a place at the bar, the two detectives caused a minor stir as they high-fived and back-slapped their way through the crowd. A little coaxing and a bit of intimidation got them two seats in the vicinity of where Moran wanted to be. Before they sat down, he gestured over to one of the female bartenders.

"Hey, Sylvia," Moran said with a boyish grin, "you didn't go setting off any fire alarms today, did you?" he asked.

"Why?" she asked.

"Because you're looking pretty hot."

Jimmy Egan glanced at him with a look that said "how lame was that?"

"Don't mind him, Syl," he said. "He's a victim of self-abuse."

Men found her alluring, especially Moran. She was tall and thin-waisted, with long blond hair, and large breasts that seemed to sway whenever she moved.

With a toss of her hair and look that could be open to interpretation, Sylvia said:

"So, what's it going to be, Eddie?"

"Oh, you know . . . what I usually want."

She smiled at him knowing what he wanted wasn't on the menu. "Okay, and that would be . . . what?"

Moran plucked down a crisp one hundred dollar bill in front of her.

"What's that for?" she asked.

"The usual . . . you know, two pints of Beamish with a couple of shots of Concannon . . . you know—the usual."

"Well, yesterday, the usual was two pints of Guinness and two shots of Jamison."

With smiling eyes Moran pushed the hundred in her direction.

"That was yesterday," he said. "Today's another day," letting the moment fall into some type of obscure innuendo.

"Wise ass," she replied as she wrote down his order, then walked away murmuring something he couldn't hear.

"You know, Jimmy," said Moran, "I like watching her walk away. You know what I mean?"

"Yeah, Eddie, I know what you friggin' mean . . . already. How come you're always hitting on her? You know she's married," Egan said, as he popped a toothpick in his mouth from a dispenser that was sitting next to a bottle of ketchup.

"Yeah, I know, but you know, I kinda like the challenge. I like living dangerously."

"Oh, yeah, well, you could end up fuckin' dead."

Moran put a big hand on his partner's shoulder and said, "Do I look dead to you?"

"Only from the neck up," Egan replied, shrugging the shoulder Moran's hand was on.

Even though the bar was busy it wasn't long before Sylvia returned with their order.

While she was placing Moran's drinks in front of him, he said:

"Hey, Sylvia, who do you like better, Irish guys or Italians?"

She knew better than to answer him, but decided to do it anyway.

"Well, my husband's Italian," she said with a shrug.

"Oh, is he now? Well, you know what they say about Italians, don't you?"

"Okay, what?" she asked.

"They're just Jews with muscles," replied Moran as he threw back a shot of whiskey John Wayne style.

She knew the two detectives for a long time and their brand of humor was definitely out of touch with the times. So, she never took anything they said seriously—although, she had to admit she found Moran attractive, but never contemplated going any further than some harmless flirtations. Besides all of that, he always over-tipped her a lot.

With an insidious little grin she leaned over the bar and said:

"You know, Eddie, I can't argue with you . . . because my husband's got a very big muscle between his legs . . . you know what—he likes to flex it every night."

Before she left, Moran called after her, "Whoa . . . that was a blow. Wasn't that a low blow, Jimmy?"

Egan didn't bother to answer him. He was too busy trying to get the attention of a detective he knew from the "two-oh."

"Yo, Larry," he shouted. "How are things over in homicide?"

The man answered back, "Just about as good as they are in vice, without the graft."

Egan pretended to laugh at what had become a standard cop joke: how vice cops were always "on the take." Egan shot back with a rejoinder of his own. "Hey, Lar? What do you call an African-American ghost?" Not waiting for an answer, Egan said out loud, "A spook."

The detective told him he was a racist. Egan shook his head, "No, I'm not," he said. "I'm just a disappointed Republican."

A man sitting next to Egan said, "Hey, 'Stand-up.' How many cops does it take to change a lightbulb? Only one, but he's never around when you need him."

Egan looked at the man and said, "Cop jokes aren't cool. Did you hear the one about the Chinese couple who had a retarded baby and they named him Sum Ting Wong?"

Egan pretended to laugh at what he had just said, then turned away from the guy to talk to Moran. Standing close to him was a fireman he knew by the name of Sipinski.

"Hey, Joey," said Egan.

"Hey, what?" answered the fireman as he leaned away from the bar to get a better look at the detective.

"You know why Polish people end their names with the letters 's-k-i'? Because they can't spell toboggan."

The fireman snickered as if he thought the comment was funny. "That's pretty good, Jimmy," he said as he slapped Moran on the back. Moran looked at him then said:

"Hey! Joey. Don't look at me. He's your friend, not mine."

"Oh, thanks a lot. With friends like him, who needs enemies?"

The three men laughed then touched their glasses in a toast to some arcane alliance.

"Hey, Jimmy. Here's one for you," said Sipinski. "What do you call an Irish homosexual?" He waited a moment for Egan to respond then finished by saying to him, "A gay-lick . . . you get it?" he said. "A gay-lick."

Egan and Moran looked at one another then burst out laughing; not at the joke, but how Sipinski actually took the time to repeat the obvious. It seemed to cement what they already thought: that Polish guys weren't the sharpest knives in the drawer.

In the midst of their jibes Egan told the fireman he would buy him a drink. The man declined saying he had to go home for dinner—his wife was waiting for him— leaving the two detectives with the unspoken thought that at least he had someone to go home to.

Before he said anything, Moran did a quick look around, then moved closer to where his partner was sitting. While doing so he nodded in the direction of the bar's front door.

"Don't look now," he murmured, "but Reno and Spielman just walked in and it looks as if they got some kind of camel toe with 'em."

While chewing pensively on the end of his swizzle stick, Egan paused for a moment, then said with a sigh:

"Yeah, I know, I saw them when they walked in. Finish up your beer and let's go see what they want. Hopefully, this won't take long and we can go somewheres else. Oh, and another thing, no jokes or any wise cracks; be professional!"

"Look who's talkin'!" exclaimed Moran as he finished up the last few swallows of what had been his third pint of Beamish.

While they moved through the bar's burgeoning crowd, they happened to bump into a sergeant in their department named Isabella Cox. She was a heavy-set black woman who was a close friend of their immediate supervisor Captain Desmond Wallace. They didn't like her and by all accounts she didn't like them.

In their opinion she was nothing but a blatant suck-up, who had made her promotion under the auspices of the NYPD's affirmative action program. In addition, they considered her to be overly opinionated and way too snarky for her pay grade.

They hated to do it, but for the sake of civility and police solidarity, they stopped long enough to exchange some insincere salutations with her. With that out of the way, they moved into the adjoining dining room. Upon entering they spied the two FBI agents with the unknown woman sitting at a table for six.

It was Tom Starr who stood up and waved in their direction. To them it appeared as if he was purposely trying to draw attention to himself and to those he was with. It was something quite uncharacteristic of him.

They had known Reno Starr and his partner Trent Spielman for five years or so. In that time period they had developed a mutual rapport for one another—the kind that bordered on friendship.

It wasn't until recently that they found out the two agents had been sent to Iraq. They had been assigned to one of the consulates as "legal attachés." Their mission was to investigate crimes perpetuated by American civilians and crimes against them.

After shaking hands with Starr and his partner, Reno introduced their female companion as a CIA agent named Lauren. It wasn't important, but it sort of bugged them that CIA types were often referenced by a single name. It was semi-understandable when you considered the type of work they did. However, it seemed a lot like spy versus spy for their way of thinking.

They spent a short amount of time getting reacquainted discussing old acquaintances punctuated by citing certain arcane references and recent events. Of course they were well aware of the fact that their conversation was being parsed under the discerning eye of their companion Agent Lauren, who sat there stone-faced seemingly oblivious to what they were discussing and yet her body language told a different story.

It was Spielman that laid out one of the reasons for meeting them at Scrumpy's. According to him they were interested in their boss Captain Wallace whom they called Tutu. Egan explained to Agent Lauren why they referred to him as that—mainly he said because Wallace was African American and his first name was Desmond. She filled in the rest by saying, "as in Bishop Desmond Tutu, the black South African political activist who stood up against apartheid."

"That's the one," replied Egan.

"I take it you don't care for African Americans?"

"I like them as much as they like me," Egan said, letting the tone of his voice convey more than his words.

Sensing their obvious irritation with one another Spielman interjected by telling Egan why they were interested in Wallace. It seemed that he was caught on camera at the site of an FBI stakeout in Montreal, Canada. He was seen in the company of a high-valued suspect by the name of Christopher Graham Bentley. They were seen getting on the same bus going to the same restaurants. In one instance they went into the same restroom.

The suspect was under investigation for dealing in counterfeit Canadian passports and stolen antiquities from Iraq. It was at that point Agent Lauren told the two detectives that Bentley was ex-British military, a captain in the Special Air Services—the SAS.

He had been asked to resign under suspicion of murder while on assignment in Baghdad. Furthermore, he had worked with certain MI-6 and CIA operatives on a few highly-classified missions and might have compromised their effectiveness—for money.

She went on to explain that after leaving the service Bentley went to work for a private military corporation called Global Solutions. He was listed as a security specialist; at least that was his formal title. In reality he was a jack-of-all-trades,—kind of a go-to-guy when something had to be done. "We think he's still in their employment and working in the US and Canada."

"Okay," Egan said to her. "I get all that. What's all . . . I mean, why us . . . Eddie and me? I mean, why are we meeting here at Scrumpy's?"

"I think I can answer that," said Reno Starr. "It's like this, Jimmy. Ever since Montreal we've had a surveillance team on your Captain Tutu."

"Why?" Moran asked.

"Well, we think he might be selling police intelligence to Global. He's in a whole lot of debt . . . kinda goes with the territory, you know."

"Is internal affairs aware of this?" asked Moran.

"No, we'd rather keep them out of it," explained Starr. "At least for now . . . we want him to stay under surveillance . . . you know what I mean?"

"You still haven't told us why we're here?" Egan said as he motioned to one of the waiters to come over to their table.

"You see, Jimmy, it's like this: you and Eddie don't like Captain Wallace."

While he was telling the waiter to bring everybody at the table a round of drinks and some menus, Egan said, "Oh! Really! What makes you think that?"

"Well," replied Starr, "we know he wrote some pretty scathing proficiency reports about you two—cost you guys your promotions, put a sizable dent in your bank accounts."

"You got that right . . . that fuckin' *mulignan*," said Moran.

Their conversation was cut short as the waiter took their drink order with Eddie Moran abstaining saying he had enough while he was at the bar.

"So, what do you want us to do?" asked Moran.

"We want you to give Wallace bits and pieces of information, that . . . we give you—sort of steer him in our direction," replied Spielman.

"What's in it for us?" asked Moran.

With a nod of his head Spielman said, "How about your promotions?"

Using the same gesture Moran said:

"We're in . . . ain't that right, Jimmy?"

Egan didn't like it, but he knew the game. So he kind of bobbed his head a few times in apparent agreement.

"Sure, why the fuck not?" he said as he opened his menu.

"Let me ask you this . . . why Scrumpy's?"

"Well, there's some people here from your precinct," Starr said, "who, uh, know us from Federal Plaza. We want them to see us together talking. We want that to get . . . back to your captain. Most likely . . . he'll start asking you and Eddie questions . . . like why you were talking to the feds without his knowledge."

"You get the picture," said Spielman.

"Fuckin' moon-you?" asked Agent Lauren.

"Yeah, in Italian it means . . . Ah! Never mind," replied Moran as he paid for their drinks.

With her eyebrows raised she answered him with a terse, "I know what it means . . . Detective."

"Oh, okay," was his only reply.

"Anyway, there's a lot more to this story," she said.

"There always is," muttered a bemused Moran.

She then proceeded to run her fingers along the edge of her glass, as if it were a crystal ball and she was conjuring up something more to say. She then went on to explain Christopher Bentley's relationship with Wallace, that they were just the "tip of the iceberg" . . . that there were other "fish to fry."

Egan couldn't help himself; just to be a smug he told her that she was mixing her metaphors. She ignored his comment then went on to tell them about two other men of interest. The first, she explained, was also a former employee of Global Solutions and possibly worked for their affiliate: the World Enforcement Bureau known as the W.E.B.

"Oh, boy!" explained Moran. "Is this going to be one of those?"

"One of those what?" Agent Lauren asked.

"You know complicated, like a pain-in-the-ass type of complicated."

"Is that a mixed metaphor, Detective Egan?" she asked.

"No, not really," he said. "It's a simile because I used the word 'like.'"

"You're pretty smart, aren't you?"

"Nah, I'm just well-informed," replied Egan with a grin.

"Hey, Jimmy," asked Tom Starr, "you got any one-liners?"

"Sure. What'd you call a chicken's ghost? A poultry-geist."

Starr smiled, but before he would say anything else, Agent Lauren said:

"Do you mind if we got back . . .."

"Jeez, I'm sorry . . . Agent Lauren," Egan said. "You were in the middle of telling us about . . . another former employee of Global Solutions."

"His name," she said, "is Anthony Robert Gordon. He uses the acronym ARGO as an alter-ego, a psychic fall guy. He was a decorated sniper with the 101st Airborne and the Rangers. In addition, he was involved with one of our SMUs."

"What's an SMU?" Egan asked.

"Yeah, well, you know, don't you, Detective?"

"It stands for Special Missions Unit," said Reno Starr, with a sideways glance at the CIA agent.

"Hold on a second . . . uh, let me get this straight," said Egan. "These guys . . . you're interested in . . . they all left the service to, uh, work for this private security contractor. Am I right or what?"

"Uh, you're right on the money, Jimmy," said Spielman.

"Ok . . . in what capacity?" asked Eddie Moran.

"Supposedly, they did just that."

"Did what?"

"Security work," replied Spielman. "Of course, we know . . . they did a lot more . . . but we can't prove it."

"Prove what?"

"Like steal a lot of money," said Agent Lauren, "while eliminating anyone who got in their way."

"What's a lot of money?" Moran asked.

"Oh, millions," said Agent Lauren.

"Okay, but I hate to keep asking . . . what's all this got to do with me and Jimmy?"

Spielman and Starr went on to explain how the three suspects enjoyed the company of high-priced hookers. The connection of course with that thought, was that they were well-known as experts in that field of vice.

"So, you want us to find out through our CI if your three suspects are in the metro area . . . am I right?" asked Moran as he reached over and took a sip of scotch his partner had ordered.

"Well, in a nutshell, that would be a yes . . . but . . . ." said Reno Star.

"But . . . what?" asked Moran.

"So, let me ask you this," said Egan, "if we find these guys, what do we do with them, hold 'em or what?"

"No, not really," said Starr. "We just want to know if they're here and where they're going . . . you know, keep them in view."

"That's it?"

"That's it," answered Agent Lauren. "So, can you help us out or what?"

"Well, we'll do our best . . . right, Jimmy?" replied Moran, neglecting to tell them they already knew that one of their suspects was dating one of their CIs.

With an air of finality, Reno Starr stood up and said: "I'm sure you will."

With that being said Spielman and Agent Lauren did the same.

They all shook hands and bid each other goodbye knowing that they would see each other again and again.

Egan and Moran sat there for a while discussing what, if anything, was said. They weren't quite sure what was what. However, they knew the truth of the matter lurked somewhere in their midst; in time they would most likely find it.

They knew that because that's what they did or at least something close to it.

Before they left Moran asked Egan what he thought of Agent Lauren. Egan told him that any guy who had sex with her better check his dick—for freezer burn.

CHAPTER 15

"Man is born as a freak of nature, being within nature and yet transcending it. He has to find principles of action and decision making which replace the principles of instincts. He has to have a frame of orientation which permits him to organize a consistent picture of the world as a condition for consistent actions. He has to fight not only against the dangers of dying, starving, and being hurt, but also against another danger which is specifically human: that of becoming insane. In other words, he has to protect himself not only against the danger of losing his life but also against the danger of losing his mind."

Erich Fromm, *Escape from Freedom*

As Egan sat back in his chair a pleasant sense of ease settled over him. It had been a long day and finally he could relax and do what he wanted—toast the end of it.

With that in mind he sipped on his first drink of the day, then proceeded to nibble on a few gourmet nuts from an ornate dish sitting on the bar in front of him. It was one of the many amenities offered to you while staying at the Dunsmore Hotel.

Unfortunately, he was there on business; he had to

meet one of its bartenders—a guy by the name of Charlie Dezara. He was a CI who had come through for him on a number of occasions. Supposedly, he had some pertinent information on a particular suspect the FBI was interested in—someone who called himself Anthony Austin whose real name was Anthony Robert Gordon.

The source of the information came from an escort girl he was quite familiar with; her name was Renee DeMarco, aka Renee Bardot. She worked for an escort service called *Laches*. It was French for "the failure to do something you should have done." He found that out by looking it up in a French dictionary.

According to Charlie, Renee was just a close friend of his. In reality, he acted as a "steerer," a conduit for her to meet some possible clients. Usually they were businessmen who happened to be staying at the Dunsmore, although he had connections at other hotels, also.

Of course like all CIs Charlie wanted something in return. This time he asked for an ounce of coke and money. A high price but one he was willing to pay, that is, if the information was as good as he said.

For some unknown reason Charlie had left before he got there. The reason being he had a family emergency. The funny thing was Charlie didn't have a family. So, obviously he had something more important than meeting him—a fact he would discuss with him the next time they met. No sooner did that thought cross his mind, when his cell phone rang—it was Charlie.

After a brief but terse "hello," Charlie said he was sorry for not meeting him. He explained how a close friend of his had been picked up for prostitution and he had to go to that precinct with a bondsman to bail her out. He asked Egan for a possible favor for which he would give him the information he wanted. Egan said "he would look into it"—code for he could make the charge go away.

Charlie then said, "The guy you're looking for works out at the Easy Street Gym," then hung up.

Finally, without so much as a handshake or a kiss goodbye, the guy paid their bill and left. Egan could sense that this was his cue; his window of opportunity. As he sat there gathering up his confidence to go over and talk to her, he remembered what Eddie would always say when they were out trolling for "scags"—looking for women they thought were an easy make. "One of the biggest mistakes a man can make is to allow his perceptions to become the object of his desires."

He still didn't know what that was all about, but it sounded philosophical enough to be remembered. So, with an air of alcohol-induced assurance, he decided to make his move. He took his drink from the bar, then slowly strolled over to where she was sitting. He stood close to the chair where the nerd had been, then settled himself into it, close enough to brush her calf with his own. He knew it seemed awkward enough, "but what the fuck, balls don't need shoes," he thought, citing another of Eddie's senseless aphorisms.

After a few minutes of protracted silence, he turned in her direction only to pause for a moment. He could distinguish the fragrance of the perfume she was wearing. It was the same type his ex-wife used to wear, Seduction.

Dismissing what should have been an obvious warning, he decided to talk to her anyway.

"I think I know who you are," Egan said, letting the tone of is voice go low and mysterious.

She turned to face him then smiled.

"Isn't that a very old line?" she asked, her voice soft, yet confident. Egan couldn't help but notice that when she crossed her legs, her skirt traveled halfway up her thigh.

Struggling to maintain the momentum of his introduction, he took another sip of his drink before he answered.

"It would be," he said, "if your name wasn't Susan Solomon."

With a slight look of surprise, she searched his face

for a name.

"Do I know you?" she asked, while turning her body away from his. The way she acted and the tone of her voice let him know he had probably gone somewhere he shouldn't have. Egan realized he had to talk fast if the story was going to go the way he wanted it to.

"I'm terribly sorry," he said. "My name is James Colin; I'm a detective with the MTA." He always lied whenever he thought a person or a situation could be problematic. "I met you and your husband at a police fund raiser about a year ago."

While readjusting her skirt, she said, "Oh! Really, well I'm sorry I don't remember you, Detective."

"Hey, that's alright. I'm the kind of guy that's easy to forget. Uh . . . your husband is Dr. Stanley Solomon—right?"

"Yes . . . he is. Why do you ask?"

"Oh, no reason . . . you know . . . just testing my memory," Egan said. "Say . . . I hope . . . I'm, uh, not imposing on you?"

"No, not at all . . . I'm flattered that you would remember me."

"Well, it's my job to remember faces and names. Besides you . . . uh, have one of those faces . . . you're pretty," hoping that she wouldn't think he was hitting on her while obviously he was. She sort of smiled then looked around the room as if she was looking for someone. He could read between the lines; she seemed to be getting a little annoyed.

So, he inched a little closer to her; sometimes you had to take charge or forget about it.

"Are you waiting for someone?" he asked.

"Yes," she said, "a friend of mine; he was supposed to meet . . . me here—around five."

Egan glanced at his watch; it was already half-past. Either she was lying or telling the truth—he really didn't care.

"I'm sorry if I ask so many questions; I guess it's the cop in me."

He then ordered two more drinks; she thanked him then reached for her pocketbook that was lying on the bar. She then proceeded to shuffle through it until she produced a gold cigarette case.

"Whoa," Egan said, "I haven't seen one of those in years."

She then removed an electronic cigarette.

"Yes, it's an heirloom . . . by the way, I hope you don't mind me asking . . . why are you here?"

"Ah, nice touch," he said as he pointed to her e-cigarette while placing a fifty dollar bill on the bar.

"Uh . . . nothing really, but to answer your question . . . you know . . . just some unfinished business—trying to attach a few loose ends. You know what I mean?"

She smiled at him while partially closing her eyes as if to say "like mind your own business . . . lady."

"Hey! You know what? We have something in common," Egan said as he took out an e-cigarette of his own.

"What flavor is yours?" she asked.

"Strawberry. And yours?"

"The same," she replied while blowing a cloud of watery vapor in the air.

"Kinda of neo-romantic," Egan answered as he did the same. "Like one of those old movie scenes from the past between Humphrey Bogart and Ingrid Bergman . . . you know: *Casablanca.*"

"Are you always so reflective?" she asked, letting the atmosphere between them fill with insinuation.

"So," she asked, "why are you really here . . . I mean if you're finished doing what you wanted to do . . . why are you still here?"

With a rakish grin Egan replied, "Maybe to meet someone like you."

She responded with a cold stare of obvious

annoyance, "I don't know what you want," she said. "You must think I'm awfully stupid or very desperate."

His eyes drifted languidly over the glass of whiskey he was holding and gazed at her with an inquisitive expression of his own. With a soft, but reassuring voice he looked at her and said:

"No, neither one . . . I think you're very pretty and maybe you might be taking a small vacation from life."

"Oh, really! And why would you . . . think that?"

"Because I saw your room key under your pocketbook and I know you're divorced."

She looked down at her handbag then removed the plastic key from where it was and placed it in one of the pockets of her suit coat.

"Congratulations, Detective. You're very observant, aren't you? And, well-informed. I often take a room at the Dunsmore . . . to get away and relax."

"Well, that's uh . . . what you should do," Egan said. "Relax."

"So! Are you doing the same?" she asked. "I mean taking a vacation from life?"

"No . . . not really . . . I'd like to—that is, if the opportunity was there . . . you know, mmmm, maybe we could take one together?"

With her eyes flashing an angry glare at the suggestive nature of his comment, Susan responded with one of her own.

"Don't you think that, maybe, we should take some time to get better acquainted?" Before he answered her, Egan held up his glass so she could look at it.

"You see this?" he asked. "The ice cubes are melting."

"So?!" she exclaimed.

"So, that's life. We're like these friggin' ice cubes . . . we're melting . . . pretty soon we'll be gone."

In an apparent huff, she replied, "Oh! Don't be so dramatic. Anyway, I still fail to see your point."

He answered her back with a cop's voice:

"Well!" he said. "Why don't you stick around and maybe you will."

"I doubt it!" was her only comment and then turned her head so as to avoid the way he was looking at her.

Egan sort of grinned at her apparent ire and then stood up to languish at the side of the bar. He then ordered one more drink for the two of them and told the bartender to give him the bill.

While he was standing there he kind of noticed how their conversation became less confrontational to increasingly familiar, with an occasional touch of sexual innuendo. For the two of them it seemed to be an arresting development of ulterior proceedings that might lead to unintended consequences.

Maybe, if he could read her mind, she might be thinking that "the heart was a lonely hunter" and subject to fruition—a consideration he was well aware of.

She told him about her husband: how he was a lying, cheating bastard. Egan was quick to concur by telling her that most husbands were lying, cheating bastards—how they didn't meant to be, but it was just the nature of the beast. He couldn't believe he actually said that considering he had been one himself.

With stifled sniffs she explained how her husband had open affairs with his patients, that he never wore his wedding ring. She said that one time in a fit of rage she threw hers away and sold her engagement ring.

Egan knew better than to try to rationalize with her so he let her vent. He made it a point to nod at the appropriate moments while pretending to be sympathetic. Of course as he was doing that he was thinking of how he was going to get her up to her room.

She got around to asking him about his life: was he ever married, how did he like being a cop, the usual stuff. He told her that he was divorced, no kids, and he enjoyed being with the MTA, but looked forward to retirement and spending his pension in Florida.

For some reason he felt a need to tell her about his marriage. He explained the essentials—how his wife left him for this wealthy lawyer she was looking for, how she loved money more than she loved him. It wasn't true, but for the moment sympathy and lies appeared to be the coin of the realm.

Egan noticed how Susan's expression seemed to change from something ineffable to contemplative. After an extended moment or so, she took a drag on her e-cigarette then told him she was sorry.

"Honestly," she said, she had to agree with his ex-wife's choice of taking money over love. In the end it was far more practical.

He pretended to laugh and go along with her assessment of his ex-wife's choice. His hope was to hide the pain that lingered from the memory of losing her.

In the midst of discussing their hurt feelings and what they should do about them, it became apparent, at least to him, what they ought to do. He suggested that maybe they should go up to her room and possibly find some comfort in one another's arms, or revenge.

Of course, she knew what he really had in mind, and thought, "oh, what the hell." He was good-looking and she hadn't had any in a little while. However, there was just one thing.

"Uh . . . before we do that," Susan said, "I just want you to know, that I know some cops on the NYPD."

Egan wasn't at all sure where she was going with that statement, so he said:

"Oh! Is that so? Okay, so name me a few?"

She answered his question with a short list of people he didn't know, then ended with someone he did: Desmond Wallace.

Egan turned away from her to regain his composure. He then turned back and shrugged his shoulders telling her he didn't know any of them.

"Well," she said, "you might be wondering why I brought all of that up."

"Yeah . . . you could say that."

"Well, Captain Wallace told me cops often have drugs on them."

"What for?" Egan asked, knowing the answer, but dying to hear what Wallace had to do with any of this.

"You know," she said, "to give to criminals so they would snitch on another criminal."

"Could be . . . I mean, I've heard of it."

"Well," she said.

"Well, what?"

"Well, do you have any on you or what?"

"Could be," replied Egan as he nodded his head while rocking his body back and forth.

"So, you know the rest . . . I like to get high . . . booze gets boring—you know what I'm saying?"

"Uh, I get the picture."

"So, why don't we go up to my room and get high together," she said as she placed a hand on his thigh very close to his junk. "You know I could pay . . . I have money."

"That's okay," Egan replied. "Why don't you go up first? I'll follow you up later."

"You aren't going to run out on me, are you?" she asked, her eyes searching his face for the response she was looking for.

"Hey! No way," Egan said. "I've got too much invested in you," as he showed her one of their empty glasses.

She smiled tentatively, as if to say . . . "we'll see," then walked away.

He knew he had to wait around a while, pop a "get sober pill" and drink a large glass of water. No sense going upstairs if you couldn't do anything when you got there.

While he was paying their bar bill, Egan reflected on what she had told him. The fact that she was using cops as her private dealers—pretty fuckin' smart, he thought, and safe, too.

"Well, time to rise to the occasion, at least once, anyway"—drunk or sober, he could always do that.

Egan followed the path Susan had taken that led to the elevators and the room she was in. After what seemed like an eternity in the elevator, he finally made it to her room, then knocked on the door. When she let him in, he could tell she had been crying and her mood had changed drastically.

She stepped away from him as he approached her. She told him she couldn't go through with it—she felt she was making a big mistake—then turned her back to him and said:

"Maybe, it would be better if you just left."

Egan swore at himself for getting involved in such predictable bullshit and would have gladly walked away if he could. However, he knew he had to find out what she was up to and her entanglements with Wallace and the other cops. All he needed was a little time. So, he went up behind her and gently wrapped his arms around her waist.

With an apprehensive sigh, she leaned into his caress and said:

"Please, don't . . . I can't."

He then kissed the space behind her ear and whispered seductively, "If you just try you'll find it's easier than you think."

She turned and put her arms about his neck. With her eyes tightly shut, Susan kissed him forcefully. Egan could feel her mouth start to open and her tongue searching for his. He became aware of the heat from her body as the heaviness of her breasts melded against his chest.

Slowly, he maneuvered her towards the hotel bed then laid her down with him resting by her side. Using eagerness and ardent fervor as their guide, they began to explore one another, whose direction seemed to be taking them, where they wanted to go.

Suddenly, without warning, Susan sat up, then slapped Egan across the face. Like water on fire, her anger extinguished the passion between them.

With her eyes brimming tears, she looked at him and said:

"I'm sorry; I just don't want you to think I can be used."

While trying to fight back the wave of rage that rushed over him, Egan exclaimed, "Hey, I'm sorry, too."

Hoping to evoke the response she wanted, that maybe he would slap her back or call her names, she said:

"Are you mad at me?"

"Do you want me to be?" Egan said, as he rubbed the side of his face, pretending that she had hurt him. He had dealt with nut cases in the past; the best thing to do was to stay calm.

"No . . . maybe—I don't know," she stammered, turning her head to avoid his gaze.

"Well, I'm not . . . call me crazy—but, maybe, that's what I needed."

Thinking he would have said something else, she replied:

"Well, what . . . do you mean?"

"Oh, nothin' really," he said as he stood up to straighten himself out.

"You said you weren't mad at me."

"I'm not!" exclaimed Egan as he walked towards the door.

"Then, where are you going? . . . I don't want you to leave—what about my stuff?"

"We'll see one another again."

"No, we won't . . . you know we won't."

"Oh, yes, we will . . . uh, trust me," replied Egan as he waved goodbye while letting himself out the door making sure it slammed behind him.

He didn't know why he left; he should have stayed but his ego must have got the best of him. He'd think it over later on when he wasn't so buzzed.

Anyway, fuck it, like they used to say in the corps, "Sometimes discretion is the better part of valor." Besides, he didn't' have any condoms on him, anyhow. God knows who that crazy bitch was last with; probably Captain Tutu and he wasn't into no interracial sex.

He rode the elevator down to the lobby and on the way he sort of patted himself on the back.

All in all, he thought, it wasn't a bad day. He got a lead on Reno Starr's Mr. ARGO and a big break on dear old Captain Wallace. To finish it off, he wasn't through with Susan Solomon, not by a long shot he wasn't.

CHAPTER 16

Since his return to NYC, Gordon had met with Chris Bentley and his partner Tojo Grimaldi. True to the contractor's code neither of them asked where Gordon had been or the circumstances that surrounded his departure. Of course, if they wanted to know, he would have told them.

He was briefed on the possibility of some future interventions; as of yet, nothing had been formulated or agreed upon. As always Bentley told him to lay low and to not get involved in anything that might draw undue attention to him. It was a piece of advice he should have listened to, but as usual, boredom and restlessness got the best of him.

So, to while away the hours, he arranged to take some private martial arts classes at the Easy Street Gym. Gordon was sure it would be a rehash of what he already knew, but as most guys who practiced the arts would tell you use it or lose it. In other words, train hard or get your ass kicked.

All had gone well for a few weeks until he began to feel as if he was being watched. It seemed to him that no matter what time of day he was there, the same two men would show up. Although, at times only one of them would come in, hang around, and then leave, they never bothered him, but yet he could feel their presence. He found out through his martial arts instructor they were both NYPD. The larger, heftier of the two was called "Gloves," the other was referred to as Detective Egan or Jimmy.

The truth of the matter was the Easy Street was one of those fitness emporiums that catered to the politically correct. The set-up was if you had the money you could become a member, whether you were straight, gay, man or a woman or other—the gamut. However, they did have one rule which everyone appreciated: no kids. It also had the reputation as a place to meet and cheat, all under the guise of health and wellness.

In addition to that, Gordon noticed more than a few drug deals taking place, as well as some expensive swag changing hands. What didn't make any sense was why would anyone take the chance of getting busted with the cops being so open as to who they were—unless they were in on it, or they were trolling for possible CIs while giving immunity to anyone who cooperated. It also answered the question of why he would often see the cop they called Gloves or his partner sitting in an unmarked car outside the gym entrance.

Whatever the reason, he didn't care; all he knew was it made him too nervous to stick around to find out. On the other hand, he decided that before he left, he would finish up with his instructor on a few of the finer points of Krav Maga, the Israeli fighting system that was the zeitgeist of self-defense.

On the day before Gordon planned to leave, he was hitting the heavy bag in an effort to coordinate his footwork with a few of his punching techniques. In the midst of what he was doing, he stopped to watch a couple of female mixed martial artists enter the ring. It appeared to him to be an impromptu sparring match between two professional fighters who were known not to like one another—so, the specter of animus hung over their encounter.

The issue that made it unusual was that one of them was a transgender that had undergone reassignment surgery giving him a functional vagina. Her name was Gloria George whose real name was Douglas George Raggi. The controversy was did George have the right to fight in the female division of the MMA. In the world of political correctness she did, but in reality, George was still a man. He had a man's strength, speed and temperament, and the technical fighting to go with it.

To Gordon, George was drop-dead gorgeous with big tits, six-pack abs and a heart-shaped ass. He knew if given the opportunity to fuck her, he couldn't. She was still a guy and that would make him a de facto homo. However, what made her so tantalizing was she had a woman's body with a man's mind on how to use it.

When the two fighters entered the ring they were dressed for the occasion: in a suit of protective gear. The ensemble included head and chest protection, as well as shin guards, with the addition of over-sized boxing gloves. Gordon could well understand their concern for caution since each of them was capable of shortening the other's career.

As he stood there watching them, a man came up beside him and said:

"How's it going, Anthony, or do they still call you ARGO?"

Before Gordon had a chance to respond, the man leaned into him and muttered, "I told you we would meet again—didn't I?"

Gordon didn't bother to glance in his direction. He knew the man's voice and remembered where he heard it last.

"So, how you doin' . . . Tommy?" replied Gordon. "Or . . . are they still calling you . . . Reno?"

With that exchange, Starr placed a hand on Gordon's

shoulder and murmured, "You still working for Global?"

Gordon countered by moving away; as he did, he made it a point to look down at his shoulder and brush at it. He then pointed to his ear and said, "Sorry . . . I can't hear you—too much noise."

Starr knew the game between them, so in a very loud voice he said, "You still working for Global?"

Gordon shook his head, "No!" then asked, "You still working for the FBI?"

In the interim Gordon's mind raced ahead wondering how in the name of God did Starr ever find him at the Easy Street? More than that, how did he know he was in New York City? Where did he slip up? He had been so fuckin' careful to cover his tracks.

Feeding on the tension between them, Reno moved closer to where Gordon was standing.

"You know, Tony," he said, "my offer still . . . stands."

"Is that so?" answered Gordon. "And what would that be?"

"Ah . . . you know, the one I gave you in Iraq . . . you know—help me and I'll help you."

With a sarcastic expression, Gordon asked, "Really! And what kind of help do I need?"

Before he answered, Starr glanced around to see if anyone might be close enough to listen in on what he had to say.

"You know," he said, "you tell me about Global and I'll see you don't go away."

The two men knew they were just wasting one another's time, but Starr had succeeded in doing what he had intended—putting Gordon on notice that he was on to him. He knew Gordon had to be asking himself a lot of questions like how did he get found out.

Ignoring the obvious that Gordon would never cooperate or tell him anything he didn't want to, he said:

"So, why you in the city?"

Gordon turned and looked at him.

"Oh . . . I don't really know . . . could be I like the restaurants."

"Cute," replied Starr, "Oh . . . uh, there's something else . . . tell your friends I said 'hello.'"

"Okay, I'll do that . . . just as long as you do the same."

"Yeah," Starr said, "and who would that be?"

Gordon pointed at Moran and Egan who were on the far side of the gym talking.

Starr shook his head and smiled, then pointed at the two women in the ring.

"Hey," he said, "you ever wonder why a couple of good-looking babes like that would want to punch each other in the face . . . like it's a man's game, that MMA stuff."

Gordon rubbed the side of his jaw as if he was contemplating a response.

"No, not really," he said. "I guess it might be they're . . . cuntfused."

Starr laughed then said, "Cute . . . hey, you still as good as you thought?"

"Well," replied Gordon, "there's a way for you to find out . . . or, are you too busy worshipping the ground you walk on?"

"Whoa, not me," said Reno.

"Oh, yeah . . . well, who did you have in mind?"

Starr pointed in the direction of Eddie Moran who was staring at them.

"Cute," said Gordon. "Answer me this, I thought you guys in the Bureau . . . were supposed to be brave, courageous and bold?"

With a look of ambivalence, Starr glanced around then patted Gordon on the back.

"Only when we have to," he said.

Gordon glanced over in Moran's direction then back at Starr.

"Well," he said, "you know, Tommy, one of these days you might just have to do that . . . and guess who's going to be there? Me."

Starr leaned in close to Gordon, almost face-to-face, their eyes locked in a stare-down.

"I sure the fuck hope so," he said. "I mean it would break my fuckin' heart if you weren't."

As he drifted away, Gordon stopped then looked over his shoulder and said, "Hey, Reno . . . who said you had a heart? You gotta be a man . . . to have one of those."

In turn, Starr just smiled at him, then slowly raised his arm, extending the middle finger of his fist.

Gordon then proceeded to walk in the direction of a bench where his gym bag was laying on the floor next to it. Once he was there, he started to remove his protective gear from it, putting each piece on as he did. The stuff was still clammy from the previous time he used it, making him even more incensed than he was already.

He wasn't in the mood to fight Moran, but his anger and the thought of kicking this cop's ass was too much to pass up; besides, he would think of Starr every time he hit him.

The trouble was he was in the process of having the tattoos on his chest removed, so, to hide the fact, he always kept his t-shirt on. The other thing was that area of his chest was very sensitive; if Moran hit him there, he would be in some serious pain. So, for more padding he decided to use his Easy Street towel under his rib-and-chest protector.

It was then that he figured out how Starr knew where he was. He remembered the last time he was with Renee they were at the Langley Hotel. He had spent some time in the bathroom, so she must have gone through his gym bag and saw the logo on the towel then told someone.

The question was, why? She didn't know his real name or who he was, but somehow Reno had figured it out.

He didn't have time to think about it at the moment, but he would, and when he did, Renee might need medical attention. Right now, he had to take care of someone called Gloves Moran. Why the guy wanted to fight him he didn't know, probably Starr had something to do with it. The other part of the equation was why he was doing it. The only thing he could point to was pride and anger and the thought of knocking the shit out of some overweight cop.

The other part was Moran was a lot older than he was, at least by ten years, and from what he heard a boozer. He knew not to let any of that sway him; there were plenty of old men who drank that could kick his ass, so he had to beware of Moran.

The art of fighting in the ring was speed, endurance and being a well-trained tactician. He knew Moran was most likely an accomplished boxer, so he wasn't going to stand in the center of the ring and trade punches with him.

No, he would use his skill in Muay Thai, the art of the eight limbs. It was called that because you used punches, kicks, elbows and knee strikes to counter your opponent. The style came from Thailand, mostly used as a contact sport; however, it had been incorporated in other forms of martial arts.

When he entered the ring, the same small crowd was still there that had witnessed the sparring match between the two female MMA fighters. Gordon didn't like it. He wasn't there to put on a show, but knew that's just what he and Moran were going to do.

He could see Reno Starr and Detective Egan standing close to Moran's corner. The sight of them made him feel vulnerable, as if he was outnumbered; there was no one in his corner except himself—a situation he had often faced, and yet, never could get used to.

Since they hadn't agreed upon any rules and no one was there to officiate what went on between them, it was a street fight. Gordon knew even with protective gear both of them could get seriously hurt.

When he went to the center of the ring to touch gloves with Moran, he asked him straight out if he still wanted to go through with it. Moran didn't hesitate; instead, he just stared at him through the centerpiece of his headgear, the part that covered his nose. He took his time to respond, letting the moment drag on.

"What do you think?" he said. "Tough guy."

Gordon stepped back and spoke through his mouthpiece, "Okay . . . let's do it . . . hey, I almost forgot—good luck."

Moran turned and looked back at him and said in a distinctive, but graveled voice, "Fuck you."

As the two men circled one another, Moran pawed at Gordon with a left jab while rivulets of sweat creased his face. Gordon knew Moran was trying to feel him out—a typical boxer's ploy used as a way of seeing how your opponent moved. He noticed something else: Moran was already starting to sweat profusely and they hadn't even started.

He decided to target an area on the outside of Moran's upper thigh of his left leg. The anatomical significance was it housed the lead element of the sural nerve that controlled foot movement. With that thought in mind, he then swiveled on his front left leg and whipped a vicious roundhouse kick using the shin of his back leg. In Muay Thai the shinbone was the weapon of choice. It acted as a club that carried far more impact than the top of the foot used in karate.

The technique appeared to have little or no effect on Moran. However, Gordon knew if he did it enough, "Gloves" would start to crumble. With a sense of enraged urgency, Moran charged at Gordon throwing a flurry of rights and lefts that landed heavily on his shoulders and arms. Inadvertently, one of those punches hit Gordon in the vicinity of a tattoo sending a powerful stinging sensation across his chest.

In an attempt to get Gordon on the ropes, Moran tried to clinch with him. Gordon was fast enough to slip away; as he did he landed an uppercut on Moran's jaw that staggered him.

Gordon could hear the people around the ring shouting out words of encouragement for Moran to "kick that s-o-b's ass." Well, he thought, so much for bipartisan support. He then unleashed a flurry of his own consisting of a series of elbow strikes and kicks.

From out of nowhere Moran landed an overhand right to the side of Gordon's head—the force of which was absorbed by his headgear, but still powerful enough to send him reeling backwards.

He knew he had to shake off the effects of Moran's punch and to clear the cobwebs from his head. So, in a moment of desperation, he wrapped his arms around Moran's chest, dug a heel behind his back foot, then fell forward, sending the both of them to the mat.

Gordon landed heavily on Moran's chest knocking the wind out of him. As he lay there gasping for air, Gordon proceeded to punch him in the head. Since there were no rules, what Gordon did was totally acceptable, but not to Agent Starr or Detective Egan. The two of them jumped in the ring and yanked Gordon off their friend, then shoved him aside.

"Nice fight," said Egan. "Why don't you hit the showers . . . me and Eddie got business."

Gordon backed away relieved that Starr and Egan had stepped in to end the fight. Moran was a lot tougher and stronger than he thought.

"Yeah . . . sure," he said, "whatever . . . you say . . . I got to get going, anyway."

Starr went over and grabbed Gordon by the arm and said, "I'd get the fuck out of NYC . . . if I were you."

Gordon looked down at Starr's hand, then pushed it away.

"Well, you're not," he said. "That's the second time

you touched me . . . you think you're a big man. Well, there's a lot of room under that bus."

Gordon rushed headlong from the ring and ran towards the men's locker room. When he got there, he tore off his protective equipment, t-shirt, shorts and boxing shoes, then shoved all of it into his gym bag.

He wasn't prepared to take a shower; he just wanted to get the fuck out of there. Within minutes, he put on his street clothes, then left the Easy Street Gym as fast as he could.

When he finally hit the sidewalk, the cool air and street noise never felt or sounded better. As he walked towards a subway entrance, Jimmy Egan pulled up alongside of him. He rolled down his passenger side window and yelled out:

"Hey, you need a ride?"

"No, thanks, boss," said Gordon. "I like the subway."

"The subway's a dangerous place."

"Well," said Gordon, "I'm a dangerous man."

Egan smiled then waved to him as he pulled away.

Gordon felt the cell phone in his front pocket begin to vibrate. It was a text message from Chris Bentley. All it said was, "You're on."

CHAPTER 17

In a furious blur of sight and sound, Fulton Bates watched as a subway train roared past him. The air from the onrushing cars left him with a pleasing sense of exhilaration and impending doom.

After the train had gone by, his eyes shifted to the edge of the platform. His only thought was how easy it would be to take a few quick steps and all his misgivings would blissfully end.

Bowing his head, Bates cupped his hands around a match and lit a cigarette; he knew it was against the law, but didn't care. After a few deep drags he tossed it from where he was standing to the tracks below. He then rammed his hands into his coat pockets and searched for a piece of chewing gum.

As he stood there staring straight ahead, Bates pulled nervously at the collar of his jacket, shifting his weight from one foot to the other while chewing diligently on the wad of gum in his mouth. His behavior might have seemed peculiar somewhere else, but in New York City he was just another over-stimulated commuter waiting for a train.

When his fare finally arrived, Bates felt unable to move, as if he was being held back by some unseen hand. With a surge of capricious resolve he propelled himself forward then stepped into the unyielding crowd of the subway car.

When he reached his stop, Bates pushed his way through the door with the rest of the throng and then followed along as they marched towards the turnstile exits.

He climbed the subway stairs that led to the street. Out of breath he emerged triumphantly into the daylight. He felt the cold air penetrate his lungs as the veil of claustrophobia fell from his face.

The sun had just begun to set as he walked down Fifth Avenue. This was his favorite time of the day, neither daylight nor darkness. The incandescence of electric light seemed ineffective, a lot like his life, he thought, as he trudged along.

The idea of having to ride the subway everyday weighed heavily on his mind. Along with that imposition was the depressing realization he had to go to work just to pay the bills.

He had been out of prison for a year and still couldn't cope with the outside world. To him prison was less complicated, more predictable, and at times he wished he was still there.

As he passed by the different storefront windows, he made it a point to stop and look at the holiday displays. It was Christmas time in the city and he enjoyed looking at the toys and the mechanical Santas.

Christmas was a time for children; it was the children he missed the most. Pressing himself up against the glass his thoughts shifted back to what the prison psychiatrists told him: whenever he began to think of children, he was to focus on something else and squeeze the electric buzzer he kept in his pocket. The buzzer gave him a noticeable tingling up his arm; it was supposed to serve as a form of bio-feedback and a physical reminder not to go there. The mild shock brought back memories of endless group sessions with the prison shrinks and other men like him. It was society's vain attempt at trying to desensitize them from their lust for children.

In prison, the other cons called pedophiles "short eyes." They were considered the lowest of the low and the most hated offenders in the joint. He had been in protective custody the entire time he was in. To put him with the general population would have been suicide or worse.

Bates turned his head without meaning until his eyes rested on a small boy standing by his mother. He watched as the two of them looked through the window at the animated elves who were reenacting a toy-making scene from Santa's workshop.

The little boy's smiling face and bouncing exuberance was too much for him to bear. He could feel a sense of urgent desire take hold of him. He turned away and proceeded to walk on, all the while squeezing the buzzer in his pocket as a sudden revulsion for his past life swept over him.

He had never been like other people. When he was a child he had been diagnosed with a learning disability. They called it attention deficit disorder. School was an insurmountable task; it seemed he could never achieve what the other children could. In a period of desperation his parents took him to a special clinic where a group of child psychologists performed a battery of mental tests on him. They were determined he was "incapable of any sustained concentration." One noted clinician informed his parents that in his opinion their son had little if any ability to develop cognitive skills. Their general diagnosis was that he might have some form of neuro-hormonal dysfunction or may have suffered oxygen deprivation at birth. The only positive development was the specialists felt he exhibited fine muscle coordination with an unusual aptitude for music. It was then that his father decided that he should pursue a musical career and sent him to the best music teachers in New York City.

After years of piano lessons and endless hours of practice, he achieved the status of child prodigy. He would later find out that those noted clinicians had also determined he had definite homosexual tendencies. His parents were advised to monitor his social interactions very carefully in the event that he might become predatory or overly submissive.

Unfortunately, his father's business affairs fell on hard times. He lost a small fortune in real estate and plunges in the stock market. Bates remembered how his father anguished over their misfortune blaming himself endlessly. He always felt that his father's untimely death from a cerebral hemorrhage was the direct result of his financial stress. His father left them a fortune in life insurance: $5 million—a sum that would have taken care of his mother and himself if she hadn't remarried.

His stepfather was quite handsome, charming, but a heartless, fucking bastard. He remembered how he squandered his mother's money on inane business ventures, boats and lavish homes.

Another memory plagued his thoughts, the man abused him when he was ten-years-old and even until his early teens. He made him strip naked and then beat his buttocks with a riding crop. Sometimes he would have him suck his cock while he watched the two of them in a mirror. What he didn't know was he did the same to his mother.

What was disturbing was the fact that when he thought about it, he had to admit that many times he enjoyed his sessions with his stepfather. It wasn't until the prison psychiatrists explained to him that many times sexually abused children would often grow up to be abusers themselves.

Suddenly, he found himself hyperventilating—a condition that would often occur if he let his emotions overwhelm him. Bates pulled a small paper bag from his coat pocket and then began to breathe into it. The sudden abundance of carbon dioxide normalized his respiration and calmed his composure.

Looking up at the street sign, Bates realized he had turned around and walked two blocks in the wrong direction. He hailed a cab and told the driver to take him to the Player's Café on 86th Street. He had been working there as their house pianist for only a month and didn't want to be late.

As they crossed Seventh Avenue, Bates saw the apartment building he lived in as a child. Parked on the street in front of the entrance was a limousine. He watched as a uniformed chauffer opened one of the car doors for two well-dressed men. A feeling of envy crossed his mind as he saw the two of them go into the building.

Bates told himself they had to be gay. He could always tell when someone was gay or not. If you asked him, it was the way they walked, their mannerisms and the way they looked at one another.

A smirk creased the corners of his mouth when he thought about the new gay lifestyle. How they could get married and behave as if they were just as normal as any other married couple. They still didn't understand that no matter how accepting society was, it would never be the same for them—especially, not the same amongst men who were ultra-straight, the homophobes who saw gay men as weak and untrustworthy.

Bates pressed his back against the seat of the cab and marveled at the naiveté of people. Someday the world would realize that everyone was just some nameless little dog licking at the bowls of acceptability while seeking the fantasy of self-esteem.

When he walked into the café, Bates passed by the bar. As he did, one of the bartenders reached out and handed him a drink. He thanked him and then filtered through the bevy of regulars who were often there on a Friday night.

He stopped long enough to say hello to Sal Vincent, the owner of the Player's Café and a wanna-be gangster who always dressed in black.

"You're late," said Vincent as he pointed to his watch, a gaudy hunk of gold studded in diamonds.

Bates smiled then feigned an apology by raising his glass in apparent acceptance to Vincent's observation, who thought all his employees were late and deserved less than they got.

As he began to play, Bates scanned the room hoping to find someone of interest. After a few minutes, he saw the same handsome man from the night before.

They shared mutual smiles then nodded at one another as a form of introduction. He felt uncommonly pleased; immediately his thoughts turned to the possibility of some future conjugal tryst, one that was mutually satisfying to both of them.

He knew the man was straight; he could tell just by looking at him, probably bi-curious, out looking for something different. A lot of straight guys were like that. Well, certainly he could help him out in that regard. The thought left him wanting for what was sure to come, an "introduction to the ineffable."

As he played, Bates acknowledged the presence of the usual patrons, making sure to pay special attention to his admiring gay friends and closet queens. Secretly, he detested homosexual bitches; they were so predictable, affected and overly obsequious. He sighed at the thought of them, but knew they put money in his jar, so he smiled dutifully in their direction.

From his corner table, Gordon watched as Bates gave his best impersonation of Liberace, or, at least a facsimile thereof.

Anyway, he had to concede to the fact that the guy was talented, an excellent pianist, even if he was a homosexual, pedophile, faggot bastard. Of course, to say that wouldn't be politically correct, even if it was the truth.

When he leaned forward, Gordon felt the weight of his Automatic pressing against his ribs; it was a cold reminder of why he was there. As he watched Bates play, Gordon reflected on the events that led to the contract on the man's life.

As it was told to him, someone by the name of Mark Durant was a single parent whose wife and daughter were killed in a car accident; he was left alone to care for his only child, his son, Mark, Jr. In an attempt to help him cope with the loss of his mother and sister, he thought his son might learn to play an instrument. The thought was that the discipline may provide a constructive diversion for the boy's feelings.

Durant's friends told him about a very popular piano teacher who was just marvelous with children; his name was Fulton Bates.

Every Sunday, Durant would take his son to Bates' Manhattan apartment for piano lessons. His son seemed to be totally taken with the man and looked forward to going there. As the months passed by, Durant left his son with Bates for extended lengths of time. In effect, he was using him as a babysitter and a surrogate parent.

It was this type of unquestioned trust that Fulton fostered in the parents of the children he seduced. Gordon sipped his drink and thought over the convenience of the scenario. It was like bringing the chickens to the fox, just for safekeeping.

As if that wasn't enough, Bates also used drugs to make some of the boys more willing and the event more satisfying. It was after one of these all-day Sunday sessions that Durant returned to Bates' apartment to pick up his son, only to learn the boy had been taken to Bellevue Hospital and was pronounced DOA.

The toxicology report showed a large amount of cocaine in Mark's body which brought on a massive heart attack that killed him. A subsequent autopsy revealed traces of semen in the boy's rectum which matched Bates DNA and blood type. This was enough evidence for a jury to find him guilty of rape and child molestation that led to the victim's death.

In a plea bargain the judge gave Bates seven years, but due to overcrowding at his facility, he only did six. In addition to his sentence, Bates had lost a wrongful death suit and had to pay Mark Durant $200,000. The $200,000 was all Bates had left of his inheritance.

During his trial, it was revealed that Bates was a member of a group called NAMBLA which stood for the North American Man/Boy Love Affair. The organization provided him with legal assistance and some of its members showed up in court to give him "moral" support.

Upon his release from prison, Bates returned to New York City, registered as a sex offender, used the name Emerson Lavell, had some plastic surgery, dyed his hair and found work as a piano player.

What intrigued Gordon wasn't Bates; it was Mark Durant, the father. He didn't have the money or the influence or the connections to hire high-priced shooters; however, his brother did.

His brother was Joe Durant, a well-known senator from New Jersey. He was the type of politician who embraced "special interest groups," and, of course, he was all too willing to help them out if they needed his assistance, which of course they paid for. One of his slogans was "you're in the know when you vote for Jersey Joe."

The Lowe brothers were in the know; they were one of the senator's biggest supporters. It wasn't much of a stretch to say they would do anything to have a sphere of influence over such a power political figure. The future of Global Solutions and the WEB depended on lucrative government contracts.

Of course, he didn't know, but Gordon figured Joe Durant must have discussed his brother's tragic situation with the two of them and how much he would appreciate it to see Fulton Bates get what he deserved. The brothers Lowe, being who and what they were, could easily accommodate such a request. Of course, it was all speculation on his part, and yet, it fit.

Another part of the contract was how he became involved in it. Originally, the arrangement had been given to TOJO, his partner, one of Conrad Lowe's most trusted "employees." Grimaldi was his mentor in Iraq when they both worked for Global Solutions as "security experts."

Grimaldi knew his life's history of the things that had happened to him in the past. How he had been kidnapped by the terrorist group the FARC, the Fuerzas Armadas Revolucionarias de Colombia—in English: the Revolutionary Armed Forces of Colombia. He was only twelve at the time, a common occurrence in the early 90s. He knew how a few of their soldiers tried to rape him; they didn't succeed, but the experience left him emotionally scarred.

It was around that same period of time his father had been killed in an ambush while trying to find him. His mother paid his ransom and sent him to the U.S. to live with her brother in Queens. It was there that he learned how easy it was to kill.

Gordon leaned forward and sipped at his whiskey; the memories still lingered. He knew that TOJO was well-aware of his hatred for pedophiles and for homosexuals in general. Therefore, he knew that if he presented the right proposal to him, he couldn't refuse. They would split the contract money, $50,000 a piece, plus expenses. He would pull the trigger and TOJO would do some of the legwork.

Gordon sat back in his chair and thought about it; not a bad deal, especially for his partner. He took all the risks and his good friend played it safe. So, what else was new he said as he finished up his drink.

That wasn't the problem; it was how the thing was to go down. It was another contract that called for him to be up-close-and-personal, something he swore he wouldn't do, especially after the "werewolf debacle."

Whoever wanted Fulton Bates dead wanted a close-up picture of him with a gunshot wound to the head. When Grimaldi told him that part, he told him to go fuck himself.

However, when he thought it over, he changed his mind. He didn't want to pass up the money, and besides that, it gave him the opportunity to put a pedophile in the ground. When you looked at it, it was sort of a win-win situation; at least, it appeared that way.

It was time for him to get acquainted with his target. Gordon glanced at his watch; it was Fulton's break time, and he was up at the bar talking to what looked to him as a fairly attractive woman.

"Well," he said to himself, "I guess there's no accounting for taste." Obviously, she didn't know who or what she was talking to. Maybe, she didn't care. A lot of women thought homos were interesting. Anyway, whatever their story was, it was time for him to get acquainted with the "illustrious" Mr. Bates, or with his "aka Emerson Lavell."

He paid for his drink with cash—credit cards in his line of work were a definite no-no. He left the tip on the table and then strolled around the club until he found an open seat close to where Fulton was standing.

It wasn't long before Bates turned away from the woman he had been talking to, reached over to where he was sitting and touched his arm.

"Excuse me," said Bates with a convivial smile, "I don't mean to bother you. Have we met before? Do we know one another?"

Gordon flashed him an accepting smile, "Well, if we had, I would have remembered," then shrugged his shoulder in a gesture of passive enticement.

"Well, let me introduce myself," said Bates, "I am Emerson Lavell."

"Oh, I know who you are," Gordon said as he shook Fulton's hand. "I was here last night." With that being said, Gordon watched the woman Bates had been speaking with slowly turn and walk away. Too bad, he thought. Under different circumstances, he was sure he could have made her day.

"Yes, you were," replied Bates in almost a lyrical tone of voice, "and you sat right over there." He pointed in the direction of the table Gordon had been sitting at the night before.

"Well, Mr. Lavell, you certainly are very observant, aren't you?" said Gordon in an effeminate manner.

The secret to every ruse was to act sincere and to understate the obvious. "Why, thank you, Mr. . . . I am sorry, I didn't quite get your name," replied Bates.

Gordon leaned forward making sure to place a hand on Fulton's arm. "I'm terribly sorry. My name is Anthony Austin; my friends call me Tony."

"What a nice name," Bates said, thinking that the name was probably made up. Most straight guys used some other name when they were on the "troll for trouser trout." He didn't care; the guy was super gorgeous, very good-looking, with a to-die-for body-builder's physique.

While gazing over the edge of his glass and looking into Fulton's eyes, Gordon said, "Well, that's because I'm a really nice guy."

"I'll bet you are," said Bates in a breathy sort of way. "May I call you Tony?"

"Certainly," replied Gordon. "I mean Anthony is . . . kind of formal between friends."

"Are we friends, Tony?"

"I think we are; at least, I hope we can be," said Gordon, letting his voice say more than just words.

As Bates inched his way closer to where Gordon was sitting, he said, "You know, Anthony, I mean, Tony, I must tell you that I've seen you before. Do you live in the city?"

"Well, kinda, I guess," answered Gordon, "I'm over in Brooklyn—Cypress Hills, Highland Park area. Do you know it?"

"Do I know it? Of course, I know it," said Bates, placing his hand on Gordon's thigh. "I live in Park Slope; that makes us almost neighbors." Gordon tried not to cringe at his touch, but forced himself not to pull away.

Bates looked at his watch, "My break is almost up. Why don't I give you my business card?" Bates then placed the card on the bar in front of Gordon. "Call me anytime. I mean that, Tony. Anytime."

"Thank you, I will," replied Gordon as he puts Bates' card in the pocket of his suit jacket.

Off to his side he saw Sal Vincent ambling in their direction. "Hey, Emerson," he said, "you're up," then pointed at his watch.

"Don't forget. Anytime," said Bates as he walked away.

Vincent leaned into the space where Gordon was sitting and said, "You don't look like the type, but fuhgeddaboudit; he's not your kind. You know what I mean?"

As Vincent slipped away, he turned back and gave Gordon the "toot-a-lou" sign with his fingers, then blew him a kiss. Gordon couldn't help but think that the man needed to talk to the muzzle of his Automatic; if he did, he wouldn't be blowing any more kisses.

It was raining hard when Gordon left the Player's Club, so he decided to take a cab to where he had parked his car. The car wasn't his; it was TOJO's. He had loaned it to him for the express purpose of getting what he wanted: a quick completion of the Bates' contract and to collect his share of the money.

Driving around in cars wasn't his thing; they were convenient, and yet at times they could become highly problematic. The thought of having an accident, mechanical problems or being pulled over by the cops was something he could do without; it made him nervous just thinking about it.

He preferred mass transit or cabs. The trouble with that form of transportation was the use of video cams, recorders and the very inconvenient memories of people. If there was one thing he didn't need, it was to be remembered, recognized or filmed. Anonymity was the key. If that wasn't possible, then a good disguise was the next best thing. This time that type of situation hadn't presented itself.

While he sat in the car contemplating his next course of action, Gordon watched with bemused interest as the wiper blades swept the rain from the windshield. How apropos, he thought, almost metaphorical, when something or someone got in the way, all you had to do was push it, or them, aside. Maybe, that's what he was: a human windshield wiper. With that thought and others going through his mind, he felt the cell phone in his jacket pocket begin to vibrate.

Gordon knew who had to be calling him since only he and one other person had that number and that other person was his partner TOJO "The Baker" Grimaldi. According to him, he got his nickname "the Baker" when he was living in Palermo, Sicily. He was working in a bakery owned by some local Mafioso. The guy had him making and baking loaves of bread, then filling certain ones with packets of heroin wrapped in condoms. Those particular loaves were marked and then sold to customers with the right code and had paid in advance for some very expensive *panne*.

Gordon answered his cell phone in the usual way by saying, "Who is this?"

The voice on the other end shot back, "Who the fuck do you think it is? You're grandmother . . . smart ass. You know, Anthony, smart people don't swim too good . . . you understand *finocchio?*"

Gordon had to laugh at what Grimaldi said to him or what he alluded to. It was one of his Sicilian aphorisms that wise guys end up wearing concrete shoes. And, the fact that he called him a "faggot," was especially amusing when you considered the circumstances; the pejorative would seem to be right on.

Gordon countered TOJO's statement by saying, "*oh scusa don chiavare, por favor,*" or loosely translated as "excuse me, sir beggar, please." Gordon took pride in his ability to be multi-lingual; he was fluent in Italian, Spanish and Arabic.

He and Grimaldi would use Italian dialect to express the heat of the moment or to emphasize a point. Mostly they used it to insult one another in a friendly sort of way.

"So, what's the story?" asked Grimaldi. Gordon thought his partner's tone of voice still had that raspy Italian quality to it. The kind that made him sound like a character from some gangster movie.

"How did it go?" he asked.

"Better than we expected," replied Gordon.

"Ah, *strafigo*; better than we expected . . . well, that's good enough . . . so, when?"

"Probably sometime tonight," answered Gordon as he turned down the volume on the radio.

"That soon . . . huh . . . that's if everything works out . . . you know what I mean."

"Yeah, I know what you mean . . . one more thing."

"What's that?"

"I've got a new plan."

"Oh," replied Grimaldi, "I didn't know we ever really had one."

Gordon let out an audible sigh then went on to explain what he was going to do. How he was going to wait for Bates to leave the club, then pick him up as he was walking towards the subway. The excuse being it was raining, so he thought he'd give him a ride back to his apartment in Brooklyn.

"Sounds pretty good so far, then what?" asked Grimaldi.

Gordon went on by telling him if Bates accepted the ride, he would try to convince him to go on to his house in Greenwich, Connecticut.

"I didn't know you had a house in Connecticut," said Grimaldi.

"*Minchia, Ma che, sei scemo* . . . it's a fuckin' story . . . Jesus H. Christ, get with the program, will ya?"

TOJO laughed, "Sorry, Antonio, I am a little *udriaco*, you understand?"

"Yeah, I know," groaned Gordon, all the while dismissing TOJO's excuse of being drunk: TOJO was an actor and would often play dumb or drunk just to have you lower your guard. It was a common practice in their line of work to use subterfuge or any other ploy to get what you wanted, and his partner was one of the best.

"Anyway, forget about it . . . are you listening?" said Gordon.

"I'm listening, I'm listening . . . you *romp I palle* . . . you pain in the ass."

"Listen to me; if Bates goes for it, I'm going to take him to a place I checked out before. It's a street with a lot of woods with little or no police surveillance."

"What happens then?"

"What do you think?" questioned Gordon. "I'll talk him into getting out of the car."

"What if he won't go?"

"Then I'll force him out . . . shoot him . . . take his ID, his money and cell phone, make it look like a robbery."

"Then I drag his body deep into the woods; *finite*. Hey, he's biodegradable."

In a voice low enough so you could scrape the floor with it, Grimaldi said, "Sounds good. When you are done, call me; let it ring three times, then hang up. Then call back and do the same. Don't call me back; I'll call you." He finished by saying *capisce*, understand, I'll call you. "*In bocca, al lupo*, goodbye and good luck."

Gordon was left with the all too familiar feeling he had grown accustomed to: he was on his own.

In the pensive atmosphere of his mind and only the sound of his windshield wipers slapping the time, Gordon waited. He had parked his car next to the curb on the side of the street he knew Bates would use to get to the subway.

It wasn't long before he saw him in his side view mirror. He was holding an umbrella kind of bent forward in the direction of the elements, and ultimately in the direction of his fate.

Before he decided to open the passenger side window, Gordon held off until Bates was semi-parallel with that side of the car.

"Hey, Mr. Lavell," he shouted. "Hey, Emerson, it's me, Anthony Austin. You need a ride?"

At first Bates hesitated. When he recognized who it was he scooted over to where Gordon was parked, popped his head through the open window and greeted him with an enthusiastic "hello." He then folded his umbrella, shook it a few times, then opened the car door and slid inside.

"Well, well," exclaimed Bates with a smile.

"This is a nice surprise. I thought I would never see you again . . . say, this is a really nice car. What is it?"

"Series 6 BMW."

"Is it expensive?"

"Kind of, depending on what you consider expensive. I was waiting for you to leave the club; I sort of followed you."

"Why?

"Ah, I have to be honest with you, Emerson . . . I had you on my mind . . . it was raining really hard . . . so, I thought I'd . . ."

"So, you thought you would give me a ride. How considerate of you," replied Fulton in a tone of voice that could best be described as feminine. It was an affection he acquired while learning to survive in prison with men who would sooner kill him then look at him. He found out in prison the more female you became the more valuable you were, especially if you willingly dispensed sexual favors to those who would protect you.

"Well, I have to admit something to you," said Bates as he positioned himself closer to where Gordon was sitting.

"Oh, and what's that?" asked Gordon as he looked out his window at his side mirror for coming traffic.

"Ever since I saw you at the club, I wanted to give you a ride," replied Bates, using that moment to slide his hand along Gordon's thigh, stopping close enough to his crotch to make him alter his position. Within the same motion, he leaned in closer so he could kiss Gordon's shoulder; it was a gesture of submission—something he often did with men he wanted to become "familiar" with, not unlike a dog bowing to his master.

Not accustomed to homosexual etiquette, Gordon called up his sense of professional tolerance and refrained from chopping him across the throat. He remembered to take a deep breath and then recalled one of his favorite aphorisms:

"An emotion was unfulfilled intention where action was delayed; while anger created self-reference of imagined behavior in a self-satisfying fantasy."

In the meantime, the strains of "Something Stupid" came through the speakers which only added to the idiosyncrasy of the moment.

At a standstill as to what to do, Gordon said, "uh, I have to be honest with you, Emerson . . . I was . . . I mean, I had you on my mind. Could I ask you a question?"

"Go ahead," said Bates, "ask away. I love questions."

"Ah . . . would you mind . . . instead . . .?"

"Instead of what?"

"Would you mind going to my place tonight instead of me driving you to Brooklyn?"

"Your place," replied Bates with an inquisitive look, "and where pray tell is your place?"

"Greenwich."

There was a pregnant moment of silence as Bates mulled over Gordon's request.

"Greenwich, you mean as in Greenwich, Connecticut?"

"That's the place," replied Gordon with a laughing kind of smile. "I have a home with a Jacuzzi, and two fireplaces, one in the bedroom." If there was one thing Gordon knew about homos: they loved money. Gay guys couldn't resist a man with a big wallet or a big dick, preferably both. But either one would suffice, he reckoned.

"Well, that just settles it. You must be rich or you're just trying to bullshit me into sucking your cock. Of course, you know, I would do that for you anyway. You know I don't expect reciprocation. I'm a sub.

"Sure," said Gordon as he nodded his head trying to look enthusiastic, "so, I guess that's a yes . . . like you'll go with me to my house?" trying to add supposed innocence to the proposal.

"Don't be silly. How could I ever say no to someone like you? There is one thing."

"Oh, yeah? . . . I mean, what's that?" Gordon asked as he pulled away from the curb into a passing parade of cars.

"I don't have a change of clothes."

"Clothes," Gordon replied, "oh, I don't think you have to worry about that."

"Why is that?" asked Bates with a smile.

"Because I don't think you'll need any," said Gordon as he squeezed Bates' thigh.

Fulton took Gordon's hand in both of his and held it up to his mouth and kissed it. Gordon put his index finger between his lips. As if on cue, Bates opened his mouth and began to suck on it in a blatant display of fellatio. He did that while watching Gordon try to drive the car with one hand and the other stuck in his mouth.

When Gordon finally wrested his hand from Fulton's face, he called him a fucking asshole and for him never to try anything like that again. He wanted to say and do a lot more, but for the sake of the contract and the fifty grand, he kept his mouth shut.

At first Fulton felt highly incensed at Gordon's show of anger, but then thought about it and apologized for the indulgence.

They drove along for a mile or more in a contrived state of silence with Fulton waiting for Gordon to get over his supposed snit. He still didn't understand what his problem was; it wasn't as if they had gotten into some type of car accident. Fulton tossed it up as some sort of heterosexual display of masculinity coupled with their silly relationship with cars.

It was something he couldn't relate to but went along with anyway. Why not? It was a free ride. And, like they used to say in jail: it ain't nothin' unless it's free.

It wasn't long until they reached 96th going over the FDR Drive, then over to Bruckner Boulevard and onto I-95 North.

Gordon finally decided to break his silence by telling Bates about his life. How he was born in Bogota, Colombia, his father was German and his mother was Colombian, how he had moved to Queens when he was twelve, went on to NYU after high school. He had earned a master's degree in English and that he inherited a lot of money after his father died.

He continued to tell a lot about himself, most of it was true, knowing that Bates would never get the chance to repeat any of it anyhow.

Dutifully, Bates sat there pretending to listen to what Gordon was saying all the while not caring or believing half of what he heard.

What he really wanted to talk about was what Gordon could do for him: like sex, money, and most of all, the possibility of establishing a long-term relationship. One that would take him out of fuckin' Brooklyn into a lifestyle that was more conducive to his wants and needs. On their ride along I-95 Bates took out his iPhone and told Gordon he wanted to take a picture of him so he could send it to a friend of his in Brooklyn. Without hesitation, Gordon snatched the iPhone from Bates hand. He knew if he ever took his picture and sent it to his friend the entire operation would have to be scrapped. A situation he wasn't about to let happen.

With his mouth open in a state of momentary confusion, Fulton sat there staring at him, then in a show of anger, used his fist to pound on the dashboard.

In an attempt to assuage Bates feelings, Gordon promised him that he could take all the pictures he wanted once they got to his house.

"Fuck you and your house, too," hissed Bates as he stomped his feet. He told Gordon he wanted to go back to Brooklyn. He was tired of his "phony-ass attitude of pretending to be bi-curious."

Gordon felt something like this might occur so to be prepared, he brought along a few Thai-sticks (a high-potency cannabis of seedless marijuana tied around the center most stalk supposed to be kickass weed). If there was one thing he knew musicians loved it was to get high and he was sure that Fulton wouldn't be an exception.

He handed one of the joints to Bates who immediately calmed down a little. He smoked two of them. However, every time he took a hit, he would offer some to Gordon, who had to decline citing the fact that he was driving.

He told Bates he'd love to get high with him in his Jacuzzi when they got to the house.

"Yeah, yeah," said Bates. "How come everything we're going to do is when we get to your house? Fuck that, we should stop somewhere, and I'll show you what I can do."

Gordon gave him a few sips of brandy from a silver flash he had stowed away in one of the cars many compartments. With that, Fulton finally stopped talking and went to sleep.

When they finally arrived at the Greenwich Avenue exit, the atmosphere between them had become, at best, somewhat tentative. Gordon wasn't used to dealing with the mercurial emotions of a gay drama queen, and Bates didn't like Gordon's strident attitude.

In an apparent huff, Bates turned in Gordon's direction and told him he had changed his mind, that he was sorry—he wanted to go back to Brooklyn, that it just wasn't working out between the two of them.

With a discernable sigh, Gordon nodded his head then pulled over to the side of the road.

"I understand," he said, his voice heavy with apparent dismay. "Is there something I could do or . . . I mean I really want you to go with me . . . like my house is only a half-hour away in Glenville."

"Well, you know, you don't have to beg . . . I mean if you really want me to go with you . . . like you could always buy me."

"Buy you?"

"Sure," said Bates, casting Gordon a presumptive smile as he ran a hand over the center console. "You can afford it. Think of it this way, I would be your, uh, your own personal little whore. You could do whatever you want with me."

Bates was sure Gordon would explode. He was the type all macho and all. He would probably swear or slap him or force him to do something humiliating; men had done that to him before.

Gordon knew he couldn't quit now; they were so close, and then he could end this charade once and for all.

"Okay," said Gordon. "How much do you want?"

A wave of disappointment washed over Bates' fertile mind. The answer wasn't what he expected. He was sure Gordon would become physically violent, or at least try to do something to him.

Of course, all of that would probably come later, most likely within the confines of his bedroom. He could see the two of them in bed, the fireplace glowing in the dark, their bodies wet with sweat, casting shadows on the wall.

He envisioned Gordon behind him using his belt against the cheeks of his ass while he lay there naked and exposed, his wrists tied to the bedposts. The thought of succumbing to different forms of abuse left him quickening with desire wishing that they were already there.

"Well," he said, "how about all the money in your front pocket?" pointing to a discernable bulge in Gordon's pants. "Or is that just your dick?" he asked.

"Don't you just wish," replied Gordon while delving into his front pocket for a wad of cash he kept on hand since he couldn't use credit cards or checks to pay bills with.

He handed the money to Bates who promptly took it from him then slowly counted it.

"Wow! Tony . . . 2500 . . . jeez, you must really, really want me to go home with you."

As much as he hated Bates, he had gotten to know him. It was hard to take someone out when you knew them. Mentally, he shrugged his shoulders; still, that just the way it was.

"You know, Tony, you don't have to be so fuckin' serious. I was just kidding you . . . I mean . . . here," said Bates, handing the money back.

Gordon looked at the money and then at him. "Keep it," he said, "I've got more."

Bates rejected the offer and put it in the glove compartment in front of him.

As they drove along, Bates asked Gordon if Anthony Austin was his real name or just some alias. Gordon countered by asking him if Emerson Lavell was his real name.

Before he said anything, Bates looked away then glanced out the passenger side window.

"Wouldn't you like to know," he said softly, then turned back to face Gordon and squeezed his arm.

"Boy, Tony, you sure got some big arms; you must work out a lot."

"Enough to get by," replied Gordon.

"Enough to get by what?"

"Whatever I have to."

"Oh, okay . . . well, I tell you what, I have to get by," said Bates.

"What's that?" asked Gordon.

"Peeing . . . how about you?"

"I guess so . . . I know a spot not far from here . . . kinda out of the way."

"Good," answered Bates, "I like out-of-the-way places. Hey, you know what?"

"What?"

"Maybe, when we're there . . . you know . . . maybe, you and I can do something in the car."

"Maybe," said Gordon.

"Well, you know what I always say, don't you?"

"What's that?" murmured Gordon, not taking his eyes off the road.

"Anytime, anywhere," answered Bates, using his feminine voice.

"That goes for a lot of things."

"What did you say?" asked Bates as he turned up the heat button on the console.

"Ah, nothing, nothing at all," replied Gordon, annoyed with himself that someone like Bates could get to him. If you would have asked him, he would have said he thought that he was better than that. The idea left him feeling angrier than he already was.

The thought of putting him away became more appealing as they drove along.

"We'll be there in a few minutes," said Gordon while turning down the street he had planned on.

"We're here," said Gordon as he drove up on to a small patch of ground close to a group of trees.

"Thank God," answered Bates, "because I really got to go."

As soon as he turned off the car, Bates jumped out and walked into the darkness.

Gordon was quick to follow, making sure he stayed a few feet behind. With the lights of the car turned off, the surrounding area was quite dark. However, the light from a distant street light provided enough illumination for Gordon to see Bates standing in front of him urinating to his bladder's content.

He had already taken out his silenced Automatic when he came up behind Bates who didn't turn around or stop what he was doing.

"Wow, did I have to go," he said out loud.

Gordon had placed his hand and the Automatic he was holding in a plastic bag. The reasoning was when he shot Bates he wouldn't have to go searching for a penlight for the spent cartridge.

The only thought Gordon had was finally the moment had arrived. He raised his hand and slowly pulled the trigger; the gun jumped in his hand. There was no sound other than Bates as he fell to the ground.

Gordon stood there for a moment watching Bates moan as he lay face-down on the ground. He then walked up to him, slipped the front of his shoe under his chest and rolled him over.

"Why, Tony, why?" said Bates as he reached up with one hand only to have it fall back across his chest. His voice became weak and his words trailed off so Gordon couldn't hear what he was saying.

He then bent down on one knee and grabbed the front of Bates' jacket, pulling him up so they faced one another.

In a voice as cold as the ground he was kneeling on he said, "You want to know why? I'll tell you why, you son-of-a-bitch, because my name is not Tony Austin, that's why. And you are not Emerson Lavell, that's why. You are Fulton Fuckin' Bates and you are worth more to me dead than alive."

It was at that point that Gordon realized he was shouting at a corpse. He released his grip and let him fall to the ground. Gordon dragged Bates' body luggage style into a secluded area of the underbrush to the place he told Grimaldi about.

He then shot him twice in the forehead. After doing that he used an instant digital camera to take a few close-up photographs of Bates' face and the bullet holes in his head. He would give the pictures to Grimaldi who would pass them on to whoever wanted them, thereby fulfilling the conditions of the contract.

Gordon reached into the breast pocket of his suit jacket and withdrew a small vile of chicken blood which he poured on Bates' clothes. He them removed the man's wallet, wristwatch and two rings and put them in a neat pile next to his body. After doing that, he pulled down Bates' pants and underwear to his ankles. He then took two large sticks which he set over Bates' genitals in the sign of the cross. He then took two tarot cards out, one that stood for justice and the other for the devil, putting one of each in Bates' two hands.

His reasoning was simple: to make the crime scene look as if it was a ritual killing. No matter how it played out, Gordon knew it would cast doubt on the motive.

When he drove back to Manhattan, Gordon felt satisfied with the outcome; it couldn't have gone any better. However, he was still aggravated that someone of his caliber had been used to kill a low-life like Fulton Bates.

He thought over how he had to have TOJO's car sanitized so as to remove any trace of Bates' fingerprints or DNA. He would have to have his clothes incinerated including his shoes and gloves. Reluctantly, he knew he had to have his Automatic destroyed, even the silencer. Anything that was at the crime scene had to be destroyed, even the tires on Grimaldi's car.

He had a safe house to go to in Manhattan, an apartment that belonged to one of Bentley's contacts. He had a lot to think about, but Fulton Bates wasn't one of them.

CHAPTER 18

"Sex is like a snowstorm. You never know how much you will get or how long it will last."

— ARGO —

While he was sitting at his kitchen table counting out the money Grimaldi had given him for the Fulton Bates job, Gordon debated whether to have a drink or not. He never drank alcohol during the day; nevertheless, on certain occasions, he made exceptions—today was one of those exceptions. Standing in front of him next to stacks of one hundred dollar bills was a bottle of Irish whiskey. It was a gift from Chris Bentley for what he said was a job well done.

Anyway, to quote one of his favorite poets Oscar Wilde, he could resist anything but temptation. So, he poured himself a small amount of the Irish into a glass filled with ice. He took a sip then picked up a stack of hundreds and once again began his count.

While he was doing that, he contemplated how much he disliked his employment. He then thought about the alternative and how much money he was making and all the things he could buy. With those thoughts acting as a chaser, Gordon took another sip, closed his eyes and said:

"Ah, fuck it."

He then thought over the plans for his next involvement; from what he was told, it would be somewhere in Brooklyn. He was to be a back-up shooter for either TOJO or Chris Bentley. As of yet, it wasn't a green light, just a feasibility study.

With nothing left to do but sit around and wait, Gordon figured that maybe he would give Renee a call. He was in the mood to give himself a present and she made a helluva gift. Furthermore, he needed a night out, a little let-loose time, and who better to do it with than her. To make matters more agreeable, he needed to know how Starr had found him out and what connection Renee had with him or the NYPD.

If she didn't want to tell him anything then maybe the feel of a silencer pressed against her temple might change her mind. He knew there were two overriding motivators: money and fear, with fear taking the lead.

Without a doubt Gordon knew he would never "knock her off"; that wasn't his style. He didn't do women or children—not even for money. However, there was a slight hesitation that crossed his mind: Did prostitutes really count? A distant voice told him "presumably so" with the caveat "depending on the circumstances."

Gordon reached into his back pocket and pulled out his wallet. He folded it open and found her business card nestled amongst the many. He dialed her number then waited for her answering service to pick up. The voice on the other end sounded like an invitation to a wet dream.

Gordon left her his alias, Anthony Austin, and the cell number of a throw-away phone. The idea being, if she gave it to the cops or whoever and they tried a reverse look-up, they'd end up with "nada." He then settled back and waited for Renee to call him.

He also figured that she knew his true identity; Tom Starr probably told her who and what he was. He didn't care, but if he was going to have anything to do with her or conduct any business in NYC, he had to know.

It wasn't long before the throw-away cell phone rang; it was Renee. In a syrupy tone of voice she asked him if he was Anthony Austin or not. He answered her with an emphatic "yes." She then went on to ask him a barrage of questions:

Where had he been? How come he hadn't called? Was he in town and where? Etc., etc.

He sure as hell wasn't about to tell her any of that. Instead, he gave her the usual line of bullshit: he had gone away on business and he missed her a whole lot. When he thought about it, he did miss her—at least certain parts of her.

Gordon went on to say he was thinking of taking her out to dinner and some place they could dance. He told her how he had purchased a new suit and wanted to show it off.

She asked him what kind did he buy. Gordon told her it was a Baroni, and what they called a jet-black sheen with a tone-on-tone shadow pinstripe. He went on to say that he was thinking of wearing a black shirt with French cuffs and a black tie.

The reason he mentioned all of that to her was he knew Renee really appreciated men's clothing. Say what you wanted about her, but she just wasn't some run-of-the-mill "*puttana*." The girl had taste, or at least what passed for it.

Renee told him she had just the place to go; it was in Manhattan at a situation called Stage 8. It had excellent food, a small but intimate dance floor and a very cozy bar. The waiters were all gay and the club girls were extra friendly.

It was for members only, but the public was invited with the members getting the best tables as well as substantial discounts on food and liquor. She saved the best part for last and told him she was a member.

He asked her when and where and would there be anyone else at their table?

She told him that she had a friend who had just flown in from California and would he mind if she came along? Before he had a chance to respond, Renee said that her friend was an adult film star.

He couldn't say "of course" fast enough, all the while extolling how much he admired adult film actresses and how they were his favorite kind of "thespians." Renee knew what he had in mind, maybe a little *ménage à* **trois** at the end of the evening. "Hey," she thought, it would mean less work for her and possibly the chance to enjoy what she did for a living.

As for Gordon, he envisioned the night ahead and where it would end up. Hopefully, he mused, with the three of them in some hotel with him swallowing a bottle of Viagra.

He met the two women at the restaurant which turned out to be far better than what he expected. It was ultra-chi-chi with muted colors, spotlights over what appeared to be expensive paintings, heavily stuffed chairs and a single rose as a centerpiece on each table.

Renee's friend turned out to be quite a stunner, with high cheekbones, a thin nose and bee-stung lips. In addition to that she had a gorgeous blond ponytail that went all way to the middle of her back.

She was wearing a black dress with a slit up the back and seams on her nylons. Better than all of that, she had a really great set of tits. To round out the fashion show, Renee had on a mocha-colored suit with a short jacket and a tourniquet for a skirt.

Gordon forgot about why he was taking Renee out to dinner; instead, he concentrated on the time at hand. He loved women, good times and great food. However, it was ambience that put him in the right frame of mind so he could enjoy it all.

After they were seated, Gordon ordered a bottle of champagne; nothing fancy, just an ordinary $300 of bubbly.

Gordon thought the menu was varied with some interesting specials. He decided it would be easier if he ordered for Renee and her girlfriend who had introduced herself as Leslie St. Cyr. He didn't believe that was her name, but who was he to cast dispersions on someone else's use of an alias.

He thought for their appetizers they would go with the Asian gravlax and ginger shiso vinaigrette. After a slight deliberation, the girls chose the roasted monkfish with sweet potatoes and orange lumen vinaigrette for their entrée.

He wasn't a fish person, so he went with the dry-aged prime sirloin, broccoli rabe, Barolo butter and tomato marmalade for his entrée.

They spent the shank of the evening talking and dancing with intermittent sips of wine. The girls texted incessantly while they ate, with frequent trips to the ladies' room to snort a few lines and pee.

Gordon didn't care; his mind was on what they would do after they left Stage 8. He made it a point to dance with Leslie. He loved the feel of her body next to his and the smell of her perfume.

At different times through the evening Leslie told him about her life—how she had gone to college in Wisconsin to study drama, then went to Hollywood to pursue an acting career. The rest of her resume was somewhat predictable—how to make ends meet she had gotten into porno and pole dancing in strip clubs. On top of all that she had become temporally addicted to cocaine.

Gordon had heard it all before; he felt sorry for her, but knew many women had an unconscious desire to become self-destructive.

At the end of the evening Gordon did something he

hardly would ever do: pay the bill with a credit card, instead of cash. It really didn't mean much since the card was in the name of his benefactor—Anthony Austin. However, it was a paper trail, something he tried to avoid.

The cab ride to the hotel was disturbing with Renee and Leslie passionately kissing him while they played with his junk. The end result being he had a constant hard-on through most of the trip, as well as a case of blue balls that left him walking funny as they entered the lobby of the hotel.

After they entered their hotel room, Gordon flipped on one of the room lights. Its warm glow seemed as a welcoming response to their admittance. He then walked over to a nearby closet and hung up his suit jacket.

With the ease of someone who had done this before, he settled into one of the upholstered chairs next to the bed. He had Renee and Leslie take up a position in front of him. The two women said nothing, letting him direct their actions and the degree of what he wanted them to do.

Gordon proceeded to undue the buckle of his belt, pulling it free from his pants. After doing that, he took a moment and unzipped his fly, then released the top button of his trousers.

With a look of serene sexiness, Renee and Leslie followed his lead and started to undress. Renee stepped aside allowing Leslie to be first. With a slowness of purpose, she removed her dress, tossing it aimlessly on the bed.

Her eyes never faltered from Gordon's steady gaze. She was wearing a black push-up bra, the same colored garter belt, panties and nylons. Her shoes were basic black with spike heels; the whole ensemble was a picture of what Gordon had in his mind—erotica.

Leslie then walked over to her handbag that she had left sitting on a chest of drawers and removed a pair of dark-framed glasses. She had been told that men fantasized about blondes, with ponytails, wearing glasses—especially if they were half-naked.

Not to be outdone, Renee did the same and slowly removed her suit jacket, one button at a time. When she was through, she placed it next to Leslie's dress. With her thumbs hooked inside the waistband of her skirt, Renee slowly wiggled it down past her thighs letting the skirt fall around her ankles. With the deftness of a dancer, she stepped away from it. She had done all of that without taking her eyes from Gordon's watchful stare. To finish what she had started, Renee reached behind her and unhooked her bra, then pushed the straps from her shoulders. She took the bra in one hand and dropped it at his feet.

Gordon couldn't have been more entranced; he loved watching women undress. To him it was a conversation without words, the height of innuendo. He knew from the start that his money had been well spent. It followed that old maxim: you get what you pay for.

Gordon could sense it was time to start the show; to him sex was a physical fitness test with blissful results as the prize. He motioned for Leslie to come over to him and kneel at his feet. She knew the rest and pulled his pants open while helping push them to the floor. She then drew down his underwear letting his burgeoning cock go free.

He held it in one hand and watched as she worked her mouth towards it. It wasn't long before she could go all the way to his balls without gagging. Gordon marveled at her ability to do that, considering he had a pretty big dick—at least that's what he had been told. His assumption was that with all her porno experience she had perfected her ability for performing "deep throat."

He knew he couldn't let her continue or he would lose it and he was determined to get his money's worth out of the evening's activities. He pushed Leslie's head aside and told Renee to kneel down next to her. Always compliant, Renee did as she was told, but before she started to give him head, she rolled a condom down his shaft. It was something she knew Gordon liked. He said it changed the sensation, plus she didn't have to swallow his semen.

Gordon let Renee go on until he got to the point where he thought he was going to cum, and then told her to stop. She removed the condom, stood up and went to the bathroom to flush it down the toilet.

While she was there, Gordon instructed Leslie to lay across the side of the bed with her feet on the floor and her arms out in front of her. He stood behind her with his belt in his hand and smacked her voluptuous ass—not too hard, just enough to get her attention. He wasn't into spanking women, but sometimes it seemed like the right thing to do.

Leslie knew her part and moaned seductively, all the while telling him to hit her harder. As he did that, she flexed the muscles of her buttocks and tightened the ones in her back.

Gordon grabbed her ponytail and pulled her head back. He could see her profile in the mirror above the chest of drawers. She looked so enticing Gordon knew he couldn't wait; he had to fuck her.

He pushed her panties to the side and slowly let himself inside of her. After doing that he started to pick up speed. With piston-like precision, he watched his cock slip in and out of her well-shaved muff. As he did that, he told her to talk to him; the words didn't matter just as long as she repeated what he told her to say.

Renee stood by his side kissing his face then working her way down his body until she was on her knees next to his thigh. She waited for him to pull out of Leslie and then turned to put his cock in her mouth.

The scene became pornographic with Gordon fighting to control himself; within minutes he knew he couldn't stop. So, he pulled out of her and jerked off sending a stream of cum over her ass.

He then threw himself on the bed next to her, his

chest heaving and his heart pounding. Leslie kissed his face telling him how good he was, that they had the rest of the night ahead of them. He wished she hadn't said that, it was something he didn't want to reflect on.

Renee lay on his other side kissing his shoulder while gently massaging his balls and stroking his semi-flaccid penis. Gordon hovered somewhere above his altered state of mind and contemplated the thought of having to do this again.

As if on cue he could hear his cell phone vibrating on the table next to the bed. He knew who it was, the perfect excuse to end his sexual excursion into porno land. When he picked it up there was an encryptic message telling him that TOJO had been injured in a car accident and for him to come to their predetermined rendezvous.

He told Renee and Leslie he was sorry that he had to leave, that he had an emergency to attend to. The two women told him he was crazy, that they didn't believe him, that he should stay. He begged their forgiveness; he would make it up to them, but duty called. They told him what he could do with his duty.

Gordon dressed as quickly as he could, kissing the two women as he did; it was awkward but doable.

When he finally left the hotel and caught a cab to Brooklyn, he was once again ready to ply the wares of Leslie and Renee. Unfortunately, he knew in the world of sexual fantasy timing was everything and the moment could never be revisited.

Gordon hailed a cab in front of the hotel. He told the driver to take him to an all-night diner in Williamsburg. As they drove along he kept a watchful eye behind him. He wanted to see if it was the same car that had followed him from Stage 8 to the hotel—it was.

The obviousness of the tail couldn't be misconstrued; Renee had told someone in the NYPD or FBI about her date (with him). Whoever that person or persons were couldn't be too bright, considering they were using the same vehicle for the same purpose or maybe they just didn't care.

So far his plan was working well in finding out just how much influence Renee had with those agencies. He had told Chris Bentley to send him an encryptic around 1:30 in the morning so he could use it as an excuse to leave Renee and her friend. Furthermore, he wanted to see if anyone was waiting for him—they were. The thing that bothered him the most was the injury to TOJO; it would fuck-up the progression of the feasibility study.

Gordon told the cabbie to drive slow and not to make any sudden turns. He wanted the car that was following (behind) them every chance to do so. He had given the driver a couple of hundred bucks for the ride and his cooperation to go along with what he wanted him to do—which, of course, he did.

When Gordon entered the diner he found a booth next to a window, ordered breakfast, then sat back and tried to relax. He planned on sticking around for an hour or so, then walk over to the subway station and catch a train back to Manhattan. He knew once he hit the city he was home free.

While he was enjoying his sausage and cheese omelet, backed up with a cup of black coffee, he looked up to see Tom Starr walking towards him. All he could think of was *chinga tu madre* (Spanish for fuck your mother).

Starr smiled then sat down across from him and said:

"Hey, how you doin', Tony?"

Gordon tried not to show how he felt. He knew he had to stay cool; it was the only way to handle a situation like this.

"Oh, I'm doin' just fine," Gordon said. "I always like a little '*agida*' when I'm having breakfast. You want like a cup of coffee before you go?"

"So, you want to talk or what?" Starr asked.

Gordon gave him his best "fuck you" look. "You gotta be shittin' me?" he asked as the waitress poured the two of them their coffee and gave Gordon his check.

"Well, you might want to hear what I have to say."

"I doubt it, but try me anyway."

"Here it is," Starr said as he took a sip of coffee then leaned forward and said.

"The NSA cracked some of your encryptics. We know you're working for Global."

"So?!"

"So, here's the deal: you and your two friends, T.J. Grimaldi and Christopher Graham Bentley . . . well, we want you to work for us."

"*Minchia*!" Gordon exclaimed (an Italian word used as an exclamation of surprise—literal translation: penis.)

Gordon looked around to see if anyone might be watching them.

"Hey! We know you three are doing something with the Muslims. The Muslim Brotherhood have lost five of their top imams . . . one was car bombed, the other four were shot . . . long distance."

"Easy!" Gordon said. "Maybe before we go any further, you take out your RF trans-corder (radio frequency transmitter detector combination tape recorder detector designed to be worn during a face-to-face conversation which vibrates in the presence of hidden recording units—small as a pack of cigarettes) and I'll take out mine,"

Starr smiled, reached into his coat pocket and placed his unit on the table; Gordon did the same.

"Now . . . as you were saying," said Gordon.

Starr explained how the agency was being squeezed from up above on how to shut down any terror cells in the US—how they could do things the agency couldn't.

"Like what?" Gordon asked.

"Well," Starr said, "you know . . . like take them out."

"Mmm . . . I'm listening," Gordon said as he turned his head from side to side.

"Let me make this easier," Starr said. "You know

about the 'Whitey' Bulger case up in Boston?"

"Yeah, I know of it . . . what about it?" asked Gordon.

"You know how John Connolly made a deal with Bulger to tell him all he knew about the Mafia in Boston, to give him a day-by-day narrative?"

"Yeah."

"Well, Connolly told Bulger if he did that he would arrange it so 'Whitey' . . . could do what he wanted without any interference from the agency . . . he got a pass."

"Okay . . . so, what you're saying is me and whoever I'm with do our thing with the Muslims . . . and you and yours . . . look the other way."

"Kind of . . . here's something else: we pay you."

Gordon sat back, took a sip of coffee, cocked his head, made a soft whistling sound and said in Italian:

"*Non credo a una parola di tutto questo.*" (It was Italian for "I don't believe a word of it.")

"*Fiducia di me,*" said Starr. (Italian for trust me.)

"Okay," replied Gordon. "So, like where do we go from here?"

"Reno" took out one of his business cards and placed it on the table in front of Gordon.

"Call me," he said. "You will get my answering service . . . just say green or black . . . green is a yes—black is uh, no. *Capisce?*"

Gordon nodded his head.

"*Bene,*" said Starr as he stood up to leave, putting his RF trans-corder in his pocket.

"Yeah . . . see you around," replied Gordon as he put his RF in his jacket pocket.

"Hey, Tony," said Starr as he walked away.

"Yeah?" answered Gordon.

"Nice suit."

CHAPTER 19

Gordon lay against the headboard of his bed, his back comfortably supported by two large pillows. The evening seemed unusually cold as a slight draft sent an arrow of chill through the room. Pulling a blanket up to his chest, he reminded himself why he didn't like roadside motels, they were unpredictable. As he stared at the television, Gordon thought over the reasons why he was there.

On the bed by his side was a loose-leaf notebook containing the details of his present piece of business. As Gordon opened the book he looked down at the picture of the man he was planning to kill.

He had followed him from New York City to a small town outside the city of Binghamton in upper New York State to a place called Valonia Springs, population under a thousand. It was the kind of place where everybody knew one another, but didn't admit it. Not a great place to visit he thought sarcastically, but a great place to hide. While studying the man's picture he scanned the rest of his notes then reflected on their significance.

Richard Carroll Spencer was known as the "Werewolf Rapist of Syracuse." The moniker came about due to his use of wearing a werewolf Halloween mask while committing a series of burglaries and rapes.

Gordon turned to a particular page and looked at one of Spencer's victims, Veronica Lorraine Carter. She was the daughter and only child of Helen and John Carter. He was better known as Buffalo Carter because of all the property he owned in the city of Buffalo. Helen Carter was well known for her charitable acts and laudable graciousness. The Carter story wasn't unusual, just another case of a family destroyed by crime.

For a moment Gordon stopped reflecting on the case then asked himself: when was a crime ever sensible? Shaking his head, he laughed at himself for asking such a rhetorical question.

Spencer was accused of raping Carter's daughter in May of 1992. In that same year he was also accused of raping five other women in the Syracuse area.

Veronica Carter was everything to her parents, the type of child every parent dreamed of. She was an honor student at the University of Syracuse, an accomplished violinist, and a member of the women's track team. She had it all, he thought, as he looked at her picture: sparkling blue eyes, beautiful blonde hair with a perfect face. Her popularity on the campus of the University of Syracuse was well known.

Shortly after reaching her senior year Veronica convinced her father to buy her a home in the suburbs of Syracuse. As always, her father could not say no. The home was lavish, two fireplaces, a hot tub and five bedrooms. The only thing it didn't have was a security system.

She was famous for her extravagant parties, inviting the campus elite and the socially prominent. It was after one of the parties that Spencer gained access to the house. He found an unlocked window and let himself in. As he searched the home he found Veronica sleeping in the master bedroom. Wearing his signature werewolf mask, Spencer sat on the edge of the bed, then calmly placed his hand over her mouth.

"Wake up, sleepy head," he whispered in her ear while pressing a knife against her throat. Frozen with terror, she did nothing to resist, but lay there acquiescing to his commands. Spencer moved with well-rehearsed quickness, binding her hands behind her then covering her mouth with duct tape. After completing that part of his scenario, he pushed her nightgown up over her head, then slowly fondled her body. Taking his time with her he decided to bind her ankles and search the rest of the house. As he left the room he said to her, "Don't go away, I'll be right back; don't let the bedbugs bite."

Spencer methodically made his way through the rest of the rooms. While doing that he discovered Veronica's closest friend, Virginia Musante, sleeping in one of the guest bedrooms. She was the daughter of a very prominent neurosurgeon in the city of Syracuse. Spencer performed the same procedure on the Musante girl as he had done to Veronica.

According to the police report, Spencer went back and forth between the two rooms— raping and torturing them at his leisure, then left without taking "anything of value." Gordon stopped reading and thought about the statement "anything of value," as if their bodies were nothing but dog shit.

Veronica left Syracuse University and moved to Buffalo to live with her parents. There she was placed in intensive psychiatric care to battle her overwhelming depression. Finally, in the fall of 1994, she committed suicide by taking an overdose of sleeping pills.

Unfortunately, the Musante girl didn't fare any better. After the dismissal of Spencer's case, she moved to Florida, changed her name and finished her college education. While driving home from Florida, she was killed in an automobile accident.

Gordon shook his head with detached disgust, and then reached behind himself to fluff up his pillows. Putting his notebook aside, he lit a cigarette and then opened a can of diet soda. After a short while, Gordon decided to read his notes again. He didn't know why he spent so much time reflecting on the case. His only thought was by doing that he might make a better decision on what he should do.

It was the confession of an inmate at Attica Prison by the name of Justin "Pretty Boy" Rhodes that led to Spencer's capture. Rhodes knew of the Carter and Musante rapes. He saw a chance to cut a deal for a reduced sentence if he informed on Spencer. So, he gave as much information to the state attorney's office as he could recall. Rhodes went as far as implicating himself in a number of unsolved robberies that he and Spencer had done together. He would later relate to a grand jury that Spencer had bragged to him about a series of rapes he had committed in the Syracuse vicinity. Rhodes told the grand jury that Spencer told him that he had used a Halloween werewolf mask for added effect. The allegations made by Rhodes could not be substantiated by additional testimony or evidence. The grand jury dismissed his testimony as an attempt at a reduced sentence with the state.

There were other problems with the case against Spencer; first was the fact that Spencer never ejaculated when he had sex with his victims. Without semen samples there were no conclusive blood tests or DNA testing. In addition to this there was the use of an improper search warrant by the Syracuse police; they were trying to locate photographs that Spencer had allegedly taken of his victims. The case against Spencer was finally dismissed due to lack of evidence. It was these legal atrocities that helped Gordon convince John Carter to seek justice elsewhere.

Gordon remembered how he had followed the Carter case for a year after Spencer's dismissal. During that time he contacted Carter, introducing himself as ARGO, while proposing the idea of eliminating Spencer.

Carter vehemently declined the offer, stating he

wanted nothing to do with the scene. It was during that time that Carter received a picture of his daughter bound and gagged, lying naked on her bed. The picture was the final abomination; Carter agreed to have Spencer murdered. He also agreed on the amount of $200,000— half down, the remainder to be paid after the hit. Carter also wanted Gordon's assurance that he would have complete anonymity. Gordon complied with his wishes, assuring him that he had nothing to fear, thinking how incredible it was that a man of Carter's intellect would believe such a lie.

Revenge made people irrational, irrational enough to believe almost anything. Gordon sat back scoffing at the idea of anonymity. Didn't Carter know the first thing anybody did when caught in a criminal act is to make a deal?

With a feeling of contempt for the stupidity of the human race, Gordon left his bed and paced about the room. As he did this, he reflected on his business arrangement with Carter. The plan was simple, yet somewhat ingenious. Gordon told Carter to use an attorney named Morton Lapinski for his business deals. Carter informed him that Lapinski's law firm could do the closing on a large shopping center he wished to purchase. When Carter paid Lapinski's firm for their legal services, he would include the money for the Spencer contract.

Gordon smiled to himself as he thought over the irony of the deal. The entire procedure would be a write-off for Carter's corporation.

After everything was completed Lapinski would do what he had done in the past; he would take a percentage of the contract money for himself and then transfer the remainder to an offshore numbered bank account that Gordon had set up.

Putting aside his thoughts, Gordon went to the window of his motel room. As he stood there looking out at the parking lot he noticed a man and a woman walking from their car towards the motel. They would stop every few feet then kiss. With an envious smile, Gordon whispered to himself, "Never underestimate the power of love; better yet, the power of expected sex."

Mentally snapping his fingers, Gordon's thoughts shifted back to Spencer and where he could be. With a gesture of frustration, he hit the table next to him with his fist sending an ashtray clattering to the floor. Ever since Spencer had moved from New York City to Valonia Springs he was having a difficult time tracking him. To make matters worse, the son-of-a-bitch was living with his sister Margaret and her dog. He hadn't seen Spencer or his sister in the last three days, or the dog he thought; curiosity was wearing a hole in his cautious nature. He could feel his frustration compromising his lack of restraint. Contracts were a source of constant pressure; it was never simple, he thought, like you see in the movies.

Gordon knew what he had to do; he would investigate Margaret Spencer's home. Gordon thought over the situation. If he found Spencer with his sister it was going to be dicey. He would kill Spencer, tie up his sister, then steal whatever he could. The police would think it was a robbery that went wrong.

With this in mind, he decided to prepare for the occasion. He opened a large suitcase and placed it on the bed. Gordon removed the following items: a black utility jacket and matching pants, a pair of steel-toed assault boots, and a bullet-proof Kevlar vest compliments of the NYPD. He couldn't decide on whether to use his .35 automatic or his 9mm automatic. Picking up both pistols, he held one in each hand then chose the automatic. His decision was the 9mm automatic gave him more firepower—not as much stopping ability—but more bullets. As he held the automatic in his hand, he attached a silencer to the muzzle, thinking that "silence" would be the key to the operation. His next item was a pair of night vision goggles. Gordon knew he would be in darkness so the goggles would give a definite tactical advantage. He then took a roll of duct tape thinking how it would be a pleasure to use it on Spencer. The last few items were a Gerber fighting knife, a black ski mask and a pair of skin-tight leather gloves. As he surveyed his equipment a slight feeling of trepidation crept through his mind. He hated this ninja stuff; too many things could go wrong. On a job like this Murphy's law was the rule not the exception. Gordon sat in the darkness of his car sipping a cup of black coffee, thinking of what he would do next as he listened to the haunting melody of Ravel's "Bolero."

He had strategically parked his car in a cul-de-sac at the end of a road that crossed in front of the Spencer home.

The car was shadowed by two large hemlocks that were part of an island of trees that bordered their property. Even in darkness Gordon could see the outline of Margaret Spencer's home silhouetted against a clouded sky. He estimated the distance from where he was parked to the home to be no more than 100 yards.

Opening the glove compartment, Gordon removed his night vision binoculars. The binoculars gave him a much greater range of vision than his goggles. Scanning the house and the surrounding area he searched for any sign of activity.

After an hour of surveillance, he detected no sign of movement. He then decided it was time to make his move. Reaching down by his side, Gordon picked up his ski mask and placed it over his head all the while thinking what to do with Margaret's dog.

On a previous surveillance, he saw her German shepherd tied to a line in her backyard. Gordon knew the key to a successful entry of the house was to neutralize the dog. He preferred to kill the animal outside the house rather than in. It would be much easier and less risky. So far he had not seen the dog or detected any movement within the home. Contemplating the thought of killing the shepherd bothered him. He didn't like killing animals; it was bad karma. Animals were far better than most humans, but sometimes you had to do what you had to do.

Mentally shrugging his shoulder he lifted his automatic from its holster then threaded a silencer on its muzzle. Slowly he pulled back the slide then let it go. With an ominous click he chambered a round. Placing the pistol back into its holster he took a sip of coffee then swallowed two amphetamine pills. He knew the combination of the coffee with the speed would increase his stamina and heighten his awareness. Gordon put the binoculars back into the glove compartment then slipped his night vision goggles over the ski mask.

He had taken the precaution of disconnecting the courtesy lights of his car. This enabled him to open the doors without being seen. Taking a deep breath, he slowly exited the vehicle and then slipped into the night while he quickly made his way into the darkness of the woods.

It had rained during the day giving the branches a slick, icy wetness. As he navigated his way through the trees, a frosted mantel of moistness covered the ground leaving him with an uneasy awareness to the sound of his own footsteps.

Gordon followed the wood line to the backyard of Margaret's home. From where he stood he saw no sign of the dog. Using a small barn as his cover he swiftly crossed the distance from the woods to the back door of the home. With the aid of a small pocket light clutched in his teeth and the use of an electronic lock pick, Gordon opened the door. As he crossed the threshold into the kitchen, the unmistakable smell of decaying flesh tinged his nostrils. From his past experiences Gordon knew the smell had to be human. He stood motionless in the pitch blackness of the kitchen listening for any sound or movement. Slowly, he removed his automatic from its holster and held it in front of him.

Common sense told him to turn back; however,

curiosity and the desire to fulfill the contract made him move on. In the muted green light of his night vision goggles he could see his breath. Keeping with his cautious nature, Gordon crept slowly along the kitchen wall through a doorway into the hallway. Like a predatory animal he measured every footstep. Off to his left was a large dining room, then a living room. The only discernible sound was the slow tick of a grandfather clock in an alcove at the end of the hallway.

He then stood motionless at the bottom of a staircase leading to the second floor. Taking a deep breath he slowly started his ascent. Halfway up one of the wooden steps creaked loudly, sending a shiver of apprehension along his spine. As he swore to himself, he envisioned a scene from an old horror movie.

In the subdued glow of a space heater, Richard Spencer lay quietly in his bed smoking a cigarette. He didn't like having to live in the cellar, but his sister insisted that was where she wanted him, so he obligingly followed her demands. "Well," he thought gleefully, "I guess I changed her mind."

With the shadows of the darkened cellar drifting about him, he suddenly heard an unfamiliar sound in the kitchen above him. Instantly, he knew someone must have entered the house. A shot of adrenaline coursed through him as the hairs on the back of his arms bristled.

Spencer slowly left his bed, then reached for a baseball bat that lay by the side of his bed. He had affectionately called it his "meat tenderizer." Leaving the confines of the cellar, Spencer walked up the steps to the kitchen. He could hear whoever it was on the stairs leading to the second floor.

With deliberate anticipation, he decided to wait in the alcove at the end of the hallway. Satisfied with his decision, Spencer smiled inwardly knowing the intruder had no choice but to come back down and face him.

As he waited in the darkness, Spencer thought the

intruder must have discovered his sister and her dog. "No matter," he said to himself, "whoever it is will receive the same fate." He then thought about his sister Margaret, how she never stopped questioning him. She was always looking though his things. She found the pictures of the girls and threatened him with the cops. Spencer remembered how he hit her with his fist then her stupid dog attacked him. He recalled the feeling of how he split that old dog's head open with the bat then he did the same to that old bitch. Nodding his head with approval at what he had done, he worked his hands along the shaft of the bat. It was comforting to know he would soon use it again.

Gordon's macabre fascination with the eerie and the unknown gave him the impetus to go on. As he reached the second floor, a dull ache in his hand made him realize he was holding the grip of his pistol too tightly. He stopped walking, took a deep breath and then consciously rested his hand. Glancing at the luminous dial of his watch, Gordon saw that it had taken eight minutes to walk from the kitchen to the second floor. An uneasy feeling of the unexpected questioned his every movement. While he inspected the second floor, opening one of the bedroom doors the pungent smell of decaying flesh overwhelmed him.

In the glow of his goggles he could see a woman and a dog laying side-by-side on a canopied bed. As he drew closer, Gordon saw it was Spencer's sister Margaret. He scanned the room hoping for some apparent cause to their death. A flood of questions ran through his mind. Foregoing a closer examination of the decomposing bodies, he turned to leave the room. Suddenly, the phone by the bed rang shattering the vacuum of silence. The sudden sound acted as an engine of fear causing him to run down the corridor to the stairway. Keeping his pistol in his right hand and the banister in his left, Gordon moved as fast as he could down the flight of stairs. When he reached the bottom step, a shape leaped from behind a wall of darkness.

Gordon felt a stinging blow across his forearm causing his hand to go numb, sending his pistol clattering to the floor. Ignoring the pain, he swung his fist into the face of the attacker sending the man backwards against the wall. With fear-injected quickness, Gordon grabbed at the bat. Both men crashed into the grandfather clock shattering the glass door. Gordon tried desperately to drive his knee into his attacker's groin. Missing his mark, he glanced off the side of the man's leg, cutting his knee on a jagged piece of glass from the door of the clock.

Each man pulled, shoved and cursed as they fought their way along the hallway.

The two men stumbled into the dining room and fell across a table which crashed to the floor. Gordon fell across Spencer, landing heavily on his chest. Quick to take advantage of his position, he pushed the bat towards Spencer's throat. As he did this he whispered through his clenched teeth, "Die, you motherfucker, die."

Spencer responded with the same guttural voice, "Not yet, you son-of-a-bitch," then started to push him off.

With a fleeting sense of astonishment, Gordon realized that his assailant had a chance of winning. Releasing his hold on the bat, Gordon jumped to his feet and lifted one of the dining room chairs. Without hesitating, he swung the chair to where Spencer lay. As he attempted to do this, he lost his balance, smashing the chair harmless to the floor. As he staggered sideways, Gordon watched Spencer rise to his feet and then raise the bat above his head.

"Whoever you are, you're dead meat, motherfucker," Spencer shouted as he swung the bat angrily in the darkness.

With the help of the night vision goggles, Gordon finally recognized his attacker was Spencer. He thought it was Spencer as they were fighting, but in the confusion and darkness, he wasn't sure.

As they stood there each man tried to catch his breath. Gordon reached down to the floor and picked up a vase, then threw it at Spencer, striking him in the chest. Spencer let out a low grunt as he staggered backwards.

"You dirty piece-of-shit," he said, his voice strained with rage. "You think you can hurt me? Well, think again, you son-of-a-bitch."

"I just did, Richard," Gordon said as he maneuvered for a better position to attack Spencer.

"Who are you?" Spencer yelled as he stood looking vainly in the darkness.

"ARGO."

"What the fuck is an ARGO?" asked Spencer.

"Good question, scumbag," replied Gordon as he reached for his knife.

Spencer swung the bat at the sound of his voice.

"I'm the guy who is going to kill you," Gordon said as he reached for a broken part of the chair.

"Yeah, well, you just try," growled Spencer. "You just try."

"I've got a message for you, werewolf man," said Gordon as he angled for a better position to attack from.

"Yeah, well, I got one for you: eat shit and die."

"Uh, Richard," said Gordon mockingly, "sticks and stones, sticks and stones."

"Fuck you, asshole."

Gordon did not reply choosing silence as a weapon. Gathering his strength, he rushed at Spencer jamming the broken chair into Spencer's stomach. The sudden force of the attack sent him backwards into the hallway. As he stepped back, Spencer slipped on a small area rug and then fell backwards against the hallway wall.

Crashing to the floor, he yelled with frustration, "You're dead, you're dead, you fucking bastard, you're dead." All the while Gordon watched him struggling to get to his feet.

"I don't think so, werewolf," said Gordon as he dropped the chair and kicked Spencer solidly in the ribs. He felt his steel-toed boot hit with a deep thud. Spencer gasped loudly, dropping his bat to his side as he clutched his ribs. Gordon bent low slashing at Spencer's neck only to miss and cut his shoulder.

Spencer let out a shrill scream that echoed in the hallway.

Gordon stood back looking at Spencer, watching him struggle to his hands and knees.

"You're skating on hell's ice, Richard, and it's real thin," Gordon said as he positioned himself to kick him again.

"Fuck you," said Spencer, his voice barely audible.

"Uh, Spence," said Gordon, his voice cold and menacing, "you remember Veronica Carter, don't you, Spence? Well, she told me to give you a message and here it is." Gordon drew away from him where he was, then kicked him squarely in the side of his face, sending him over on his back. He watched Spencer put his hands to his head, then roll from side-to-side in pain. Gordon knew it was time to end the life of Richard Carroll Spencer.

Slowly he lowered himself to where Spencer lay, then reached out and grabbed his hair with one hand as he plunged his knife into his chest just above the collarbone, piercing an artery and one of his lungs.

Gordon could see Spencer trying to say something, but all Gordon could hear was a loud hissing sound as he watched Spencer's life exit his body.

Standing over his body, using a tablecloth from the dining room table, Gordon wiped the blood from his knife. He then remembered he had to go back into the alcove to retrieve his pistol. As he walked back to where Spencer's body lay, he stood over him. Taking a moment to gather his thoughts as he placed the gun in its holster, he said, "I guess you can't change the past, Spence, but you can change the conclusions."

CHAPTER 20

"The inherently seditious nature of the Muslim Brotherhood's agenda and its incompatibility with western civilizations' governments is typically obscured in the Free World by the assertion that the '*Ikhwan*' only seeks to achieve its objectives through non-violent means."

— "Mapping the Muslim Brotherhood in America"

To Gordon, the advent of Tom Starr and the FBI did little to change his routine. Although, it did supply him with an overall sense of relief to know he didn't have to worry about the agency or the NYPD.

He still continued to have sporadic meetings with Chris Bentley, TOJO and now Agent Starr. It went without saying how he felt about Reno and the FBI. He didn't like or trust either of them, but money talks and bullshit walks, so he went along to get along.

As for how Reno felt about him, he figured his sentiments were pretty much the same as his—if not hateful, at least contemptuous.

In accordance with their newfound relationship with the FBI, Global Headquarters had Chris Bentley and his team scrap the feasibility study they were working on for one the FBI wanted them to do. All business and communications between the FBI and Global were to be conducted exclusively through face-to-face meetings between Gordon and Tom Starr. It was stressed that Agent Starr's identity should be unknown to the members of his team.

Due to the fact that secrecy was of paramount importance, no e-mails, voice messages or written orders were used; this made their plans and communications slow and laborious.

The person of interest the agency wanted a feasibility study on and perhaps "removed" was a Muslim cleric named Mohammed "Alim" Elbarasse. The name Alim in Arabic meant "the one who knows." The idea of assassinating him was never really discussed, but remotely inferred and open to their interpretation.

Supposedly, Elbarasse was the head of an obscure but all powerful entity within the Muslim Brotherhood called the American Islamic Trust Fund (or the AITF).

It controlled 80% of the titles/deeds of mosques, Islamic schools and a variety of Muslim-owned businesses. Another part of their influence was they promoted and financed the "proper" conduct of certain prestigious Muslims.

Moreover, the AITF helped recruit perspective candidates to the Islamic cause. As to Elbarasse, he was also the imam of a mosque called the Islamic Cultural Center of Brooklyn, giving him additional *gravitas* within the Brotherhood.

The obvious assumption had to be the FBI wasn't interested in the AITF's legal transactions, only in their "nefarious" ones and who, according to them, Elbarasse was the mastermind.

He lived in the Sunset Park, Bay Ridge area, a predominately Muslim enclave of Brooklyn.
However, to the non-Muslim citizens of those boroughs the Brotherhood had bestowed an unknown consideration

to them. They were considered "*dhimmi*" meaning a "protected person" under sharia law. A law the Brotherhood followed to the letter.

In accordance with the Quranic verses and Islamic tradition, Jews and Christians were to be regarded as "people of the book." They were to be afforded a special status under a theoretical contract called "*dhimma*" or "residence in return for taxes."

Supposedly, they were allowed to engage in practices that were forbidden to Muslims. However, for this benevolence they were to pay the "*jizya* tax" which no one did. It was, of course, to be considered for some future social arrangement; the Islamic caliphate or the Islamic dominance of the world.

In a sense the Muslim Brotherhood could be seen as a religious mafia, with extortion as part of their theocratic practices.

Unfortunately for them, Gordon and his associates had a belief system of their own; one that held dire consequences for those who happened to be objects of their enmity.

It was Chris Bentley who summed up the Brotherhood by stating that they were the embodiment of "hypocrisy," and the personification of "verisimilitude." To further that assessment, Max Geiger doubled-down on Bentley's statement by saying the MB's were no better than any other radical Islamic group—how they would cut the heads off of children to further their cause of Islamic domination of the world.

He went on to tell them that a number of Muslims were black so the correct name for them would be "Mo-Negs" which meant more Negro than Muslim. It went without saying that everyone on the team laughed and used that term and others whenever they had to say something about radical Islam. The name was blatantly racist and politically incorrect, but so were the Islamo-fascists.

To Gordon and the others the only thing the Islamos respected was the muzzle of a gun or a bullet in the head. It was up to somebody to stop their murderous intent, so God and destiny chose them.

It was Gordon who told the team that the agency was willing to pay 50,000 a man for their "assistance." He said he couldn't really formalize the terms of the agreement, but was sure if anything came up, he would work it out.

He also pointed to the fact that they were still on Global payroll and were being paid to the tune of 3,000 a week, tax-free. It was an arrangement that neither the FBI nor any other governmental agency was aware of. So, maybe it would behoove them to play ball and do "the right thing."

In addition to the feasibility study on Elbarasse, Gordon said that his contact wanted to know if they could "penetrate" a warehouse in Bay Ridge.

He also said if they accepted this additional assignment, the agency was prepared to pay them another 50,000 apiece. To a man, they thought the proposal was more than fair and would gladly take whatever the FBI requested of them.

Gordon went on to explain that the warehouse was being used as a mosque called the Islamic Center of Brooklyn. Therefore, it was deemed a religious sanctuary and no government agency could obtain a search warrant without showing probable cause.

Bentley got a laugh out of the men when he said, "That was a formality they didn't have to bother with."

The warehouse was a veritable fortress with bars on the second and first floor windows and two steel doors at the entranceways. The garage door was made of corrugated iron with a surveillance camera above it. It also had at least two security guards present at all times.

Reno told Gordon it was extremely important that the agency and the NYPD gain unimpeded access to the warehouse. He also told him that they hadn't been able to obtain a search warrant or arrange an inspection under some phony pretext to do so.

It was TOJO Grimaldi who thought of a way to do that. He proposed that they have a member of the team pose as some type of homeless guy who carried shopping bags of clothes. In one of those bags would be an IED (Improvised Explosive Device) strong enough to blow one of the steel doors off its hinges. Grimaldi said he would detonate the bomb from some advantageous point, preferably in a car parked on some street.

The bomb would give the police and the FBI their just cause to enter the warehouse and evacuate whoever was there. In turn, it would provide them with the time and the wherewithal to do whatever they wanted.

The team was never informed on what it was they were after, nor did they care. Their only concern was that they were paid and the mission was a success.

They called the plan Operation "Ramadan," (Ramadan being the ninth month of the Islamic calendar and the holiest month within that year. It was a time when every devout Muslim fasted completely during daylight hours.)

To make the whole thing more of a game, the team decided to use call signs for each member. Chris Bentley's call sign was Car. TOJO was still TOJO, Gordon was ARGO, Max Geiger was called Counter and Trevor Jacks was called Cracker.

As silly as it sounded, call signs were a good cover whenever the used their cell phones to contact one another. As part of that verbal charade, they used arcane jargon with certain words and references known only to them.

It took more than awhile to get it together, but finally the night arrived for the team to earn their money.

It was Max Geiger who had volunteered to play the role of the homeless guy. He had spent a week dressed in his disguise prowling the neighborhood the warehouse was in. He did that so when the time arrived for them to go into action, his presence around the warehouse wouldn't create suspicion. He wore dirty clothes, a scruffy beard, and a long-haired wig he stuffed under a wool knit hat.

Gordon and Chris Bentley would be sitting in a car on the same side of the street the entrance to the warehouse was on with Max curled up inside the doorway, pretending to be asleep. In this way they could stay in visual as well as radio communications with him due in part that he was wearing a micro walkie-talkie inside his jacket.

They were also there in case he needed assistance in handling any of the locals who might be passing by and wanted to hassle him.

As for Grimaldi and Trevor Jacks, they would be stationed in a van not too far from the warehouse. In Grimaldi's hand was a remote detonating device in the form of a cell phone. He would use it when Geiger radioed to him a pre-arranged command to "send the music."

He and Jacks were told to "stick around" until after the explosion just to make sure Geiger had been successfully extracted from the so-called AO (area of operation).

In the aftermath of the explosion what happened next was to be expected. The NYPD and the guys from the FBI rushed headlong into the warehouse telling three security guards, who appeared to be in some sort of daze, they had to leave. As it turned out, they weren't devout Muslims and were high on K-2 (synthetic marijuana).

Although there wasn't a fire, the FDNY was next on the scene spending most of their time berating the "lookie loos" to stay back or face arrest.

True to form the team went their separate ways without knowing where the others had gone. Subsequently, they were left with nothing to do but sit on their hands and wait by their cell phones for Chris Bentley to get in touch with them.

Of course, the news media spent every waking hour speculating on who to blame—with most of them pointing a finger at the probability of some unknown right-wing group of racists as the transgressors.

Others said it was most likely a Jewish group hell-bent for revenge over the synagogue bombing in Williamsburg. A few countered that idea by saying it could be a group of dissident Shias who had an outstanding grudge against the Sunnis.

Since no one was injured in the explosion, interest in the event quickly faded away.

For two weeks after the warehouse explosion, Gordon kind of waited by the phone, hoping Chris Bentley or Reno Starr would get in touch with him.

While he was doing that, he decided not to roam around Manhattan looking for "something to do." A practice he knew that would often get him into trouble. This time he thought he would go monk and sort of sequester himself away from the world, or do whatever he thought monks did.

At best his daily regimen was eclectic; it included a diet of salads, broiled fish with lots of lemon and butter, fruit, bottled water and no alcohol. To further his agenda he went for a few western-styled yoga lessons, long runs on a treadmill, hot showers followed by a loofah body scrub and deep tissue massage. All of it done in the comfort of his yoga instructor's apartment—she was a Swedish women in her mid-40s named Astrid.

She had that iconic Scandinavian look: tall, blue-eyed and blond. To round out her appearance, she had a thin body with large breasts and a muscular stomach. The thing that got to him was her manner of speech. She had an accentual lilt to her voice that left him thinking in ways he shouldn't have. Although, it could have been because she wore a t-shirt without a bra, and yoga pants that left nothing to the imagination.

Whatever it was, he didn't hit on her. He stayed

professionally aloof. Nevertheless, there was one massage session that could have gone sexual, but he held himself back; a fact he was proud of.

To his dismay, his daily routine was altered by a text message from Reno Starr. It was a series of dashes, slashes and zeroes—a bunch of gobbledy-gook, unless you had the code to decipher it.

The message called for him to go to a place they had met before, at an office building the agency was using as a safe house.

It was in Manhattan on Lexington Avenue and Irving Place. He was to be there at 6:00 pm in room 609 on the 6th floor. The last time they met was on the 7th floor; however, the room was mis-numbered and identified as 609. A mistake that left him more suspicious of Reno's intent and purpose.

Contrary to their previous encounters Gordon found Starr to be more sociable, a condition he always seemed to avoid. He also had something there he never had before—food.

There was a large pizza with everything on it, cans of soda, a pot of coffee and a bottle of Sambuca. The only thing Gordon could think of, it was there ostensibly to celebrate the success of the mission.

Whatever the reason for the festivities, he couldn't care less. He was there to pick up a knapsack that contained $100,000—the second half of the money that was owed to the team for the warehouse job.

Starr pointed to the knapsack and said:

"You know what this is?"

"I got an idea," Gordon replied, as he picked up a slice of pizza from the box it was in. He then popped open a can of soda and sat in a chair close to Starr's desk.

"Hey, help yourself," Reno said while he pulled a chair from behind his desk and then sat down facing Gordon.

"I don't have to tell you . . . do I? That you and your

team did a hell-u-va job . . . you know what I mean . . . a hell-u-va job."

"Yeah, thanks," replied Gordon. "Say, I don't mean to be rude, but I got some guys that are waiting for what's in that knapsack."

"Hey, I understand," Starr said, "but maybe you should stick around for a minute or two before you decide to leave—you know."

"Okay, but like what for?" Gordon asked, as he put down the pizza slice and wiped his hands on a napkin. He stood up and walked over to the bag, looked inside and then brought it back to where he was sitting.

"So, as you were saying," said Gordon, as he closed the knapsack.

"Well, for starters," replied Starr, "that Elbarasse thing, the feasibility study, forget it for now."

"Why?" Gordon asked, as he took a swig of soda and then wiped his lips with the same napkin he used for his hands.

"We got . . . I mean, the agency has something far more important . . . much more important, could be very beneficial to you and your crew."

"I'm listening . . . like how much more?"

"Oh, about a half-a-million more, assuming you and your guys can pull it off."

"Half-a-mil . . . huh," said Gordon. "That's a whole lot of 'can you pull it off.'"

"I know. Let me clear things up for you . . . You know any of these four guys?" asked Starr, as he showed Gordon four photographs he pulled from a manila folder.

"No, can't say I do."

"How about this one?" Reno asked as he pointed to a photograph of Orlando Stokes.

"You worked with him in Iraq."

"Could be, but I don't remember."

Starr stood up and walked over to the table with the pot of coffee on it, poured himself a cup and then added a shot of Sambuca to it.

"So, you don't remember . . . too bad," Starr said. "Well, he worked for Global Solutions or its affiliate the World Enforcement Bureau . . . to our knowledge—so did you."

"So, what's that got to do . . .?"

"Here's the deal, Anthony. We found two drones in the warehouse plus a couple of empty gas cylinders . . . five AK's and about 5000 rounds of ammo."

"Okay—so?" replied Gordon.

"We found recipes for making sarin gas and these four pictures."

"So, you think that Orlando and these . . ."

"Yeah, we think their part of a sleeper cell; Orlando is a convert. He changed his name to some Muslim one and is part of a mosque we've been watching."

"What do you want us to do?" Gordon asked.

"Find out what, where and how, and stop it by all means necessary."

"What makes you think we can do that?"

"You know where Orlando is and what he's up to—I know it . . . and so do you."

While he was putting the knapsack over his shoulders, Gordon said:

"Let's get one thing straight . . . I don't know jack and if I did . . . well, I doubt if I'd tell you."

"Maybe so, my friend, but you would for five times what you got in that tote bag . . . if not that, maybe for something else."

Gordon sort of grinned at Reno and said, "You think so . . . well, stick around and find out."

"Heh . . . I'll do that, but before you leave . . . you know what, Tony?"

"Fill me in," replied Gordon.

"Do the right thing," answered Starr.

Gordon stopped at the door, hesitated and then slowly turned towards Reno. "You got something else to say?" he asked.

"How about we know you and your pals are still working for Global or the W.E.B. . . . There's something else I almost forgot," said Reno, as he snapped his fingers.

"Oh, yeah? What's that?" Gordon asked.

Starr gave him the look and then rubbed the back of his neck as he spoke.

"Do you know a guy by the name of Richard Carroll Spencer, aka The Werewolf?"

"No . . . should I?"

"Well," said Starr, "your DNA says you should."

With a feeling of consternation hitting him in the pit of his stomach, Gordon didn't answer back; he just turned and walked out the door.

CHAPTER 21

"Another conditional assumption of power is the belief of exemption from normal rules and laws, even the laws of science and nature. Risk is viewed as remote, minimal, or easily managed. The patient may dismiss or actively distort evidence indicating risk, even when overwhelming, because of the firm belief in being the 'exception.'"

Cognitive Therapy of Personality Disorders — Aaron T. Beck, Arthur Freeman

The afternoon sun had just found its way through one of the windows of David L. Greenberg's private office. Its radiance seemed to bother the solemnity of one of the two men who had been sitting there waiting for his arrival. With an annoyed sense of purpose, he left his chair and went to the window, then adjusted a wooden blind so darkness would prevail.

"I was hoping you would do that," said Irwyn Roth. "That sun was starting to get to me. I would have done it myself, but I don't like to touch anything in David's office. You know how . . . temperamental . . . he can be."

"Yes, well, the senator will have to be a little more tolerant of the mundane," said Rabbi Jacobs. He then looked at his watch and said:

"I wonder where he is. It's already 1:15; he was supposed to see us at 12:45."

"You know how it is," Roth said. "He's a busy man, and you and I are just cogs in a . . . very big wheel."

While he was about to sit down, Jacobs glanced at Roth, nodded his head then said:

"You're right . . . but sometimes cogs need to be . . . respected."

Suddenly, the door behind them swung open. With an air of nonchalance, David Greenberg strode in. He was followed by the long reach of one of his security men who closed it as he went by.

Without acknowledging the presence of Wyn or Rabbi Jacobs, David L. walked past them and sat down at his desk. He then lit a cigarette. As he did, he flipped a switch on a panel in front of him, which in turn engaged an exhaust system that would clear the air in the room.

It also turned on a secret tape recorder that would take down everything that was said. He would then listen to it at some later date for the express purpose of understanding the level of communication between himself and others.

He didn't worry about Wyn or the rabbi having a recording device of their own since they had been checked out prior to entering the mansion and once again before they went into his office.

"Well," Greenberg asked, "what do you have for me?"

"I've got something for you," replied Jacobs. "The three men I requested, Bentley, Gordon and Grimaldi, are being used for purposes other than what I agreed upon."

"I see," said David L., "and what are these three men doing . . . that you feel so . . . put out about?"

"Maybe, I can answer that," answered Roth. "According to what I've been lead to believe, they've been taking care of a few domestic matters—what you might refer to as 'internal concerns.'"

"Is that so?" said Jacobs. "And, who are the beneficiaries of these domestic matters?"

"I believe . . . for some VIPs . . . that they are, uh, necessary for the success of the . . . operation."

Greenberg was well aware of who these so-called VIPs were, but would never disclose their identity or their purpose.

"Well," said Jacobs, "answer me this: was Clifton Van Dameer a domestic matter?"

Roth looked at David L. for some indication as to what he should say—there was none.

"Could be," he said. "I really don't know." He then removed a few Kleenex tissues from his jacket pocket and blew his nose.

"Do you have a cold?" Greenberg asked.

"No, just allergies."

"You know you should see someone about that," replied Greenberg. "Uh, getting back to those three men Levi asked about . . . are they going to be available in the near future?"

Greenberg didn't know who they were and didn't want to know. He wasn't interested in how or what field agents did, only in the results of their activities.

"I believe so," Wyn said. "I mean at least that's what I was told."

"Really," replied Jacobs, "who told you that?"

"You know, I really can't say . . . I, uh . . . don't know who he is . . . probably someone from Global."

Jacobs sat back in his chair, glanced at David L. and then back at Wyn.

"It doesn't matter," he said with a look that let the two of them know he didn't believe what they were saying.

Greenberg stood up from his desk and walked over to the same window Jacobs had previously gone to. He stood there for a moment, then spread a couple of wooden slats on the blind and peered out at the view below.

"You know," he said, "I read in the paper about an explosion in Dearborn, Michigan. It seems some imam was killed in his car by a bomb. Is that something I should know about?"

"Well, we talked about him at our last meeting," Jacobs said. "I had the impression you wanted Global to green light his demise."

"I don't remember saying anything about him . . . no matter . . . I'll look into that at some later date."

"I understand your concern," replied Jacobs. "Anyway, you know how it is; we give Global the money and a name—they do the rest."

"Speaking of money, do you know how much we've spent with Global?"

"Oh, I'd say around two million or so," replied Jacobs. "Unfortunately, garbage removal is very expensive these days."

"Yes, it is," said David L. "Well, the real figure is more like 2,340,000 and change. Mind you, I'm not complaining . . . I just hate to spend money."

"Sorry, about that," replied Jacobs. "I really don't keep an accurate account of your money. I'm like Wyn here; I'm just a go-between."

"Of course, you are," said David L. "I understand your position between Global and myself. I also understand your stance between me and your country. Speaking of which, are they still interested in my campaign?"

"Very much so—they're more interested in you than anyone else on the planet. If and when you become president, you could change the fate of Israel."

"I hope so," said David L. "It's good to know somebody cares about my campaign."

Roth stood up from his chair, looked at David L. and said:

"I beg to differ with you; I'm certain your constituents care."

"Maybe . . . think you could convince them to contribute more to my campaign?"

"I think they feel you have more than enough money to finance your campaign."

"Nobody . . . has ever . . . had enough money."

"Amen to that," said Rabbi Jacobs.

The three men talked for an extended period of time, more than they would usually do. Greenberg asked questions of Jacobs and Wyn as to the morality of what they were doing.

Jacobs told him that morality was a two-way street. If your enemy doesn't practice it, why should you?

Wyn quoted Oscar Wilde, citing the passage:

"That morality is simply the attitude we adopt towards people we dislike."

Both Greenberg and Jacobs laughed at his comment saying, "Ain't that the truth."

While he was lighting one of David L.'s cigars, Jacobs said, "You know what they say . . . morality without wisdom is as useful as a mirror to a blind man."

"Well, well," replied David L., "I didn't know you and Wyn were so . . . philosophical."

"We're not always monochromatic," said Roth.

"Are you saying I am?"

"Of course not . . . you're what you might say . . . diverse."

"Okay, but don't you really mean impetuous?"

"No, not really; I would say you're impulsive."

David L. smiled at his one-time friend, then raised his hand palm up.

"Uh . . . enough already," he said. "I get your point."

He knew Wyn was being diplomatic because he was being paid a small fortune to help facilitate the success of his secret war, or, as he thought of it, "an insidious cabal." Lately, however, Wyn seemed to be somewhat overly zealous in his new-found role of implementing his own sense of justice. A mystery when you considered the austerity of his business background. Most likely his zeal came from the feeling of having command of raw-naked power, a known aphrodisiac for the weak and unconcerned.

While Wyn and David L. were standing there talking, Jacobs decided to go over to Greenberg's million dollar desk and crush out his cigar in one of David L.'s ornate ashtrays. He then went to a table that had been set up with a small array of various brands of bottled water, some glasses and a bucket of ice cubes. He opened a bottle poured the contents into a glass, then added a few ice cubes. Before he took a sip, he held the glass up and peered at it as if he was looking for something.

"Anything wrong?" asked David L.

"No, I was just wondering if it was half-full or was it half-empty."

"Am I missing your point?"

"Not at all; it was just an answer or an observation. I was just thinking; will the glass ever be full or will it always be half-empty?"

"Unfortunately, Levi, time is at a premium, so if you don't mind, can we get on with the meeting?"

"Of course, Senator," said Jacobs as he placed his glass on the table.

"I would like to discuss the disposition of someone . . . we talked about . . . at our last meeting," said David L. [Disposition was code for the possibility or removing a person of interest.]

"And, who would that be," asked Jacobs, "since we often talk about a number of people?"

"Do you remember how I mentioned a certain Iranian woman who is married to a state senator named Hakeem Sasala?"

"I remember her," said Wyn. "She's Lydia Sasala. As a matter of fact, I did some research on her and her husband—with Levi's help, of course."

"I'm listening," said David L.

"First off, she and her husband are devout Sunni Muslims. She's the head of some ultra-radical group called the 'Arab Americans for Peace and Justice.'"

"That's one helluva misnomer," said David L. "There never was an Arab for peace and justice."

"You're right, but nevertheless, her group has been giving large sums of money to the governor's political action committee, that gives her or them a lot of clout with his honor."

"What else?" said Greenberg as he was walking back to his desk so he could sit down.

"My friends," said Jacobs, "have investigated her and her husband . . . they feel they may be the sponsors of a sleeper cell." [Friends was code for the Mossad]

"How's that?"

"It seems her husband Hakeem owns a farm in upstate New York in a place called Petersburg; it's about 30 miles outside Albany. According to my sources, there's been a fair amount of activity at the farm."

"When you say activity, you mean like . . . Muslim extremists, as in the Muslim Brotherhood?"

"Possibly. Could be al-Qaeda or even ISIS for that matter."

"Are you working on it?"

"We're working on it."

"We're having a meeting with one of Global's field agents," said Roth.

"When?"

"Next week some time."

"Well, you and Levi have been doing your homework."

"There is another matter," said Jacobs.

"That is . . . what?"

"We have the name of an important 'Hawala; you know him—Gilbert Norwell." [Hawala: Arabic for money changer]

"You're not the only ones; the FBI considers him to be a money launderer for the Brotherhood."

"Do you think he's a possible person of interest?" said Jacobs.

"Not right now, but look into it . . . Excuse me for a moment, I have to make a phone call. Are you two hungry?"

Both men said yes with slight nods of their heads. David L. picked up a phone on his desk, hit a button, then said:

"Yes, I'm ready now. You can bring the cart around."

Roth and Jacobs knew the cart would have a number of different gourmet sandwiches, a few bottles of expensive wine and a whole lot of money. The money would be held in a locked compartment on the cart. The actual cash was in an indestructible bag made of Kevlar. The amount would vary between $200,000 to $300,000. There was another item in the bag: a GPS guidance system.

It also had an electronic digital combination lock on it that could only be opened by someone who had the right sequence of numbers. If someone tampered with the lock a packet of red dye would explode and destroy the cash.

All of this was told to them by David L. He also let them know how much cash was in the bag by writing the number on a piece of paper.

The idea was that either Jacobs or Roth would act as a courier and transport the bag to a state park, dig a hole, cover it up and leave it. According to David L. some unknown someone would use a tracking device to find the bag, dig it up and then bring it somewhere else.

The whole elaborate scheme was to keep everyone involved guessing who, what and where Greenberg's insidious cabal would lead them.

There was a knock on the door letting the senator know his sandwich cart had arrived. Greenberg opened the door by pushing a button on his desk. One of his security men pushed it in then left without saying a word.

All three men had a sandwich or two with Wyn opting for three, and more than one glass of wine. As usual they talked while they ate with David L. asking both men why extremism was on the rise in America. He was fascinated by the psychology of fanatics, especially Muslim fanatics.

It was Levi Jacobs' field of expertise and he went on in a long explanation of how it was a quest for personal significance. It was the motivational force for violence, especially amongst the Islamo fascist.

Terrorism is not a "condition" he explained, but a process. There are many pathways into and through radicalization; each pathway is affected by various factors. Many of these so-called pathways, he said, can be viewed not as the product of a single decision, but the result of a process that gradually pushes an individual towards a commitment to violence.

"Is this from some paper or book you read?" asked Greenberg as he poured himself another glass of wine.

"Yes, I've studied many treatises on the subject . . . there are many theories on radicalization. As one social psychologist said: 'There is nothing so practical as a good theory.'"

"I like it," said David L. "Do you have anything to add, Wyn?"

"Just a few things: for one, most recruiters for radical Islam seek to identify the most-likely candidates. They usually use inducements such as opportunities for advancement and recognition within the group."

"Irwyn is right," said Jacobs. "Most social scholars say recruiters use motivational frames to convince potential participants to become operational by . . . I forgot."

Roth and David L. both laughed. It seemed that Jacobs was getting a little tipsy.

"So, how do we stop these recruiters?" asked Greenberg.

"Use the same methods they use—the social fucken media," said Jacobs. "Give the potential candidates an alternative . . . try to steer them in another direction."

"Or, maybe remove the recruiters," said Greenberg.

"That's the direct approach."

"I like being direct; it's easier."

"Well," said Wyn, "I guess we stay the course."

"Do you have any of these so-called recruiters in mind?"

"I do," said Jacobs. "There this one imam, a Muslim cleric in Brooklyn. We have it on good authority he's a proselytizing little bastard."

"Well, whatever you decide to do, consider it done. I guess we can say this has been an informative meeting . . . at least, I feel that way."

Roth and Jacobs both agreed and told David L. they looked forward to the next meeting.

"Oh, one last thing: are you satisfied with the conditions of your employment?"

Both men nodded their heads while murmuring that they were more than satisfied.

"Uh, Levi," said Greenberg, "I would like to speak to Mr. Roth alone. Uh, so we'll see you at some later date then."

"Of course. Good day to both of you," said Jacobs as he walked towards the door. When he got there he looked back and waved goodbye. With that being done David L. buzzed him out.

"I've been meaning to ask you," said David L. "Have you been . . . quiet lately?"

Roth knew what Greenberg was referring to: his feelings towards young girls.

"Yes," he said. "I've put that behind me."

"Alright! Then, I guess that's all that can be said. Don't forget the bag."

"I wouldn't dream of it. Oh, how's the family?"

"Good, very good. Make sure you read over your coordinates."

"Well, until we meet again—I'll stay in touch."

Greenberg let Wyn out, but wondered why he asked about his family—he never did before. There was something else. He knew Roth better than anybody else. He had been acting strange, kind of secretive, as if he knew something, but wouldn't let on what it was.

CHAPTER 22

ISNA HEADQUARTERS

Plainfield, Indiana

"Allah is our objective. The Prophet is our leader. The *Qur'an* is our law. *Jihad* is our way. Dying in the way of Allah is our highest aspiration."

— Motto of the Muslim Brotherhood.

"We love death more than you love life; that is why we will win."

— ISIS Fighter

Standing in a room on the second floor of the headquarters for the Islamic Society of North America was a tall, distinguished-looking man. His name was Rafeeq Hassad; he appeared to be in his early 50s.

His dark beard and deep-set eyes gave him a striking resemblance to Osama bin-Laden. It was a perception he was well aware of and at times engendered that impression in how he dressed and spoke. In the same likeness as

Osama, he had been well educated in European schools and used his family's considerable wealth to further the Islamic cause.

Gathered in front of him were a small but select group of men know in Arabic as *"naquibs"* —the translation being: people of the faith; or any type of leader. These happened to be imams from various mosques throughout New York City. They were from the faction known as Shiites as opposed to being of the Sunni denomination—a key factor as to how they followed the canons of the Koran and the Muslim law known as "shariah."

Except for the Muslims residing within the United States, they were devout enemies. They had been that way ever since the death of Mohammad and the inception of the religion itself.

Rafeeq was a *"masul,"* the titular head of their branch of the Muslim Brotherhood—the *"Ikhwans"*; or, the Brethren of Purity. At this particular meeting he wore the traditional *thawb*: an ankle-length robe with long sleeves. His headwear was similar to what Osama would wear—a white turban wrapped around a cap called a *"kalansuwa."*

With an imperious wave of his hand, he began to speak to them using a strange blend of Arabic and English. "There are those among us," he said, "who are practicing in their own form of *jihad*. They are doing this without consideration for our goals—*insha'Allah*—if Allah wills it. We must never forget that of our devotion to the '*dawah*,' of converting the '*kaffir*'—the infidels—to Islam.

"As you know, since the incident in Brooklyn, the government has used its power against us. Furthermore, those that support our beliefs are angered at such acts of violence. To make amends we must be outright and vocal in our condemnation of such behavior."

A slight murmur of unrest spread across the room. Each imam knew what Rafeeq was referring to, and indignant at his level of hypocrisy. His exploits as a purveyor of terrorist activity was more than well known.

They were also aware of the efficacy of the synagogue bombing in Williamsburg. It was certainly questionable and probably counterproductive; however, they felt compelled to confer to its intent. It was in that realm of concern that had led them to Rafeeq. They wanted him to explain how to carry out Holy Jihad while maintain a favorable image in America. His explanation was simple: he told them to "think strategically," that actions must translate into political gains. If violence was carried out by various cells then they should be admonished by respected groups of Muslims throughout the United States.

The idea was to wage an informational jihad to use the words of deceit—"the *taqiyya*"—to infiltrate and convert. They had to lull the enemy into a false sense of tolerance and security.

Rafeeq was often referred to as the Deceiver or "*Makara*." The word is very strong having the connotation of sly or cunning. In sharia law Allah was considered "the greatest deceiver."

The person who is a "*Makir*" is a person who outwits someone else to cause them harm. In reality that person schemes evil. He only reveals the opposite of what he plans to do. Amongst those of the Muslim Brotherhood, "perfidiousness" had religious significance.

"As you know," Rafeeq said, "Americans are slaves to their so-called political correctness. They will explain away any malevolent conduct as an aberration of whatever group they wish to support."

It was that type of verisimilitude that was pleasing to the ears of the imams.

"Tell us more of your thoughts," said one. "Do you have a plan?" asked another.

"I do *insha'Allah*—if Allah wills it," answered Rafeeq. "We must use all our resources within the media, as well as our political friends to help mitigate and promote what we do. For example, we must use someone like our 'good friend' Gilbert Norwell."

The imams glanced at one another then nodded their heads in the affirmative. They all knew of him and were familiar with his political sentiments. He was an important Republican conservative whose wife happened to be a Muslim—a fact that raised the eyebrows of his friends and enemies alike.

However, it was his position against big government and tax reform that gave him notoriety. In addition, he was the founder of an unlikely consortium called "The Independent Muslim Finance Group". The organization had put together an array of successful investments that funded various Islamic endeavors. It was that fact, as well as his relationship with Hamas and other Islamic groups, that gained him acceptance within the *Ikhwan*.

Another of Norwell's attributes was his position within a powerful lobbying group called "Meridian Strategies". He was its chief operating officer and owner. The firm held sway over many Republican politicians and some Democrats as well.

It was that type of naked political influence that led to the charges of terrorism being dropped against his good friend Ahmad Abbas Mirza. He was the leader of the American Islamic Council and a major contributor to certain political action groups that Norwell controlled. It was men such as Norwell that gave the Brotherhood the expectation for the final triumph of an Islamic America.

Rafeeq fell silent as he stared out at his audience. Then, in dramatic fashion, he slowly raised his arm and pointed to the back of the room. In dutiful unison the imams turned their collective heads to see what he was pointing to. It was the black flag of jihad hanging from a pole attached to the wall—the flag of the Islamic State and the purveyors of the truth: the *Dawah*.

"I am thirsty," Rafeeq said, his voice low and menacing as he pointed towards the window. "I am thirsty for the blood of our enemies—the *jizya*—the non-believers. I am thirsty for the blood of those who would defile the Holy Koran and the teachings of the prophet Mohammad—peace be upon him."

One of the imams jumped to his feet and shouted "*Allah Akbar*"—God is great. The others murmured "*Hamdullah*"—all thanks go to him.

"What must we do?" some of them asked.

"You spoke to us before of drones," said another.

Rafeeq raised his hand his palm facing them. "Yes," he said, "it has already been done. I have purchased one from the country of Panama. It will be brought into the United States through Mexico then to our compound in the State of New York."

"Who will fly it?" a young imam asked.

"No one," Rafeeq answered. "That is why it is called an unmanned aerial vehicle. However, to answer your question: I have a man . . . a Christian; he is a '*bokhesh*' (an asshole in Arabic). He will teach one of our own on what to do."

"What is the target?"

"The target . . . where else," answered Rafeeq, "but New York City."

A stunned silence swept across the room until one imam stood up and announced:

"Yes, Rafeeq is right! It must be New York City."

"When?" they asked

"I do not know . . . soon—*insha'Allah*."

Amongst the imams was a man named Ahmad al-Zaki. His mosque was the Dar Al-Tawheed in Brooklyn. It also served as a safe-house for those willing to do the work of the Brotherhood. It was also a place to hold small personalized meetings known in Arabic as "*usra*." It was there that they interviewed perspective members who could be judged as to the extent of their velleity.

As anyone would know, wishful thinking and commitment to action were separate issues.

His thoughts started to drift from what Rafeeq was saying to that of his son Akram and his relationship with a man named Orlando Stokes who said his Arabic name was Jamal Al-Jaber—his only evidence of that was a New York State driver's license.

He claimed to have converted to Islam while serving time at the Texas State Prison in Huntsville. It was a common occurrence for men of color to do that and to change their name to a Muslim one. To most people Jamal's assertions would be proof enough to vouch for his identity.

Since the synagogue bombing of Temple Beth and the subsequent investigations by the NYPD and the FBI, the Brotherhood "requested" that the imams of New York City be extra vigilant and to be suspicious of every new face they encountered. To Ahmad that suspicion fell directly on Jamal mainly due to his radical stance on the faith. He also asked too many questions concerning the community and violent jihad.

When he thought it over, he had to admit that it made him angry that his son seemed to be so taken with Jamal. It was if he was under the man's spell and would be willing to do his bidding. The fact was Akram was his only child and his only living relative. All the others had been killed in the Iraq War.

He confided in him and shared his most intimate thoughts about the Brotherhood. It went without question Akram would be his heir apparent as the next imam of the Dar Al-Tawheed.

He was also a recognized leader for the Muslim Student Association at the NYU and a spokesman for the Muslim Brotherhood. In addition, he was also a community activist, as well as a proponent for a parallel society. The sentiment was one of a social order that would accommodate the practice of a single religion.

Akram was all of that and more; the only flaw in his character was that he was gay. Except for Jamal it was a secret that no one was aware of, especially his father. He knew well the gravity of his situation—to be a homosexual in the Muslim world was an inexcusable sin (*haram* in Arabic) and tantamount to social damnation.

He had resisted his feelings for years; however, with the advent of his newfound friendship with Jamal and their singular understanding, the possibility arose for him to experience what he had only dreamed of.

Jamal explained how he could arrange meetings for him with homosexual prostitutes without the fear of being found out. He also said that he could use his apartment when needed.

All he had to do was provide him with information about the community and the Brotherhood. He didn't question Jamal's interest, only his intentions, which for the most part were left unsaid. The fact that he could remain anonymous and free to carry out his duties was to all too tempting for him not to accept.

Unfortunately, he made his situation worse by making sexual overtures towards Jamal. One night, as they were driving around Brooklyn looking for a restaurant, they parked on a secluded street. As they sat there in the dark talking, he could sense that Jamal was "interested" in him. It all ended with him performing oral sex while masturbating as he did.

They never discussed the incident and yet it created a certain bond between them—a kind of smoldering tension that seemed to ignite whenever they were alone. At times they would go all the way with Jamal having anal intercourse with him. What bothered him, Jamal would never reciprocate, using his position as the dominate male as an excuse.

It was different for Orlando; he saw his relationship with Akram as a way of gaining control over him. He knew he wasn't gay, but looked upon his pretense as a way of solidifying his hold over men that were.

He had used the same ploy while working in Iraq so he could infiltrate the various Muslim organizations that dotted the landscape. It never ceased to amaze him how many stalwart Muslims were bi-curious and would secretly succumb to the lure of such spurious entanglements. Of course, it helped that he was very well-endowed, especially in prison where homosexuality was a common occurrence and seen as a means to political expediency.

He would never admit to himself or anyone else that he enjoyed the charade of being queer or its use as a road for venality. To do so would mean that he was of that persuasion, also, the thought that disgusted him. He only got involved because he never reciprocated and reviled those that did.

To him it was part of his job to entice Muslim men into compromising situations. To do this he used whatever means necessary: sex, money, revenge—anything to get the job done. Furthermore, he enjoyed taking advantage of them since that's what they did to others.

Originally, he had been sent to New York City as a liaison between Global and Christian Bentley. Another part of his job was to be a back-up for Tojo Grimaldi and Anthony Gordon. The only drawback to the assignment was Gordon; he hated the son-of-a-bitch.

He remembered how he and Gordon first met. It was in Iraq while they were working for Global. At first they became friends, then business partners, then enemies—mainly over money and a woman.

The woman was an army supply sergeant with connections to various good and services. These assets were highly lucrative and easily sold to Iraqi businessmen. She was also a part-time prostitute and a procurer for some other female soldiers; her name was Melanie Durant. He recalled how some of her clients said that she was like "sex on steroids." Her detractors called her "Dirty Durant," due to the rumor that she was a conduit for STDs because she didn't mind having unprotected anal sex. He didn't pay attention to any of it. In Baghdad talk was cheap when it came to women and their sexual conduct. To him none of it meant a goddamn thing, other than the fact Gordon wanted her for himself and the opportunity to make money off of her connections.

Well, so did he; the sex he could do without, but the money was another matter. To mitigate their differences they agreed on a working relationship which turned out well until they had a serious falling out.

Their argument was over a cache of stolen Iraqi artifacts worth at least a couple of million dollars. When Stokes thought it over he still got pissed off. The fact was it was his relationship with a certain Iraqi that led to the whereabouts of the artifacts. Granted Gordon and his team of security personnel did the actual robbery and had to kill a few Iraqis, but that didn't give him the right to more than half.

He remembered how their relationship went from bad to worse and how they vowed to settle their differences with bullets. At the time, it was a situation that was quite common in Baghdad, especially between rival contractors and Iraqi businessmen—the fact that hardly anyone was ever held accountable made gang warfare in a combat zone more than ludicrous.

In an ironic twist of events, a gang of supposed Iraqi criminals stole the artifacts from an apartment that they were using to hide the stuff in. The other part of the story was the criminals were somehow connected to Melanie Durant—a fact he couldn't verify, but smelled of a double-cross carried out by Gordon and Durant. To Stokes, he didn't care who was responsible; someone had to pay and that someone was Sergeant Durant.

To expedite the matter, Stokes paid a group of Iraqi insurgents to kill her by any means necessary; other than that he would take care of Gordon himself. As luck would have it, she was killed by the explosion of an IED while driving along Route Irish—the infamous road between

Baghdad and its airport. As for Gordon, he was transferred to Kuwait City. From there Stokes had lost sight of him until they met in NYC.

He never heard what happened to the artifacts other than there was a rumor they had fallen into the hands of some secret group of SAS operatives. His only thoughts were to satisfy the concerns of Global Solutions and if that meant getting along with Gordon, so be it. Although, if ever he might be given the opportunity to vindicate his betrayal, he wouldn't hesitate.

CHAPTER 23

On a slate gray day in late September, a strong wind swept across the financial district of lower Manhattan. In its journey it found itself hurrying along Broad Street and other thoroughfares of commerce. For Max Geiger and his partner Trevor Jacks, the wind was just another consideration in their list of concerns while conducting a feasibility study for Global Solutions.

They were part of that firm's special observation and assessments group also known as "SOG." It was their job to wait, watch and formulate a plan around their findings—a plan that could be carried out, at minimum risk, for any would-be operator. The operator or operators might be a team of designated assassins or a single sniper known by Global as a "long-range interventionist."

The object of their interest was Albert M. Shifton—the first black and openly gay executive director of the ACLU (the American Civil Liberties Union). According to various magazine and newspaper articles he was the most hated man in America. It was under his leadership that the ACLU fought against the Patriot Act, the National Securities Act and the War on Terror. In addition, he was also a close friend of certain individuals considered to be the leaders of the Muslim religion in the state of New York.

Ever since the synagogue bombing in Brooklyn, there was talk of taking out Muslims and their sympathizers. Of course everyone knew that David Greenberg's parents had been killed in the bombing. He was vociferous in his condemnation of Islam and the extermination of its radical element.

To Geiger and Jacks, politics and religion were also-rans when compared to money. To them what Shifton did or might not have done was immaterial. They were being paid a lot of money to set him up and that was all that mattered. To accomplish this they had to know his every quirk.

The first thing they recognized, he was a man of consistency. He made it a practice to arrive every business day at approximately the same time. His mode of transportation was a chauffeur-driven black limousine with the same marker number and driver. He would be let off close or near ACLU headquarters at 125 Broad Street. He would then walk from his vehicle to the front entrance of the building at that address. Once inside, he would wait for an elevator to take him up to the 18th floor to start his day.

As to be expected, he would finish work at nearly the same time every day then take the identical limousine to his apartment on 26th Street. His residence was located in the so-called flower district of Manhattan. It was so-named due to the proliferation of flower shops in that area. This led Geiger to quip, "How *apropos* was that?" The funny thing, he wasn't against homosexuals or African Americans, only against people he saw as being overly relevant.

As for himself and Jacks, he considered their position to be of "selective tolerance." So, whenever they had to alter their point of view to accommodate the sensitivity of others, it left them with a feeling of disdain for people of that persuasion.

He and Jacks often discussed their philosophy and the misgivings of their line of work. They attributed some of their feelings and behavior to their many deployments to Iraq and Afghanistan—an actuality that placed the two of them in a military hospital for observation and psychiatric care.

This led them into a medical discharge for PTSD, and for Geiger an additional diagnosis of having antisocial personality disorder. It was something they both denied and for Global Solutions a non-issue for their employment. Of the two of them, it was Geiger who had the most baggage. His condition carried him into a messy divorce, substance abuse and some minor scrapes with the law.

His partner and some other Global employees did all they could to keep him normal and in line. At times, however, he would go off the deep end and need an extended vacation, whereupon he and Jacks would catch a plane down to Cartagena, Colombia—a place where almost everything was legal. The idea being to drink copious amounts of "recreational medication," smoke some weed and seek the attention of female companionship—the best money could buy.

He and Jacks were first introduced to the place by another Global employee: Anthony Robert Gordon, who called himself ARGO. To them he seemed kind of strange but amiable enough.

They hadn't seen him in a year or more; but of course they couldn't seek him out, even if they wanted to. It was a cardinal rule if any employee of Global Solutions or the Web disappeared, or was let go, not to seek him out. The only exception being if they wanted you to.

It was said that Conrad Lowe would often send a few of his men to conduct feasibility studies on former employees. A situation you tried to avoid since what usually followed was your demise.

What made a so-called feasibility study so demanding

was not only the tediousness of surveillance, but the added burden of establishing areas of intervention. It was imperative to consider the angles of possibility without the fear of collateral damage.

To accomplish that, the operator had to take into account what kind of munitions might be used, the personnel that may be involved, and how they would be deployed. It was a difficult assignment and yet one Geiger and Jacks had done before, "albeit" in other countries. This time they were using their expertise within the United States. A fact that didn't sit well with either of them, although the rationale was the "person of interest" was most likely an enemy of the government.

They decided not to question the politics of the operation, but to concentrate on the efficacy of what they had to do. Their first concern was how to communicate with Global headquarters. The usual way was by encryptic text messages and the use of one of Global's go-betweens. This time that someone was a fellow contractor by the name of Orlando Stokes. They had worked with him in Iraq, but never really cared for him. To them he seemed ultra-restive with a chip on his shoulder. The other part being he was an Islamo convert—a condition that didn't sit well with white soldiers. His full beard and dark skin made him look too much like the enemy.

It was Stokes who took them to where they would meet their team leader: Christopher Bentley. He was a long-time compatriot of Trevor's. They had gone through Sandhurst together, served in Iraq with the SAS, then worked for Global when they left the service. A fact that allowed them benefits that only authorized U.S. citizens could obtain.

A few days after their initial meeting with Bentley, they met with him once again. This time at an obscure bar in the Bronx. It was unexpected and out of the ordinary for them to come in contact with him in public.

It was there he told them that headquarters had a

proposition for their consideration. He asked them if they would be willing to do a completion on the Shifton assignment. Of course, a completion being a hit on the person of interest—it was termed as a domestic. It came as no surprise to either of them since Global had asked that of them in the past. They told Bentley they needed some time and would give him an answer in 24 hours. The incentive would be more than three times the amount they would receive for Shifton's feasibility study.

On the other hand Bentley sort of shocked them with a proposition of his own—a so-called private matter. He explained that the target could be considered political and yet to his knowledge wasn't on anyone's "to do list." It was a point he stressed by stating the intervention was in no way connected to the company.

It was a situation they made a rule to always avoid. The reason being the law zeroed in on the motive and the people closest to it. If it so happened the police questioned or arrested the suspect of record, that person would most likely give up the killers for leniency. It was a common occurrence and one that could give any would-be hit man a severe case of angst.

Chris Bentley was another story. He was one of them—a "Shadow Soldier." He was someone they could trust; furthermore, he was their team leader, so they listened to what he had to say.

He addressed his conversation at his long-time friend, Trevor Jacks. He explained how their arrangement could be seen as more of a favor than a job. His exact words were "it would be an act of commensurate approbation, a *quid pro quo.*"

To Geiger it was just more silly palaver between two English snobs who were pretending what they were planning to do was acceptable. It was all a bunch of euphemistic bullshit to gloss over a murder-for-hire gig. Bentley went on to say that he was well aware of how busy they were with the "Shifton assignment."

So, with that in mind he took it upon himself to do his own brand of "reconnaissance"—his own feasibility study.

"The first order of business," he said was what type of delivery system they might use. He was thinking something on the order of what they used in Iraq—a Remington bolt action (MSR) or "Modular Sniper Rifle" with a fast-attached suppressor (silencer).

The ammunition might be the subsonic .300 AAC Blackout (7.62x35mm); it was a class of ammunition that avoided the supersonic shockwave, or the distinctive "crack," as it traveled towards its intended target. According to him, all they had to do was to show up and pull the bloody, fuckin' trigger.

Geiger sat there watching his partner listen to what his friend had to say, all the while nodding his head as if he didn't have anything in it. To him it looked as if Trevor might be playing Bentley along. Whatever he was doing, it sort of pissed him off.

Another thing that annoyed him was the fact that Trevor didn't ask Bentley the obvious. How much was he willing to pay and why he didn't do the job himself? He had to remind himself that within the ethos of the "profession," the money was always a matter of negotiation and it was inappropriate to question a client's "reasons." While he was listening to their conversation he got the impression that Bentley assumed that he and Jacks would take the job. It was as if they didn't have a say-so in the matter.

One thing was for sure, except for his partner, he really didn't like officers no matter what fuckin' country they came from. They all had a certain attitude—the kind that exuded an arrogance of power that gave him a "twinge" right in his balls.

He remembered what some psychologist said to him in the VA hospital: that he had an "aversion to authority." He recalled his response: he had "spent six years in the army and never disobeyed an order."

The shrink's only comment was:

"That was then; this is now."

He didn't like doctors; they had a lofty opinion of themselves, one that fit their own narrative.

What irked him was his partner's apparent servile relationship with Bentley—a compromising mindset for someone in their so-called profession. Jacks curtailed his conversation with Bentley by stating that they needed some time to think it over. They would get back to him in a few days.

Bentley acted as if he was somewhat put off at Jacks' reluctance; however, he understood their position. He then took out a pen and wrote a five-figure number on a napkin then showed it to them. After doing that, he scrunched it up and slipped the napkin into his pocket. He took a sip of scotch, smiled and said, "Maybe it would be best if you found some time to relax." He then handed Jacks a business card. On the card was the name "Renee Bardot" and a phone number.

"She's a specialist in relaxation," he said. "As a matter of fact, she's . . . uh, you might consider it a minor recompense. A part of our . . . arrangement."

It wasn't the first time they had been offered a woman as part of their payment plan. Sex was nice, but it didn't pay the bills.

What bothered Geiger was he thought Bentley of all people would know better. A woman could make a connection between him and the two of them—an unnecessary risk and one they wouldn't take.

On the way back to their hotel they didn't say much other than the amount Bentley had written on the napkin was more than they expected.

After a few days of intense discussion as to what they should do with Bentley's proposal and what to do with Shifton, they decided not to take the compilation money on Shifton—the risk wasn't worth it. Their thinking was he had too high a profile and the law would never stop investigating his death until it was solved.

The other part of their discussion was they would accept Bentley's plan. Their thinking was they would have Bentley's intervention money as well as the feasibility money on Shifton—if it all worked out as a win-win situation.

In the meantime, Geiger resolved not to query Trevor on his relationship with Bentley. He figured they had enough to think about then to add an additional consideration to the mix. Anyway, what business was it of his how Trevor felt about Bentley. It wasn't as if they were queer for one another, and if they were, so what?

With all of that out of the way, they met with Bentley once again. This time it was a place of their choosing. They picked an upscale coffee shop in Manhattan where he explained some of what he had in mind.

The "person of interest," he said, was a Muslim businessman named Samir Al-Sayyed, who, according to him, was also a member of CAIR (the Council on American-Islamic Relations)—the implication being that he probably had ties to Hamas since CAIR was a supposed supporter of that terrorist organization.

What startled them was what he said next. He told them that Al-Sayyed was the husband of his ex-wife, Adiba. He explained that she died in a very suspicious car accident and Samir made off with a million in accidental death benefits.

Jacks asked him why he never told him about any of this while they were stationed in Iraq. Bentley's only explanation was he felt ashamed and didn't want anyone to know what he was going through. The answer was believable enough, but for Jacks, not anywhere near sufficient. However, he knew his friend's mercurial personality, so he let it go.

The rest of what Bentley had to say centered on his plan for taking Al-Sayyed out. He told them Samir lived in

Bay Shore, Long Island. He was a member of a mosque in that city and prominent constituent of the ICN (the Islamic Circle of North America). A fact that would help set him up. He went on to say that he lived on a quiet street with a small patch of woods at the end of it.

After taking a quick glance around, Bentley removed a sheet of paper from his jacket. He then proceeded to draw a diagram of what he wanted to explain. He pointed to a square he designated as "the woods." He then drew a picture of a house and the area next to it as Samir's backyard.

"The woods," he said, "are the best place to see his home, mainly his backyard . . . that was or is the key."

"They key to what?" Geiger asked.

"The key to him, Sergeant," Bentley said, letting his tone of voice convey his annoyance at being interrupted.

"Unfortunately," said Bentley, "there's only one drawback. The view is hidden behind a wooden fence. That is unless you're . . . uh, high up."

"When you say high up," Geiger asked, "you mean like in a tree?"

"Precisely," Bentley replied.

"How far are these woods from Al-Sayyed's backyard?" Jacks asked while he sipped on a cup of tea.

"Oh, about 160 meters or . . ."

"Or, about 200 yards," Geiger said.

"Quite right, Sergeant, your perspicacity is uh . . ."

"Not much of a shot," replied Geiger as he stirred his coffee.

"Oh, it is," exclaimed Jacks, "if you're in a bloody fuckin' tree!"

"Rather," Bentley intoned using his comment to corroborate Jacks' observation.

"However, you might be wondering why I don't do the job on my own. Mmm . . . well, it seems my eyes have been, what, you might say are 'deteriorating.' They've been on the 'blink' ever since my last encounter with an IED."

It was a lie, but one Bentley knew no one would ever be the wiser of and it served his purpose of expedient subterfuge.

"Sorry to hear that, ol' boy," Jacks said. "I didn't know."

"Why would you? I didn't."

"Alright, already," Geiger said, "so, what goes on in this Sayyed guy's back 'fuckin' yard?"

"Well," replied Bentley, "it seems Samir is in the habit of having get-togethers at his home. Of course, that is, they're only for members of his mosque and his ICN associates. The meetings are mostly in the evening, usually on a Friday."

Before taking a sip of his tea, Jacks wiped his lips with a napkin then said:

"I take it these are all-male affairs."

"Rather," replied Bentley, "they're Muslims, ol' boy. Did you forget?"

"It was just a question," Jacks said. "You never know with these people, especially in the States."

"Ah, you just might be onto something," stated Bentley. "The American culture might change their perspective, but I seriously doubt it—Islam is too hidebound . . . sharia law and all that rot."

Geiger wasn't amused at listening to their version of British "repartee," so he decided to interject some thoughts of his own.

"Okay," he said, "I'm starting to get the picture . . . you want us to take Sayyed out at one of these meetings, right? Answer me this: what's that got to do with his backyard? Like you want us to hit him in his backyard or what?"

"Why don't you give the major time to explain," Jacks said, letting his partner know that maybe he shouldn't interrupt.

"No, never mind," Bentley replied. "Sergeant Geiger feels 'impelled' . . . isn't that right, Sergeant?"

"Yeah, that's me; I'm impelled alright . . . whatever the fuck that means."

Bentley and Jacks smiled at one another; they were used to American petulance and had learned to ignore it.

"As I was saying," said Bentley, "at the conclusion of these 'soirees,' and after the last of his guests have left, it seems Samir usually goes outside on his deck to have a 'fag.'"

"That's a cigarette . . . right?" Geiger asked.

Bentley gazed around then looked at Geiger and smiled and then nodded his head. Trevor Jacks coughed into his hand to cover his smirk. Within that same gesture, he took a quick sip of tea and then brushed off some non-existent crumbs from the table.

"As I was saying, Sayyed usually finishes his cigarette then crushes it out in a can filled with sand . . . very regimental our Samir. He then walks across his lawn to visit his dog."

"His dog?" Geiger asked.

"Oh, I'm sorry, Sergeant. Did I stutter?"

"No, sir, I just . . . you know . . . sorry to interrupt."

Bentley went on to explain by saying how Samir's dog was chained up inside a shed next to the fence. "When he goes there," he said, "he pulls the animal out by his chain then hits it with a stick until it yelps and cowers before him."

Geiger noticed that Bentley's face lost its expression and his voice changed to a different tone as if hate dripped from every vowel. He knew that Bentley, like most Englishmen, loved dogs, so Samir was more than damned.

"It will be a pleasure," said Geiger, "to put the crosshairs on that piece of shit."

"He's an Arab sergeant," Bentley replied. "That's what they do . . . it's in their bloody DNA. Apart from all that, Samir walks back to his house, has another cigarette, then goes inside through a few sliding doors."

Jacks interrupted Bentley's train of thought by

pointing to the spot on the diagram Bentley had marked as "the woods." He then asked, "Uh, what exactly is the size . . . I mean the area of these woods?"

"The area?" Bentley replied, "Oh, roughly the size of a building lot, less than a quarter of an acre. The good thing is there are a number of trees scattered about. They have sufficient foliage to camouflage your presence. I would suggest that you look over my notes. Of course, I would . . . well, I would imagine . . .."

"I would imagine," Jacks asked, "these notes of yours have been typed?"—knowing Bentley would never be so careless as to put anything on paper in his own handwriting and then leave it behind. It was a pointless question said with the express purpose of annoying his friend.

Bentley looked askance, raising his eyebrows as he spoke:

"Yes, of course, protocol being what it is." He then added, "I assume you will do your own feasibility?"

With an emphatic smile, Geiger said, "Oh, we will—that's what we do best . . . kind of . . . isn't that right, Trevor?"

"Most certainly."

"Yes, of course," Bentley said. "Uh, I . . . however, before I leave, there are a few incidentals we should discuss."

Without looking in Bentley's direction, Jacks asked, "Such as?" He then opened a packet of Sweet'N Low and poured its contents into his tea.

"Well, first and foremost I informed headquarters about your decision to forgo their request concerning Mr. Shifton. As of yet, I haven't heard from them, but I expect an answer—soon. Oh, yes, there is the matter of the dog."

"The dog? What about the dog?" Geiger asked.

"Well," Bentley said, "if it's at all possible, leave him be."

"What makes you think otherwise?" asked Jacks.

"Well, if he begins to bark or howl, do what you must; no sense of jeopardizing the mission."

"You mean we should take him out?" Geiger asked.

"If you must."

"We'll cross that bridge when we have to," Jacks said while he wiped his lips with a napkin.

Swept up in the intrigue of the moment, Geiger and Jacks felt compelled to follow through on the idea of blood for money. They researched Bentley's plan using his notes as a guide and the same car they employed for Shifton's feasibility study.

The neighborhood Al Sayyed lived in was as quiet as Bentley's notes said it would be. The woods were just the same, except for a few teenagers who frequented the place during the day—ostensibly to smoke pot, drink beer and have sex. The evidence of that being the sight of some empty beer cans, roll-your-owns, and used condoms.

After a quick walk through the woods, they found the tree Bentley had selected as the most advantageous to scan Samir's backyard. He had marked it with iridescent paint so as to be easily identifiable at night—a problem that wasn't one since they used night vision optics as standard procedure. This time they decided to go with the slip-on head strap, mission-configurable Armasight monoculars— they gave the best picture for the money.

Within a week they contacted Bentley and gave him the "thumbs-up" as to their acceptance of his proposition. What Geiger and Jacks weren't aware of was Bentley's hidden agenda. All the while he had them working on the Al-Sayyed project, he was testing them for future operations within the United States.

To help facilitate their mission, Bentley provided them with a panel truck that had removable magnetic signs. These signs advertised a well-known plumbing and heating business—in another town.

In addition he gave them a police scanner and a laptop with an unusual app. It was a GPS system that allowed them to know the whereabouts of any police cruisers that might be in their vicinity. They didn't tell Bentley they had that type of equipment of their own. It was expected that when you worked as a field operative you would provide your own tactical hardware. In Bentley's case they decided to use his gear as a backup for theirs. The rationale being he probably wouldn't need it anyhow.

Seeing that he was their team leader and well acquainted with SOG, Bentley suspected their ploy, but said nothing to the contrary. He did however give them "un-said" kudos for being resourceful as well as surreptitious.

The two men spent a few days deliberating as to the timing of the hit. They settled on the first Friday of the following month. It allowed them 14 days to work out a few details and more time to canvass Samir's neighborhood.

The most important part of their plan was settled with a flip of a coin; it was to determine who would be the shooter—Geiger won the toss. In a sense, he was the superior candidate. Jacks was a better shot, but Geiger was more agile and weighed less—an important consideration in tree climbing.

Geiger knew the lay of the land and yet he needed to climb "the tree" before the day he was to pull the trigger. He had to make sure it was as right as Bentley told them.

To accomplish this they figured he would have to go in at night, preferably a few days before that particular Friday. Their thinking ran along the lines that Jacks would drive him to the woods using Bentley's panel truck as cover.

He would wear a pair of dark gray coveralls and a "hoody" while carrying a medium-sized tool bag. In the bag was a pruning saw for any branches that needed to be cut, a short pair of tree climbing spikes, a lineman's belt to wrap around the trunk to attach to a harness hidden under his coveralls, and a small pair of range-finder binoculars to get a fix on the exact distance and spot for him to dial into.

It all looked good on paper, but the devil was in what you couldn't see. For most people the entire set-up would appear to be bizarre and quite disturbing. For Max Geiger, it was just another day at the office. To him it was the setting for an iconic sniper shot—at night, from a tree using a silencer; it didn't get any better than that.

When the completion day finally arrived they checked and rechecked the weather until Jacks dropped Geiger off at the edge of the woods. Accordingly, the forecast was exceptional—a perfect evening—no rain, very little wind and no humidity to speak of. The humidity had a way of putting drag on a bullet so as to disturb its accuracy.

The operation was going to plan with Geiger making another successful entry through the woods—this time dressed as before, he carried a small backpack with his tree-climbing equipment in it. He also carried a long, innocuous-looking box that contained his rifle.

Their plan called for him to make his way to "the tree," then discard the box before he climbed it. Before doing that, he slung the rifle across his back, with the strap pulled tightly across his chest and shoulder—textbook style.

As he climbed, Geiger stayed in constant communication with his partner using the Vox headset and Widen walkie-talkie system. When he reached the branch of "the tree" he had marked on his previous trip, he set up and waited for Jacks to tell him when Samir's guests were leaving.

For his part, Jacks had parked on Al-Sayyed's street a short distance from his home. When the time finally arrived and Samir's guests started to leave, Trevor told Geiger as much.

Geiger started to focus in and concentrated on the spot he had picked out as the area of intervention: the place he would take Al-Sayyed out—264 yards away.

Suddenly, a slight feeling of apprehension came over him, something he only experienced once before in Afghanistan. A dull tingling sensation filled his ears and he started to hyperventilate. The realization that he might be experiencing the symptoms of an anxiety attack made him pull hard on his ability to stay calm in the midst of a stressful situation.

As quickly as those feelings arrived, they left, leaving him with a deep sense of calm. Once again he was himself, although keenly aware of the power of the mind.

While peering through the lens of his riflescope, Geiger watched as Samir passed through the sliding glass doors of his home that led onto his back deck. The only thing that bothered him: he wasn't alone—he had a female with him. She was wearing the traditional head scarf of a Muslim woman, "a *hijab*"—in Arabic, the "veil." She also had on an ankle-length black dress called an "*abaya.*"

The sight of her threw him off his game as he questioned on what to do next. All of this he conveyed to Jacks who told him to stay in place and wait to see what they would do next.

Geiger settled back in his harness and watched as the two of them stood there talking. The odd thing was Samir was smoking a pipe instead of a cigarette. This only elevated his feelings as to what else would Samir do that was unexpected.

Then, without warning, a sudden wind came along strong enough to make Samir and his lady friend curtail their conversation and move inside.

Jacks told Geiger to wait and see if the woman would leave; if she did he would tell him so.

The wind that bothered Samir also moved the branch Geiger was using as a bench rest to stabilize his rifle. Fortunately, the scope he was using was an ATN X-Sight that had a built-in stabilization system. It automatically compensated the aiming point for any variation in the horizon, allowing the shooter to stay on target without changing his position.

Finally, Geiger heard what he had been waiting for: the muffled voice of Jacks telling him the woman had left Samir's and was being picked up as they spoke.

It wasn't long before Al-Sayyed reappeared on his deck. He went over to one of the railings, lit a cigarette, stood there for a while and then extinguished his cigarette in a sand pail next to his leg. It happened just as Bentley had said it would.

He then removed a wooden rod from its holder attached to the railing. To Geiger it appeared to be half of a pool stick, maybe a little shorter. Samir walked over and down the stairs toward his dog's shed, all the while tapping the palm of his hand with the wooden rod.

Geiger followed him through his riflescope placing its crosshairs on the side of Samir's head. While doing that he took a few shallow breaths then exhaled, then one final inhalation. With each passing moment, Geiger slowly breathed out then squeezed the trigger of his Remington.

The sudden recoil of his rifle let him know that his silent messenger of death was on its way. He watched as Al-Sayyed pitched sideways, his head an explosion of mist made of blood and bone. All of it captured in the virtual color of his scope.

He felt nothing but relief for a successful shot and satisfaction knowing that he had sent another Arab to an afterlife of 72 virgins.

The dog never emerged from his house. Geiger sent him a mental salute for being one tough son-of-a-bitch—a fervent wish for a better life knowing that he was free from his sadistic owner.

CHAPTER 24

"The quest for personal significance constitutes a major motivational force that may push individuals toward violent extremism. The term extremism is always exonymic—applied to others, not to yourself."

> — *The True Believer*
> *The Passionate State of Mind*
> *The Vital Center* —

When Bentley answered his cell phone, a familiar voice at the other end told him he had to speak to him "privately." He knew that was code for an urgent request to meet with him face-to-face in his hotel room. Knowing it was Orlando Stokes, he said:

"Of course—why not; I'm not busy . . . Uh, shall we say in an hour or so"—using the Arabic word "*innaha as-saah.*"

It wasn't long after he hung up, when his hotel phone rang. He knew who it was, so he didn't bother to answer it. Within minutes, he heard a slight knock at his door.

After the usual exchange of amenities, Orlando told Bentley he didn't have much time to talk. He went on by saying that the son of his imam had just told him that his father and a few other Al-Qaeda jihadist scum were planning to attack the capitol in Albany.

With a skeptical look of chagrin, Bentley asked:

"Are you sure?"

"Yeah, he doesn't lie to me."

"When?"

"Don't know, but soon—we don't have a lot of time."

"How do you know for sure?" Bentley asked.

"I don't, it's just a feeling . . . I know these people . . . anyway, to hell with all of that shit!" exclaimed Stokes.

"How are they going to do it?" asked Bentley.

"Get this—with a drone."

"A drone!!" replied Bentley.

"Yeah, a fuckin' drone! . . . Here's the rest of it . . . the thing is packed with explosives, but that's not all. Supposedly, it might be carrying a canister of fuckin' sarin gas."

"To hell, you say," replied Bentley.

"Heh, I wish . . . gimme one of those will you," Stokes said, as he pointed to the glass of bourbon Bentley had in his hand.

"Of course . . . how do you like it?"

"Like yours."

"How did they get the gas?" Bentley asked as he handed Orlando his drink.

"Probably from the three ISIS guys who just showed up at the mosque."

"How do you know they're . . . 'daesh'?" Bentley said, using the Arabic word for ISIS (meaning one who crushes something underfoot).

"How else? From the imam's son."

"And you believe him?" asked Bentley.

"Yeah, I believe him," answered Stokes nodding his head as he sipped on his drink.

"Oh, the imam wants us to give up our cell phones. The old fool doesn't fuckin' know we got spares . . . at least I do."

"Make sure you keep it charged," advised Bentley as he took out his own cell phone and plugged in the charger.

They talked for a few minutes sipping on their drinks while giving each other provisory looks of skepticism.

"Do you know where the drone is?" asked Bentley.

"Yeah, in Petersburgh, New York, 30 minutes northeast of Albany . . . in some farmhouse barn."

"How do you know?"

"Because I'm on the imam's security team," Stokes said. "He picked me and his son and four others . . . the ISIS guys; we're leaving in a few hours."

"Do you know the address?"

"Not yet, but I'll get it to you . . . somehow."

"You think the FBI or Homeland knows?" Bentley asked, knowing that the FBI was aware of the plot due to his conversations with Gordon.

"Nah," said Stokes. "The imam seems sure . . . but, you never know . . . you know how that goes."

"Heh, I have a plan," said Stokes. "You remember what we did in Iraq . . . how we hit that bank and shot the two Iraqis we wanted out of the way and then we beat up the informant so we could use him again . . . in the future?"

"Yes, I remember," Bentley said.

"Well, I'm thinking we could do something like that . . . you know, take out the imam and the ISIS assholes, then work me and the Imam's son over . . . his son goes on to take over the mosque as the new imam . . ."

"Good show . . . it will have to make do."

"Yeah, well," Stokes said, "I got to figure a way of getting you and the team inside the farmhouse without alerting the imam and his crew."

After they finished their drinks the two men drifted towards the door. While Bentley was letting Stokes out, he shook his hand and said:

"Good luck."

"Amen to that, I'm going to need it and good luck to you . . . but you know you better put a move on . . . it's gettin' late."

Bentley just smiled and nodded his head. Before Stokes left, Bentley added a postscript:

"*As-salamu alaykum*" (Arabic for peace be upon you).

Stokes responded with the Arabic phrase:

"*Wa-alaykum as-salaam*" (and on you be peace).

After the door closed, Bentley stood there for a few minutes contemplating what his next course of action would be. He reached for his cell phone and dialed an encryptic message to Conrad Lowe informing of his situation. It wasn't long before he received an answer.

Lowe replied with an end-to-end encryption that said do whatever he thought necessary to stop 'the drone.' The rest of the message stated money was no object—success was the only consideration.

His next concern was to notify the members of his team. He told them to bring their "kit" (all of their assault gear including their new bullet-resistant clothing). The rest of his message was concise; they would meet at "Rendezvous-8" (a street on the upper west side without surveillance cameras).

Within a three-hour period, Bentley was walking from his car to another at "Rendezvous-8." He explained to each man that they were on their way to a place called Petersburgh, a town 30 miles outside of Albany. He would tell them why when they got there—a common occurrence in their world of "on a need to know basis."

However, there was one person who knew more than the others, but never let on that he did, and he was Anthony Robert Gordon. Although, there was something he wasn't sure of and that was how much they were going to get paid and by whom.

It could be the agency or Global, possibly the W.E.B. If it was the agency that would mean Reno "fuckin'" Starr would be in the catbird seat as the paymaster.

It annoyed him to know that, but not as much as Starr alluding to the fact that his DNA was found at the crime scene of The Werewolf murder. Another quandary that crossed his mind was Orlando Stokes and what he might be up to. If anything, he knew time and circumstance was a bridge he had crossed before and would do it again when he had to.

As their convoy drove towards Petersburgh, Bentley received the encryptic text message he had been waiting for. It was from Orlando who told him the address of the farmhouse and how the drone and its cargo were buried in a horse stall in the barn.

With the use of a GPS, the team was able to find an obscure road off a darkened highway that led to the farmhouse. Bentley had the men park their vehicle alongside his van that was nestled amongst a cluster of trees which ran along the border of the property of the farmhouse.

With his team gathered around him, Bentley explained the object of their mission and the necessity of its success. Except for Gordon, it came as a surprise to the rest of the team, the Islamos would use a drone and sarin gas as a weapon of mass destruction.

Bentley told them to dress in their "turtle suits," a camouflage uniform made of bullet-resistant cloth, a Kevlar vest, a helmet of the same material with attached night vision. He also "miked up" each of them with wireless hands-free walkie-talkies.

With all of that "squared away," Bentley went into his van and took out their M-4 machine guns with extended night vision and detachable sound suppressor. As a sidearm, the team usually carried a 308 automatic with a screw-on silencer, although they could carry whatever they wanted as long as it had a silencer.

It all seemed far too excessive for that type of operation, but as Bentley explained, since it was an "exigent" mission, they would have to prepare for any contingencies and "muddle" their way through it.

"So, what else is new?" asked Joe Stigler, a recent addition to the team. He was a former ranger who had lost the lower part of one of his legs while serving in Iraq.

He had been fitted with a prosthesis that worked as well as if it was his own. Stigler's handle was "Stigs." He "hailed" from Waco, Texas, or Wacko, Texas, as a lot of people referred to it.

His real name was Joe, but he took to calling himself "Yates" thinking it sounded more Texas than Joe. He had been an up-and-coming bull rider on the rodeo circuit until 9-11, then quit to join the army.

A good-looking guy with a square jaw, sandy-colored hair, pale blue eyes and bulging biceps, he hated Muslims and had an overriding desire for action. To say the least, he was a perfect fit for the team who now called themselves "Bentley's Bastards."

They decided to disperse in pairs with Chris Bentley and Trevor Jacks taking the point. Following close behind were Gordon and Grimaldi, with Yates Stigler and Max Geiger bringing up the rear.

As they pushed their way through a field of corn stalks, the faint smell of fertilizer and a gentle breeze became a friendly participant in their trek towards the farmhouse.

The farmhouse lay in the distance made only discernible through the use of night vision. Its darkened silhouette seemed to cast itself as a foreboding specter against the luminescent glow of a crescent moon.

It wasn't long after the team had begun their journey when they started to feel sick. A kind of nauseousness swept over them with their eyes tearing up and noses running.

Bentley was the first to put on his gas mask. He had made a tactical decision to issue each man a gas mask along with a complement of CS grenades before they set out for their objective. (CS is a cyanocarbon whose chemical name is o-chlorobenzylidene *malononitrile*, the defining component of tear gas.) It was a classic approach to an old problem of taking out an enemy without the use of explosives or firearms.

In a matter of minutes after using their gas masks, the men recovered from the effect of whatever agent was used to bring on their symptoms. The experience put them on notice— someone had set up an IED which deployed a noxious substance instead of an explosive.

The obviousness of its intent was apparent: they wanted a deterrent, but not a detonation that might draw the attention of the police.

It was a form of battlefield deviousness they had become accustomed to while fighting in Iraq and Afghanistan. A realization that put them on alert; they were probably facing foreign trained terrorists.

It was that type of reality that plagued the FBI and the Department of Homeland Security. They knew they had to use more than politically correct tactics to stop foreign or domestic terrorists, but the law stood in their way.

When the team approached their objective, they thought it safe enough to remove their gas masks. With the situation in hand, they edged themselves as close to the farmhouse as their cover would allow.

While lying on his side, with his cell phone cradled in his hand, Bentley waited anxiously for some type of text message from Orlando.

As previously planned, it was up to Stokes to provide some way for the team to enter the farmhouse without the use of force.

From where he had positioned himself, Bentley could see the windows along that side of the house.

Each man was totally aware of what was expected of them. They knew they were "winging it," but such was the nature of what they had to do. As they used to say in Iraq, "Fuck the problem; just getter done."

It was Yates Stigler, the new guy, who crawled over to where Bentley was hiding, then sidled his way alongside of him and whispered:

"There's a security cam hanging from the roof."

Without taking his eyes off the building, Bentley whispered back:

"Yes, Sergeant, I'm quite aware of that . . . what do you propose we do about it?"

"Well," Yates said, "suppose I take it the fuck on out? . . . I mean we got these here silencers and subsonic ammo . . . nobody hear a fucking thing."

In a barely audible reply, Bentley said:

"Brilliant . . . but, be a good lad and don't muck it up."

Stigler's smile was lost in the dark as he nodded his head. He then lifted his night vision binoculars that hung from his helmet in front of him. He did that so he could peer through the scope that was mounted on his M-4.

While he was doing that, he dialed in his sight picture, took a few deep breaths and slowly exhaled as he pulled the trigger of his rifle. The team watched as the shattered pieces of the security camera fell silently to the grass-covered ground below.

As if on cue, a small but significant light suddenly appeared at one of the first floor windows—then quickly extinguished itself.

While retreating in the direction of his former position, Stigler whispered:

"Ain't that a kick in the ass?"

Bentley was quick to send Orlando a one-word text— "Wilco" (will comply).

It wasn't long afterwards that Bentley had Gordon and Grimaldi went forward to test the window and to find out what lay behind it.

He kept a sharp eye on the two of them as they advanced from their location across a stretch of open ground towards the farmhouse. It was a risky procedure, but necessary since time was of the essence and expediency was urgent. Bentley could clearly see them through his night vision goggles as they trudged along in a half-bent position in the direction of the window.

He watched as Gordon used his utility knife to pry open the window. From what he could surmise, Stokes probably released the security latch on it, but for some reason the "bloody" thing was stuck.

"A less than auspicious start," he thought, especially for an evening of unknown consequences and questionable benefits.

What came after could be described as fairly humorous, as he observed Grimaldi struggle to help Gordon through the half-open window. He did that by having him stand on his back and shoulders, then push him by his butt cheeks while Gordon pulled himself inside.

Once he had done that, Gordon did a quick scan of his surroundings to make sure he was alone. After he was satisfied that he was, he sent a text message to Bentley advising him to come ahead.

He would have used his walkie-talkie, but feared that someone might hear the sound of his voice. An irrational consideration when he thought over how much noise he made, while he was squeezing his way through the window and into the room.

With his silenced M-4 at the ready, Gordon stood guard at the doorway that had a darkened hallway as its entrance and exit.

Outside the rest of the team had filed forward in the direction of the open window. With tentative footsteps each man attempted to follow in the path of the man in front of him. This was done in the hope of reducing the chances of not setting off any IEDs or a hidden alarm system.

Grimaldi remained outside the window, so he could help each man up, until he was the last to be pulled inside.

While the team rested in place, Bentley sent Gordon and TOJO down the darkened corridor to investigate a subdued light at the end of it.

With measured footsteps they crept along. Gordon started to sense an eerie chill of déjà vu. He didn't know why; it could be the musty smell of his surroundings or the disquieting creakiness of the floorboards. Whatever it was, it reminded him of the house Richard Carroll Spencer lived in. "Hopefully," he thought, "there wouldn't be any fuckin' werewolves to wrestle with."

When they finally reached the end of the hallway, Gordon peaked around a corner doorway only to see it was just a kitchen. Over on one side of it, was an oven who's door had been left open and the light inside was still on.

Within that same period of time both he and TOJO saw and heard a man snoring from inside an alcove; he was sleeping on a cot near a rear door.

He was fully clothed and dressed in the same garb that most of the Islamos in Iraq wore. He had the obligatory full beard, a disheveled military-styled jacket and pants, a long scarf and an AK-47 lying on the floor beside him.

Grimaldi nudged Gordon in the back as he pointed towards the Muslim and then back at himself. He made the sign of pulling a trigger indicating he personally wanted to take the guy out. Gordon shook his head, but Grimaldi repeated his request with more animation and forcefulness.

At first Gordon made a gesture of noncompliance, then acquiesced with a nod of his head. He wouldn't admit to it, but he was relieved that TOJO was willing to accept the onus of the man's death instead of placing it on him.

It wasn't a moral issue that held him back, but a matter of momentary reticence and the option of not doing it.

He then watched as Grimaldi tiptoed his way across the kitchen floor circumventing a large table while trying to avoid a few adherent chairs that blocked his path. He saw him slip into the alcove and stand over the sentry, his pistol pointing at the man's head. A few passing moments went by as he observed how his partner just stood there aiming at the guy, his finger on the trigger.

Immediately Gordon realized what had happened: either TOJO had just froze the "fuck up" or forgot to take the safety off his "friggin'" gun.

It had happened to him and almost cost him his life. He remembered how he and his team were on patrol in Anbar Province and they hit an ambush; somehow he forgot to take the safety off his M-4. To this day, he didn't know why he had it on in the first place. However, and whatever the reason, for his carelessness, he caught an Iraqi bullet in his Kevlar vest and the lasting memory of how it felt.

Before he could reach out and help his friend, Grimaldi woke up and flipped the safety off his 9 and sent a silent bullet through the sentry's head.

The event left Gordon in a kind of quandary, wondering what to do next. The answer came as Bentley's voice filled the ear piece of his headset requesting him to return as soon as possible.

He responded by telling him of his situation regarding TOJO and the dead jihadi sentry. Bentley came back by saying:

"Have Sergeant Grimaldi stay in place and for him to double-back to the room" since they had a situation of their own.

Gordon thought over what had happened ever since they arrived on station; none of it seemed to be working out.

His other concern was the thought they might have to abort the operation before they destroyed the drone. A consideration that meant failure and the possibility of no further assignments and the end to the rivers of cash that flowed their way.

He then mulled over the most important thing on why they were there in the first place, and how the Islamo bastards might deliver the drone and its cargo of sarin gas. It was a possibility they couldn't let happen, and if need be, they might have to sacrifice their own lives to stop it. A situation that all of them had faced in Iraq and Afghanistan.

There was something else that bothered him as well as the other members of the team. It was a device called an IMSI-catcher, otherwise known as stingray. It was a surveillance tool that masqueraded itself as a cell tower and could trick mobile cell phones into spewing private data to law enforcement. The worse part of it was it could track your cell phone to a particular geographic location. To thwart the use of the device they used what was called a Black Hole Faraday Bag which kept their cell phone electronic signal from reaching stingray. It was all high tech to him and something he wasn't interested in. His only concern was that it worked and it shielded him from the prying eyes of the so-called law.

Grimaldi saw Gordon wave goodbye as he disappeared down the hallway. He then walked over to one of the kitchen chairs and sat down determined to wait in silent vigil as he stared into the alcove, but not at the body of the man he had just killed.

When Gordon returned to the room, he was presented with the sight of a dead jihadi laying face up on the floor. The story was while he and Grimaldi were gone, Chris Bentley and Trevor Jacks left the room to survey the downstairs area.

In the living room at the other end of the hall they found a supposed security guard sitting in the dark. He was in a chair with his back towards the door, his feet up, smoking a joint, looking out one of the windows and seemingly oblivious to his surroundings.

It was Jacks that told him that he and Bentley attempted to take the guy hostage, but he put up a fight and made too much noise, so they had to put him down.

The other thing that occurred was Bentley received a text message from Stokes telling him he was upstairs with five Islamos. He said they were sound asleep due to a special "chi" or tea he had brewed for them.

Gordon railed at the idea of Stokes having such an integral part of the operation, but "it is what it is," so he had to live with it. However, he drew cold comfort in the thought "some other place, some other time" and then he would get the chance to put the son of a bitch away—for good.

Bentley went on to explain to him and the others, how he was going to have Trevor and Max Geiger go upstairs and find Stokes. After that, they were to tie him up with whomever else he was with and wait until he and Yates Stigler got there—a daunting task when you considered what might occur while they were walking upstairs—the fear being there could be someone at the top with his finger on the trigger of an AK waiting for you.

Gordon was glad Bentley hadn't asked him; he didn't like pushing the so-called envelope. He wasn't keen on showing he had more balls than brains. It might get you medals, but it sure as hell could get you killed.

He remembered what Bentley once said to him, that he wanted to know a man well enough to be assured that they had "their . . . solicitudes down to a farthing."

Whatever the hell that meant. But what the fuck, Bentley was one of those pretentious, limey bastards. He was the kinda guy who worshipped the ground he walked on.

As luck would have it, instead of getting that job, Bentley was nice enough to give him an easy one. He told him to go down to the end of the hallway and stand guard at the front door with the express purpose of shooting anyone who tried to get in.

"Hey! Didn't he know he would of done that anyhow?"

While standing at the front door Gordon pondered the significance of the darkness around him. It was a subject he was well acquainted with since he had spent most of his military career dealing with it.

This time his poetic side saw darkness as a metaphor for radical Islam, Al Qaeda or ISIS, and the rest of that so-called ilk. When he thought about it, they were the personification of darkness. It left him and many others like him the "enemies of darkness" and the light at the end of that tunnel.

Gordon snickered at himself as the thought crossed his mind, "So, who was being pretentious, now?"

While Jacks and Geiger were getting ready to go upstairs, Bentley sent a text to Stokes. It instructed him to stay in place and not to move about. He didn't want Orlando to become a casualty of mistaken identity—an obvious concern when operating in limited light: darkness.

Stokes replied: First room on the left.

As opposed to walking upright, Geiger and Jacks preferred a slower but safer way of going up a flight of stairs. It was a special op's procedure of lying on your stomach, shoulder-to-shoulder with your guns out in front of you. The maneuver wasn't easy inching your way up, but it extinguished some of the fear of being a standing target.

The rest of the plan called for Bentley and Yates to wait at the bottom of the stairway, just in case they were needed.

When Jacks and Geiger made it to the top, they slowly walked down the unlit hallway towards the first room on the left. The plan was for them to contact

Orlando inside the room, handcuff him and then do the same to whoever he was with.

Contrary to Bentley's orders, they saw Orlando standing outside his room with his hands resting on his head. It was Geiger who first walked up to him and said in an exasperated but whispered tone of voice:

"What the fuck are you doing out here? . . . You were supposed to be inside the room . . . we woulda found you."

"Yeah, I know," whispered Stokes, "but, I got anxious just sitting there . . . waiting—for you."

"Yeah, well stick your hands out in front of you and cross your fuckin' wrists . . . I gotta cuff you."

Orlando did as he was told, then Geiger placed a plastic police restraint around his wrists and pulled it tight.

With an eye on the door, Jacks whispered into his microphone telling Bentley and Stigler it was "all clear and come ahead."

When the two of them arrived Bentley pointed to the room and whispered to Stokes:

"How many?"

As he raised his hand he used two fingers as an identifier then whispered the word: "two."

"Is that all?" Bentley asked.

Orlando turned his head from side-to-side and pointed to a door across from where they were standing, raised his hand and showed Bentley three fingers, all the while using a small penlight to illuminate his face and hands.

Stokes drew up close to Bentley and said:

"The imam's in there with his son and another guy."

"Are they sedated?" Bentley asked.

"I think so," replied Stokes in a whisper, "at least they were the last time I checked."

"When was that?" he asked.

"About a half-hour ago."

Bentley pointed to himself and Yates and then the door on the right; within that same motion he pointed to Geiger and Trevor Jacks and the door on the left.

It was Geiger and Jacks who moved first and slowly opened the door on the left. With the door slightly ajar they took a peek inside where they saw two men sleeping in the same bed. On either side of them was an AK-47 and a bandoleer of magazines. In one corner of the room was a small electric space heater that glowed in the dark.

The room smelled of bad breath and body odor leaving Geiger with the knowledge of why Orlando had waited outside in the hallway—he would have done the same.

While Jacks stood guard at the foot of the bed, Geiger slipped around and picked up their rifles. He placed them far enough away so they would be safely out of reach. As he was doing that, one of the Islamos rolled over on his side, farted, then mumbled something in Arabic.

Using his Starfire flashlight as an instrument of alarm, Jack sent its penetrating beam into the eyes of the two men.

When he did that, Geiger banged the feet of the two jihadis with the muzzle of his M-4. Using a low and menacing growl, Geiger uttered:

"Time to wake up . . . mother fuckers."

The two men reacted in similar fashion by sitting up abruptly. The mumbling Islamo put his hand up to shade his eyes from the blinding light while his friend did the same. Suddenly, one of them dove off the side of the bed searching for his weapon. His friend tried to do the same, but Geiger shot him in the leg before he could complete the move.

While all of that was going on, Yates and Chris Bentley burst into the room where the imam, his son, and the other Muslim terrorist were sleeping. They saw one of them attempt to get up from his bed and reach for his pistol on the nightstand next to him.

It was Bentley who rushed the guy striking him on the forehead with the butt of his rifle. The blow sent the man backwards towards his pillow and into a semi-conscious state. The other two remaining Islamos sat straight up and slowly raised their hands above their heads.

It was at that point Bentley turned on a light revealing their ski-masked, battle-dressed appearance. The sight of them seemed to startle all three men into an apparent state of nervous submission.

To emphasize the seriousness of their intent, Stigler went over to the older man who was obviously the imam and slapped him across the face. He then proceeded to handcuff all three of them. While he was doing that, Bentley waved his M-4 in their direction, as if he was looking for a reason to pull the trigger.

The man they thought was the so-called imam, Ahmad Al-Zaki, said, "You have no right to assault me and my companions—you need a warrant for our arrest." He added another request, "We have broken no laws and want an attorney."

With a wave of his hand and a snickering kind of laugh, Stigler replied:

"Hey! I'll tell you what . . . old man . . . you're going to need more than some fuckin' lawyer to get out of this."

Bentley grabbed the arm of the imam while Yates took hold of his son Akram. They proceeded to lead the two of them out the door and across the hall to the room Geiger and Jacks were in. The other Muslim prisoner did as he was told and dutifully followed close behind.

When they walked into the room, a light was on and they saw two captive jihadis sitting on the floor next to a chair Orlando was in.

When the imam asked why Jamal had been given a chair and not the others, it was Geiger who answered first by telling him:

"It's none of your fuckin' business, but if you have to know, it's because Jamal is African American."

The imam did not respond, but sat down with the other captives to await his fate.

Orlando wondered if Geiger and the rest of the team would be so courteous if they knew he was holding on to a secret. A secret that would make them a lot better off, at least financially.

How there was more than just a drone and some sarin gas buried in the barn, but also a box of money; it had been given to Al-Zaki for safekeeping.

As always it was his son Akram that told him of it. He explained how an important Muslim leader named Mohammed "Alim" Elbarasse gave it to his father, but he didn't know how much or where in the barn it was hidden.

The thing that bothered Orlando was not the amount or where it was stashed, but how was he going to get it without involving anyone else.

It was a hell'va fuckin' problem and one he didn't have an answer for, so he decided to let it be and bide his time. Hopeful, at some future date, an opportunity would come his way and he would take it all for himself. Besides, he had given the team the drone and the sarin gas— they'd get paid a lot of money for that. So, fuck it, he deserved the money in the barn; it was the least anyone could do.

While leaving Stigler in charge of the prisoners, Bentley huddled with Geiger and Jacks in the hallway. He asked the two of them, "Who do you consider to be the weakest of the captives to interrogate first?"

"An easy question" replied Jacks.

"I would imagine the chap I shot in the leg. It stands to reason he must be a bit . . . gammy, and in all probability . . . not thinking well enough."

With a slight laugh, Geiger said:

"Heh, a bit gammy . . . huh, you know . . . I like that . . . a bit gammy."

Bentley and Jacks just looked at one another, but said nothing. They knew Americans were somewhat daft and not to be understood.

When the three of them returned to the room, Bentley walked over to the wounded Muslim, bent over and grabbed him by his hair. He then yanked his head back and said:

"Listen to me, my bearded friend, we're not working for the bleeding police . . . you bloody wog—*ana afham*." (Arabic for the word understand.) He then went on to say:

"We're here on or own . . . *ana afham* . . . *ana afham*?"

He punctuated his words by shoving the man's head back and forth until he let him go.

Bentley knew Muslims, especially Islamos, respected physical force; and saw mercy towards a foe as a sign of weakness.

The man said nothing of any significance. He just lay there and moaned while Bentley dug his boot into his wounded leg.

The captives responded to the man's cries by shouting, "*Allahu Akbar*!" It appeared the guy was a lot tougher than they thought and wasn't going to talk.

"Listen up, you bloody bastards," Jacks yelled. "We know you have a fuckin' drone . . . tell us where it is or I swear to God . . . we'll make little girls out of all of you."

His raspy voice cut through the silence like the sound of a chainsaw in a forest. The Muslims sat there with their heads down, silent at first, then in unison chanted "*Allahu Akbar*" over and over again.

"Ah, shut up," yelled Geiger, as he pointed at his finger at them.

"You're all '*Daesh*'. You bastards like to cut the headies off babies. Well, we like to cut the balls off scum like you . . . *ana afham*?"

The imam looked up at him and said:

"We are not '*Daesh*,' we are the true followers of the prophet Muhammed . . . peace be upon him." (*Daesh* is Arabic for the Islamic State of Iraq and the Levant. It is also considered a derogatory term for the group known as

ISIS and punishable by having your tongue removed if used in their presence.)

Bentley knew when you had to deal with the likes of extreme Islamists you had to be just like them. So, to get what he intended, he had to be just as crafty and as they were and just as heartless.

Even though they knew that the drone was somewhere in the barn, they had to find out where it was hidden and if an IED was attached to it.

To do all of that, they would probably have to question each one of them individually. If need be, systematically torture them, separately or together, whatever was necessary. He didn't want to, but sometimes "you had to do what had to be done and this appeared to be one of those times."

One thing was for certain, he had to keep Orlando in the good graces of the imam's son. To do that, he had to make his interrogation look authentic. So, he had Trevor help him with Orlando; they led him from the room down the hallway to a dingy bathroom. To further the illusion, Bentley had Orlando sit on the toilet whereupon he reached down and flushed it. He had purposely left the bathroom door open, so its familiar sound would reverberate down the darkened corridor to the apprehensive ears of their captives, who considered waterboarding as a great disgrace. The worse being if toilet water or urine was used.

Even though he was in on it, Stokes didn't care for the ominous atmosphere that he found himself in. He knew the idea was to make it appear as if he had been "worked-over" so the imam and his men would give up and cooperate, but still and all he didn't like it.

Trevor Jacks told Orlando to close his eyes, whereupon Bentley tossed a cup of cold water in his face. He then tossed another cup of water in his face followed by a resounding flush of the toilet.

Jacks told Orlando to turn his head to the side, close his eyes and to tighten the muscles in his jaw. He then punched him in the face; it was a glancing blow off the side of his cheekbone. The punch wasn't hard enough to cause visible damage, but it did leave a prominent welt. He followed it up by backhanding Orlando across the mouth cutting his lip.

Bentley stepped in and snipped the pant leg on the inside of Orlando's thigh. He then used his combat knife to cut his flesh. It was deep enough so it bled profusely creating a significant stain in the area of his crotch.

After what seemed like an appropriate amount of time, Bentley and Jacks decided to take Stokes back to the room that held the prisoners. Jacks made it a point to open the door with a sudden and dramatic flair, then tossed Orlando in front of the imam and his son. Their response was to yell out *"Allahu Akbar"* over and over.

It was Geiger who stepped forward and said in a loud and threatening voice:

"Heh! What did I fuckin' tell you? . . . Shut the fuck up." He followed his statement by kicking a young jihadi named Omar in the side of his head. The guy had deep-set eyes that glistened, probably due to some type of drug. He had a full-length black beard and nose hair that seemed to intermingle with the hair above his lip.

His clothes looked unkempt as if they had never been washed and he smelled kind of rancid. Even by Muslim standards he would be considered gross.

Both Trevor Jacks and Chris Bentley sensed they might not elicit any useful information from their captives, except for one possibility—the imam's son.

They knew he was gay and from what Orlando had said of him he was weak and would most likely relinquish whatever he knew when faced with the aspect of being tortured.

Chris pulled Stigler aside and into the hallway where he told him to go downstairs and relieve Grimaldi and

Gordon. He explained how the two of them had left their positions to start searching the barn for the drone. He also instructed him to go outside as far as the road and radio back anything he thought suspicious.

By letting Stigler go, it left only himself, Trevor and Max Geiger to watch the prisoners and conduct interrogations. Bentley decided to follow his hunch and take the imam's son down the hallway to the bathroom.

When he and Jacks were about to leave with Akram, the prisoners began to yell in protest.

Geiger pointed his rifle at them and swore he would use it if they didn't quiet down.

To emphasize what he said, he pointed the muzzle of his M-4 towards the ceiling and pulled the trigger. The result had its intended effect, as bits of debris fell to the floor, the imam and his men fell silent.

When they reached the bathroom, Jacks sat Akram on the toilet. He then used a dirty towel to blindfold him. Without saying anything, Bentley tossed a cup of toilet water in Akram's face.

"Does that smell like piss to you?" he asked.

"You know where the bloody fuckin' drone is hidden . . . don't you?" asked Jacks, as he flung another cup of cold urine in Akram's face.

"No, no . . . I don't know . . . I will not . . ."

"You won't what?" asked Bentley, knowing when a prisoner starts to talk he doesn't stop.

Jacks leaned over close to where Akram was sitting, then in a sneering tone of voice asked:

"How would you like to go for a little swim in that bleeding, fuckin' loo . . . you repugnant piece of pig snot?"

"You know," Bentley said, as he jerked the blindfold from Akram's face, "this may help you think a little more clearly." He then removed his utility knife from its scabbard and held it out in front of him.

"You are aware, aren't you" he asked, "that we're all Jews?" It was something Akram would have no way of knowing, but Bentley knew it would make him cringe.

"You know what we believe in . . . don't you?"

". . . in fuckin' circumcision . . . you bloody, fuckin' wanker!" shouted Jacks, his voice one octave lower than a scream.

Akram turned his head, closed his eyes, and then uttered breathlessly:

"No . . . I will not . . . anything. I will not—I am in the hands of Allah—peace, peace be upon him."

"Is that so?" asked Jacks. "Well, for the time being, you're bloody well in our fuckin' hands now." He then put his index finger up to Akram's lips and pushed it into his mouth.

Bentley leaned in close to Akram so he could whisper in his ear:

"I know what you are . . . Don't I?" he asked. "You're 'sadj . . . Aren't you?" He used the word "sadj" which was Arabic for "peculiar" as a reference for homosexuality, because the word homosexual didn't exist in the Arabic language.

"Tell us where the drone is, you bloody, fuckin' . . . 'ubnah'" (Arabic for the word gay), Jacks said.

"I . . . I am not that."

"Oh, that's quite alright, old boy . . . ah, have it your way," said Bentley, as he pulled Akram from the toilet seat to his feet. Jacks moved in close to Akram and looked him in the eye. Without saying a word, he slowly unbuckled Akram's belt, then drew his zipper down. He then worked his pants and underwear to the floor, exposing his genitals.

"Why! Look at you," said Bentley, as he pointed his knife at Akram's penis.

"Your 'todger' is getting hard . . . you cheeky little bastard—you." He then placed the dull side of his knife under Akram's testicles and said:

"If you don't tell us what we want . . . well?"

"Well!" Jacks said with a sarcastic chuckle, "you might end up dressing like a woman . . . like a bleeding— *khawal*" (Arabic for transvestite.)

Bentley jiggled Akram's testicles as an added incentive to talk.

"No," wailed Akram, "I'm not . . . it's in the barn, in the fourth stall . . . I'm not . . ."

"Is it wired? Does it have an IED?" shouted Bentley. "I."

"Is it wired?"

"I don't know," sobbed Akram.

Bentley left Akram and Jacks alone and slipped into the hallway shutting the bathroom door behind him.

He radioed Grimaldi and told him the drone could be in the fourth stall. He didn't know if it was wired or not.

"We're on it," replied Grimaldi. "I'll call you back as soon as I can."

"Roger that," answered Bentley.

When they returned Akram to the room, they found Geiger standing next to the body of the jihadi named Omar, the one Geiger had kicked in the head.

They sat Akram next to his father who said nothing but the language of hate.

"What happened to him?" Bentley asked, pointing his rifle at Omar's body.

"Did he meet with an . . . accident?"

"Yeah," replied Geiger. "I guess you could say that . . . he sort of charged at me . . . ran into my rifle while my finger was on the trigger."

"Oh, poor show, old boy, but those things do happen."

Bentley then walked over towards the chair Orlando was sitting in. He made it a point to avoid the pool of blood that had seeped from the lifeless jihadi. He lifted Stokes up and walked him out the door into the hallway.

"I won't take time to explain the details," he said. "It seems Grimaldi and Gordon have found the drone and its cargo . . . They found something else . . . too."

"Oh, yeah?" Orlando said trying to act surprised. "Like what?" he asked.

"Like what? Oh, nothing, just a plastic box filled with money and an IED to go with it. The box was buried with the drone and the canister of sarin gas."

"Wow," Stokes said, "I guess they . . . were lucky . . . Huh?"

"Mmm, you could say that. I would imagine you wouldn't know anything about that, would you?"

Knowing the kind of person Orlando was, Bentley let his voice convey more than a touch of inquisitive cynicism.

"No," Stokes said. "I didn't know—nothin'. I mean I would have told you—you know that."

"Of course, I do . . . I was just saying . . . you know, never mind . . . you will get your share. In the meantime I'm going to bring you inside and sit you back in your chair."

"Then what?"

"Well, I'm going to duct tape your ankles together . . . then do the same to the others." He slipped a small jackknife into Orlando's front pocket.

"Do us a favor," he said, "wait an hour before you cut yourself free . . . should be easy to do since your hands are in front of you."

"What about the guns?" asked Stokes.

"We'll take them with us—be careful and we will see you when you return to the city."

All the time he had been locked up in the room with the imam and the others, Orlando had wondered what Gordon and Grimaldi were up to and now he knew: the bastards had found the money. Orlando cursed them and his luck, and yet, he knew someday he would get even, but until then, he would have to wait.

He remembered his time in prison; there was nothing else to do but wait and read a lot of books. One of them was *The Prophet* by Kahlil Gibran. He recalled a few of the passages he had memorized:

"Out of suffering have emerged the strongest souls; the most massive characters are seared with scars.

"The timeless in you is aware of life's timelessness; and knows that yesterday is but today's memory and tomorrow is today's dream."

31707698R20175

Made in the USA
Middletown, DE
10 May 2016